The
Emerald
Necklace

The Emerald Necklace

by
DIANA BROWN

ST. MARTIN'S PRESS/NEW YORK

Library of Congress Cataloging in Publication data

Brown, Diana.
    The emerald necklace.

    I. Title.
PZ4.B87493Em 1980   [PR6052.R58943]   823'.9'14
ISBN 0-312-24385-5   79-23126

For R.H.B.

Marriage is a matter of more worth
Than to be dealt in by attorneyship. . . .
For what is wedlock forced, but a hell,
An age of discord and continual strife?
Whereas the contrary bringeth bliss,
And is a pattern of celestial peace.

SHAKESPEARE
Henry VI, Part 1, Act V, Scene 5

PART I

GROSVENOR SQUARE, LONDON

Chapter I

I gazed at the perfect multi-facetted diamond he had just placed on my finger. It was set in heavy gold and was less gaudy than I had expected, though I knew it must be worth a small fortune. I wondered how Papa would restrain himself from pawning it, but then I remembered he had already been well rewarded by the diamond's donor for the privilege of conferring it upon me. With its glitter on my hand, all my hopes faded, and my marriage with Etienne Lambert became an inevitability. I felt a lump in my throat and my eyes grew moist with tears I forced back.

Lambert bent down to kiss me and I strove to hide my revulsion. He seemed to sense it, however, for rather than claiming my lips he took my hand in his and touched it with a fleeting caress before releasing it.

"You are very young." His decisive voice was softer, gentler than I had yet heard. "I shall try to make you as happy as you deserve to be."

I glanced apprehensively into his dark eyes fixed upon mine, wondering what he would do if I told him how much I detested the whole idea of marriage with him, that I loved Francis Oliphant and always would, that he lacked the youth, the sportiveness, the social status, the daring to ever bring me happiness. But I said nothing, of course, for Papa would never forgive me if I ruined his carefully designed scheme to rid himself of the mass of debts he had accumulated; nor, for that matter, would I ever forgive myself if Papa were confined to Newgate because of my refusal.

"I am sure that I shall be happy when—I get used to you," I said at last.

"Not quite the declaration of a young lady overwhelmed with love." I detected a note of bitterness in his voice despite its light tone. "But perhaps I can change that with time."

As he bowed and bade me farewell I observed that his bearing was quite patrician despite his lowly origins. And though his clothes were not of the Corinthian style favoured by Francis, his collar being distinctly low cut compared with the high points Francis sported, and he wore only one waistcoat beneath his dark blue coat, still that coat fitted his broad shoulders to perfection and he wore it with distinction. Of course, I thought indignantly, he could afford the best tailor in London, and his tailor was undoubtedly well paid for his pains, unlike those to whom my father and Francis gave their custom. I understood it was the mark of a gentleman to be in debt to one's tailor.

As Lambert left the salon into which he had been ushered with some ceremony only half an hour earlier, I remembered with acrimony the day I had first met him there only three weeks before. I had been driving in the park with Francis who had, for the first time, allowed me to take the reins of his spirited team. It had been an exhilarating experience: all that power within the grasp of my small hand, yet I had felt fully in control. I had wanted it to go on forever but the crush of carriages had been such that Francis had insisted on redeeming the reins after an all too short period, promising that another day he would allow me to hold them longer.

When I returned home I was still brimming with excitement and I rushed straight to the salon to see if Papa were in. He was, but he was not alone. With him was a stranger, tall, broad-shouldered, somehow forbidding. His forehead was broad and high. His face, though not exactly arrogant, for there was in it sagacity and intelligence, showed a slight intolerance that marked him as a man impossible to drive. There was something not altogether English about him, some foreign aspect; perhaps his dark hair which had a tendency to curl but which he combed back straight as though forbidding nature's frivolity, or his dark eyes beneath straight brows which had a discerning quality as though he knew what the mind thought before anything was said. He struck me as a man who controlled others though he himself would rarely be controlled. I found his facial expression difficult to describe. Perhaps I detected skepticism or scorn, that is until his eyes fell on my face, and then I thought there was a change, a softening, a warming. He might, I thought, have been accounted handsome by some, but he was no gay young Corinthian to attract my eye. He was decidedly over thirty, a crony of Papa's I decided, and turned away to rhapsodize on my drive. But Papa cut me short, interrupting my excited harangue mid-sentence.

"Leonora, Leonora, don't you see I have a guest. Wait! Please have the courtesy to contain your adventure until he departs. I believe you said you must go, did you not, Mr. Lambert?"

I noticed the almost plaintive quality of Papa's question, as though he were begging the stranger not to leave. It was strange to hear coming from a man of my father's standing, for Richard Fordyce, Earl of Castleford, was of England's first and oldest, though by no means its wealthiest, families.

I had never known my father to beg for anything, yet the stranger seemed to have some power over him.

Papa noticed that his guest had not replied to his question, that Lambert's eyes were fixed upon me, and he quickly apologized.

"Dear me, I have quite forgotten my manners today. Mr. Lambert, allow me to present my daughter, Leonora Fordyce. Leonora, this is Mr. Lambert, Mr. Etienne Lambert. Mr. Lambert is a—an acquaintance of mine."

"I am delighted to meet you, Leonora."

Now that he spoke for the first time, though his voice was that of a gentleman, that he was not altogether English seemed confirmed by the slight rolling of the *r* as he pronounced my name. It did not escape my attention that Papa had described the stranger as an acquaintance. I had been wrong in supposing him one of Papa's cronies, yet I had known Papa to designate others as bosom friends after less than an hour's card play together. Mr. Lambert was evidently not one of his gambling partners. I wondered why he was here at all, though apart from Papa's deferential tone it seemed of little importance.

"Run along now, Leonora," Papa bade me, "I will hear of your driving exploits later." He turned again to Lambert, "Or were you decided on your leaving?" Again I noticed a pleading note in his voice.

Lambert looked speculatively from me back to Papa.

"I might reconsider my decision, Lord Castleford, but I have no wish to deprive your daughter of describing her exploits to you. I see she is bursting with enthusiasm. Our business can wait. I now know your predicament and will call upon you tomorrow with my terms."

His tone was stiff, almost insolent, and I expected Papa to give him one of his famous setdowns. He was not a man to bear with the slightest impertinence, yet he said nothing. In fact he seemed loath for Lambert to leave. When he replied, his face reflected relief and his voice was almost fawning.

"Leonora's news can wait, Lambert. Allow me to serve you a glass of claret and let us talk now."

"Tomorrow, Lord Castleford, at ten, unless that is too early for you?"

"Indeed, no," Papa hastened to reply, though I knew he never rose until midday unless we were at Briarsmere and a day of hunting or shooting awaited him. "Ten it will be."

"Who was that, Papa?" I asked as the door closed behind Lambert.

"I introduced him to you, Leonora."

Papa clearly did not want to talk of him, yet I persisted.

"I know you did, Papa, but that does not explain who he is nor what he wanted with you."

"Don't worry your little head about it." He drew up a chair beside him. "Come, now tell me about your handling of Oliphant's team, though I don't know that I approve. That's spirited horse-flesh. I seem to remember he got that pair from Kern. Irish stock, I believe, they need a man's hand."

"Oh, Papa, don't be so stuffy. It was simply wonderful. I must have my own phaeton now, just a little one, and perhaps a team of two matching chestnuts. Can you pick them out for me? Please, Papa, be a dear. I must have them."

"You shall, my dear, you shall. Perhaps after Mr. Lambert's visit tomorrow we can go and pick them out."

I could not understand what Lambert's visit had to do with my horses, but there was no point in questioning Papa further about him. Something in the submissiveness with which he mentioned the man's name made me desist. Bother Lambert, I thought, and hoped he would not stay long so that we could go about our business. I twirled around imagining myself cutting a figure in the park in my very own phaeton. I could think of a score of people who would practically die with envy. It should be lined in blue, or perhaps lavender. Pink would be pretty but I had never seen anyone, any lady that is, driving a pink-lined phaeton. I wanted to be conspicuous, but not in the manner of those infamous Wilson sisters. No, blue it would be, a blue to match my eyes and show off my golden curls to perfection. And I would need new driving clothes to match. I would visit Madame Claudine tomorrow afternoon, after we had chosen the horses, to look over her selection.

But I did not visit Madame Claudine that next afternoon, nor for two weeks thereafter, and when I did it was for the detestable purpose of selecting wedding clothes. I say *detestable* for it was Etienne Lambert whom I was to marry.

I had not seen him the following morning when he called, for like Papa I rarely rose before noon. When I did descend the stairs, having partaken of hot chocolate and rolls in my room, ready for the excitement of accompanying Papa to Tattersall's to select my team, I found Papa pacing the floor of his study.

"Good morning, Papa," I said, kissing his cheek. "Are you ready to leave?"

He had started on seeing me, as though he had not expected me. He must have been lost in thought. Now he put his hands on my shoulders and looked at me oddly before pulling me to him and hugging me frantically.

"Oh, Leonora, Leonora!" It was almost a cry, I could not understand.

"What is it, Papa? What is the matter? Are you not well?"

I drew back and stared at him. I had often seen Papa, after a night of card playing and drinking, somewhat the worse for wear. Today he looked unwell, but in a different fashion. His face was ashen and his mouth trembled slightly, and I thought I noticed tears filling his blue eyes.

"What is it, Papa, you can tell me. You know we never keep anything from one another."

"I'm afraid that is not so, Leonora," Papa's voice broke as

he spoke. "For a long time now I have concealed from you the fact that our fortunes are in a sad state. In fact one might almost say they are nonexistent—no, not only nonexistent but, in point of fact, I must confess I am severely in debt."

"But Papa," I scoffed, "I know you are in debt. That is not so terrible for so are all the gentlemen I know."

"It is terrible when it reaches the amount to which I am down. I had always thought I would regain enough at cards to repay my most pressing obligations, but unfortunately I am dipped so low now that I am unable to repay my most urgent needs, my debts of honour. Anything else can wait, but no gentleman can ignore such obligations. And word has reached my creditors of my financial condition and I am being threatened with Newgate. *Newgate*, my dear, only think of it!"

I did, with the greatest horror. Papa in that dreadful debtor's prison, even the thought was beyond endurance. It could not be. It would not be. Briarsmere, our Dorset seat, would have to go, that was all there was. I had been born there, but there was no other way.

"Your debts must be paid, Papa, whatever the cost. We must raise the money somehow. We must sell Briarsmere." Even as I spoke the name I felt a slight sob in my voice, so fond was I of the place.

"Leonora," Papa said gently, "even the money to be gained from Briarsmere would be only a drop in the ocean. I would sell it tomorrow if it would clear my obligations, but it will not. It is not clear, you know."

Strangely I was more shocked to learn Papa could even talk of parting so easily with Briarsmere, which I had only mentioned as a last resort, than to learn that our great sixteenth century country mansion and its surrounding acres would not cover Papa's debts—a drop in the ocean he had called it. I wondered how much he could possibly owe, but I dared not ask.

"Perhaps a moneylender can help us, Papa, until we find the means of settling our difficulties. And I can sell the Fordyce pendant."

"You can't do that," Papa said quickly. "Your mother left that pendant to you. It was her last wish that you should keep it always. I cannot allow it."

"But Papa—"I protested.

"I will not hear of it. Do not speak of it again. And as for moneylenders, I have seen everyone in London. None will lend me a penny except—"

"Except who, Papa?" I suddenly remembered the stranger yesterday. "Mr. Lambert, is he a moneylender?"

"Not exactly, child, but he is a very wealthy man, a banker or something or other. He dabbles in so many areas of finance I don't quite know what he does, except I know that the amount I owe is infinitesimal to him."

"And he has agreed to loan it, Papa?" My face shone with relief.

Papa looked away and then walked over to the window and stood with his back to me.

"He has, Leonora, but he has made a condition."

"High interest, I suppose. Well, that is to be expected. If he has such money undoubtedly that is how he gained it."

"No, Leonora, he is willing to give me the sum I need."

"Give it to you, Papa. What generosity!" I stopped my effusions suddenly. Why was Papa not delirious with joy as I was? There must be a reason. "Why, Papa, why would he be willing to give away such a sum?"

"As I said there is a condition."

Papa continued to talk with his back to me and suddenly I felt frightened.

"What is that condition?"

"He has asked me for your hand in marriage." The room shrieked with the silence which engulfed the distance between me and Papa's unremitting back.

Now my fright turned to anger. Loathsome creature, I thought. How dare he make such a proposal. What utter gall. No man of honour would make such a suggestion, no gentleman. But he was a common man of trade, a Cit, who hoped to marry the only child of one of England's foremost noblemen. I hoped Papa had thrown him out on his ear for his temerity. It was almost laughable, except—except Papa was not laughing. Papa was being threatened with debtors' prison, there was nothing to laugh at in that.

"What did you tell him, Papa?" I asked finally.

Papa turned slowly, then he flicked an invisible speck of dust from the immaculate sleeve of his claret coloured velvet coat and said, still without looking at me,

"I said I would talk to you—in fact he insisted that I do so before giving him a reply."

"I see."

So Papa had been actively giving his request consideration. I found it difficult to believe he could part with me in such a fashion. Yet, of course, how could he not do so, faced as he was with such an infamous alternative. But Papa had always said I was the love of his life. He has refused me nothing. Now I wished he had exercised more restraint. I wished he had forced me to stay within my allowance. I wished that he had explained his difficulties to me. I thought of all the money I had frittered away just this year since leaving Miss Brewster's establishment for young ladies in Kensington. My presentation dress alone had cost more than three hundred guineas. It had been the most splendid gown there. *Lady's Magazine* had devoted an entire page to its description. Papa had said nothing when I gave him the account. Of course I suppose he had not paid it. It had probably been small compared with his gaming debts.

My thoughts returned to Lambert. I saw again his tall, dark figure, his taciturn face, his dark, brooding eyes, and beside him I saw the image of Francis Oliphant, fair, lithe, young, amusing—no, it could not be.

"Is there no alternative, Papa? Will Lambert accept no other security?"

"My darling, if there were would I even have considered it for a moment, would I have spoken of it to you at all? Do you know how much it pains me to speak of it now? Yesterday he had already refused me. He had been quite clear, insultingly clear, in his denial. He had said he would as soon donate the sum to a Covent Garden abbess, the insolent cur," Papa's voice rose as he recalled the moment, then he pulled himself up short. He had no wish, I suppose, to denigrate a man he might have to recognize as his son-in-law. "Then you came in and he saw you and everything changed. I wish you had not, Leonora, and yet—"

I knew what he meant, of course. He was right, it was the only way out. I swallowed hard to hide my grief. I could not bear the thought of the man, but neither could I bear the thought of Papa in Newgate. Lambert was the only alternative.

"When does he want his answer?"

"I invited him to dinner tomorrow evening. I had thought to invite your aunt and perhaps Sir Thomas and Lady Lupton, a small group to introduce him to our friends. That is, if you agree, of course."

Papa's face was pleading, his soft blue eyes clouded with shame. I nodded.

"Of course, Papa. I will make arrangements for it."

That day and those that followed were an endless nightmare for me, but I busied myself with preparations, determined to hide my feelings from everyone—everyone, that is, except Francis Oliphant and his sister, Phoebe.

Phoebe Oliphant visited me the afternoon following Papa's appalling disclosure. Phoebe had been my bosom companion at Miss Brewster's; there was no hiding anything from her. She took one look at my face as I greeted her, then put an arm around my waist and drew me over to a sofa and earnestly demanded to know what was troubling me. Dear, dear Phoebe, she had always been my comfort, my confidante, my strength. I could hold nothing from her. I sobbed on her shoulder and told her everything—everything, that is, except the name of Papa's deliverer.

"But who is it that makes such an infamous proposal?" she asked as I finished.

"Lambert, Etienne Lambert I think is his name."

Phoebe raised her pert nose in disdain and shook her dark curls.

"That Cit, Etienne St. Clair Lambert. I might have guessed. Francis has spoken of him, of his omnipotent wealth. He says he's more of a devil than a saint, and a wolf rather than a lamb. No one knows his true background but they say he's a bas—of illegitimate birth, his mother a serving wench and no telling who his father was. *She* probably didn't know if she's like others of her class. God only knows how he came by his fortune, not honestly I'll be bound. Francis says no one knows its true extent. He doubts even Lambert himself knows. But he continues to profit by the misfortunes of others, just as he is doing now. He is using you to gain a foothold in society, I've no doubt. He visits few people in society—I suspect the doors of all the best houses have been closed to him—and now he thinks to use you to open them. He's not interested in your estate, I am sure, for he owns several which belonged to others who have fallen into debt and gone to him for help. Help he will, but he gives nothing away."

Phoebe was right, I supposed. She was almost always right. Though why he should give his money away I could not quite understand. I had not known the Oliphants to give away any of theirs.

"No," she continued, "he thinks to use you in another

way. He wants children who will call one of the first nobles of our realm 'grandfather.' Perhaps he even aspires to gain a title for himself with your father's aid. If Lambert were your husband, your father would undoubtedly do whatever he could for him."

Phoebe's scornful words did nothing to comfort me. In fact they filled me with even greater dread and I burst into tears again. At once she was repentant.

"Leonora, I'm sorry. I did not mean to alarm you but I wanted to open your eyes. I admit I was incensed that Lambert thought he could buy you, that your father would think to use you as a pawn."

"But Phoebe, Papa will go to Newgate if I don't promise to marry Lambert."

"And serve him right," Phoebe said severely. At times I found her recalcitrance difficult to bear; for my part I was more inclined to tolerance.

"No, Phoebe, not Papa. He can't help gambling. He just doesn't understand financial matters, that's all."

"Then it's about time he did." Phoebe's voice was still severe. "And what will Francis do? Have you given a thought to him in all this? You know how we had always talked of you belonging to one another ever since we were small together. Francis will be broken-hearted."

"Do you not think I am as well, Phoebe? It does no good to remind me of it, I assure you. I have thought of nothing else since father spoke to me of this yesterday. You must tell him. I cannot bring myself to do so."

"But you have not yet accepted Lambert?"

"No, but he dines with us this evening. Aunt Agatha will be here and Papa's closest friend, Sir Thomas Lupton. It is by way of introducing Lambert to our circle of acquaintance, I believe. His own, I dare say, is quite low."

"Other Cits and Covent Garden wenches, I don't doubt.

It's all too disgusting," Phoebe railed. "You must refuse him, Leonora. Promise me you will."

"I cannot, Phoebe, I cannot." Again I began to cry.

Despite repeated powderings my eyes were still red that evening as I greeted our guests, and by way of explanation I complained of the chill January winds we were then enduring. I could scarcely bring myself to look at Lambert when he was announced. He greeted me formally and though he did not appear to be a particularly sociable person, he conducted himself in a surprisingly gentlemanlike manner and appeared quite at ease among his social superiors. At times I had the odd impression that he actually looked down on Sir Thomas's overbearing joviality and his wife's constant high-pitched laugh which, I must admit, also irked me. When dinner was served I watched surreptitiously to see whether he would use the wrong fork or drink from his fingerbowl, but his table manners were better than those of most of the gentlemen who dined at our table. My surprise almost amounted to disappointment.

I was terrified that he might try to propose to me there and then and I kept as far away from him as possible all evening, confining my conversation to a minimum. Aunt Agatha asked me repeatedly whether the cat had got my tongue. I felt like extending that part of my anatomy at her to prove its existence. Such unladylike conduct might have served to discourage Lambert, but it would also have earned me a great scold from Aunt Agatha and I was in no humour to endure that. I observed that Lambert got along better with Aunt Agatha than anyone else present and she seemed to enjoy his company. He did not seem to mind the fact that she was so outspoken, and for her part I presumed she was unaware of his obscure origins. I wondered whether she knew the purpose behind his being invited to dine with us that evening. For his part he made no attempt to talk to me on my own, though I was aware of his eyes upon me as I chatted with our guests. Once or twice I cast a sidelong glance in his direction and noticed that he looked unexpectedly handsome, despite the severity of his dark grey coat. Francis would certainly have adorned it with large, silver buttons or sported a brightly embroidered waistcoat beneath it, but Lambert wore only a crisp white cravat tied neatly but with no special flare and a plain pearl grey waistcoat. His white breeches were unremarkable except for the manner in which they set off his well-shaped legs. The only jewellery he wore was a signet ring of heavy gold and jade on his left hand, no fobs or chains. I wondered, since he was so wealthy, why he did not make more display of his wealth, which was the sort of thing one would expect from a person of his background. Once he caught me examining him and, as I turned away in confusion, I caught a glimpse of amusement in his eyes.

In the ensuing days I saw him frequently, always in the presence of others. Papa arranged for him to attend all the social functions to which we were invited, but only a few of these did he grace with his presence. He did, however, attend the parties and dinners given at our house on Hill Street so that I believe tongues were wagging long before the announcement was officially made in the *Gazette*. It was at one of these functions that Francis and Phoebe Oliphant were introduced to him. Even I was embarrassed at their hostility. Phoebe openly cut him and the bow Francis returned to his greeting was scarcely worthy of that name. It was hardly surprising, though, for I knew Phoebe disparaged him at every opportunity and Francis had been beside himself with rage at the idea of my marriage. There had been a great scene, ranting on his side, tears on mine, but all to no avail. Francis himself was badly in debt. He was as much given to gaming as was father and though, in due time, he would inherit his father's title to become Sir Francis

Oliphant, there was little that went with that barony; certainly nothing that could be counted upon to get us out of our predicament. I pleaded with him to forget me.

"How can you even suggest such a thing," he stormed. "You know that I will never forget you. You have been the earth, the sky, the moon and the stars to me. How could I ever forget you! I should like to call out the curmudgeon for having the indecency to even suggest the marriage. A common Cit and a bastard to boot!"

"Francis, don't," I pleaded. His anger was justified, though why he directed none of it at Papa I did not know. As for duelling with Lambert, I was not at all sure that Francis would get the best of such a match. Lambert might not be a gentleman, but nothing about him indicated that he lacked either mental or physical acumen. Francis might be hurt.

"Well, let him stay well clear of my path and watch himself carefully in my presence," Francis warned ominously.

I was thus in a state of confusion when I saw Francis and Lambert talking together that evening before we dined. I don't know what was said, I only saw a look of cool amusement in Lambert's eyes and a hot flush upon Francis' cheek.

"That buffoon!" Francis was still fuming when the gentlemen rejoined us after their port. "He had the effrontery to say that he found my coat gaudy."

I looked at Francis' coat. It was a little more elaborate than usual being trimmed with gold braid, and the cut of his high rolled collar completely immobilized his neck, making it necessary to turn the whole of his upper torso when he spoke to a companion.

"But did he volunteer that opinion?" I asked in surprise. It hardly seemed in keeping with the little I knew of Lambert to be discussing clothes.

"No. But I simply asked him whether he were going to a funeral in that drab garb of his and he replied that he preferred plainness in dress to overelaboration, and he said it in a manner that brooked little argument. The man's a boor!"

"You didn't do anything hasty?" I asked nervously, afraid the remark had precipitated the anticipated duel.

"No. He was lucky that on this occasion I controlled my temper."

As I breathed a sigh of relief I detected a slight narrowing of Lambert's eyes as he watched us talking and wondered if our fondness for one another was apparent. I would gladly have flaunted my feelings, but one look at Papa, whose gaze was also anxiously fixed upon us and then on Lambert, made me leave Francis' side to get Lambert a cup of coffee. It was the first time I had voluntarily approached him and I knew I caught him by surprise. He took the cup I offered, then he looked at me searchingly and quickly asked,

"The young man, Mr. Oliphant, is he a particular friend of yours?" I detected a note of concern in his voice.

"Francis?" I paused, tempted for a moment to admit the truth, but again I caught Papa's wistful expression. Even though I agreed for the most part with Francis' opinion of Lambert, I did not believe him enough of a cad to marry me knowing my affections were fixed elsewhere. "He's a child-hood friend. He and Phoebe, his sister, and I have spent much time together, for Briarsmere adjoins their father's estate in Dorset. If anything, it is Phoebe who is my particular friend."

"I fear neither of them likes me very much." There was regret in his voice. It was the first time he had shown concern over whether he were accepted by those of our circle. Aunt Agatha had been the only one with whom he had been affable; he had ridden roughshod over the others. I felt that his present concern must be because he knew Francis and Phoebe to be special friends of mine, friends who would visit me after marriage. I hastened to assure him that I thought him mistaken. He smiled, but neither agreed nor argued with my assessment.

The next time I saw him was in the salon where he made his formal declaration and where, against all my instincts and inclinations, I accepted him.

Chapter II

A week following the announcement of my engagement in the *Gazette*, and before the protests from my friends had subsided, we were married in an elaborate ceremony at St. George's, Hanover Square. Lambert had been against the ceremony, though not the marriage itself. I was also, but Papa had been insistent—I sensed from bravado—and I had acquiesced. I think Lambert, or Etienne as he now insisted I call him, only agreed because he believed I wanted the splendour and fuss, while nothing could have been further from the truth. I had discovered he was not a man to allow Papa to coerce him into anything. In fact Papa had been affronted when Etienne refused to allow him to put up his name for membership at White's.

"Thank you, Lord Castleford, but I have no interest in the activities of the gentlemen of that club," he had replied laconically to Papa's offer, one that Papa had gone to great pains to make. He only had offered the membership after he had taken measures to ensure that Lambert's name would not be blackballed. I saw the flush of anger rise to Papa's cheeks, but nothing more was said on the subject.

We were married, ironically enough, on St. Valentine's day, the feast day of lovers. It was also the day, Etienne pointed out, when birds were reputed to choose their mates for the year. He smiled rather wistfully and said he trusted our marriage would last for more than a season. His wedding gift to me was unexpected. I had thought he would present me with some sumptuous piece of jewellery but it was, in fact, the manuscript of a poem John Donne had written on the occasion of the marriage of Princess Elizabeth and Prince Palatine on a St. Valentine's day more than two centuries earlier. I blushed as I read the all too obvious meaning of Donne's conclusion:

> The husband cock looks out, and straight is sped
> And meets his wife, which brings her feather bed.

Only the previous evening Aunt Agatha had explained to me, in the plainest of language, just what occurred between married people. It sounded quite disgusting and the idea that this strange man would share my bed and touch my body and use it in such a manner I found positively revolting. I think my lack of response at his present daunted him somewhat, but my heart was filled with fear and dread now that the fatal, binding day was upon us and I could no longer carry on my pretence as before.

The ceremony was early and all of London was present—all of London that counted, that is,—except for two very conspicuous absences, for neither Francis nor Phoebe would take part in a ceremony which Phoebe outspokenly labelled as completely repugnant to her. Her frank declaration of my own inmost feelings did nothing to lighten my already heavy heart.

I could eat nothing at the wedding feast which followed.

Etienne must have sensed my discomfort, for he soon insisted that we leave in order to reach Dover before dark, where we were to spend our first night. From there we would cross to France in his yacht to stay at the Grand Hotel in Paris before going on to northern Italy. I had never visited the continent and under other circumstances I would have been beside myself with joy at the voyage, but now the idea of weeks alone with this stranger was daunting. I wanted only to let it pass so that I might return to my friends and my familiar London haunts.

The noise and celebration at Hill Street were at last left behind. They would, I suspected, carry on long into the night, undoubtedly with many a baudy jest at my expense. For my part I now felt completely alone.

Etienne breathed a sigh of relief as we pulled away, and took off his beaver hat and threw it across the carriage, taking my hand in his.

"Thank God that's over. You've no idea how I dreaded it."

His words surprised me. His dread could not arise from the same source as my own, but it struck me forcibly at that moment that in marrying me for the social benefits to be derived from the connection, he was taking remarkably little advantage of them. I wondered whether a sense of inferiority held him back, but I felt no sympathy with him on that score. He had chosen the connection, not me. I tried not to despise him.

He squeezed my hand and I managed a wan smile in return. He seemed to sense my uneasiness for as we bowled across the Kentish countryside through the crisp, clear air, he pointed out the dene-holes, sites of tunnels dug deep into the chalk in the days of the Romans to mine the substance. He became as excited as a boy when he spotted the flight of a martin racing through the sky, the first of the season and a good omen he foretold. The birds were called

Martinets—Little Martins—in France as a sign of affection. He spoke a great deal of the country to which we were going. Though I would have expected him to have Buona-partist sympathies—in my mind I classified both men as upstarts—still he spoke movingly of Louis XVI and his wife and their terrible fate but did not hesitate to affirm that the revolution had brought sorely needed change to France.

By the time we reached Dover, much of my anxiety had left me. But as we drew up at the ship I felt my fears return and the pallor crept back to my cheeks. Etienne accom-panied me to the parlour reserved for us and then left me while he sought out the landlord. I stood and looked out on the grey channel we were to cross the next day, worrying not so much about the crossing but about the night ahead.

A waiter came with refreshments and close at his heels was Etienne.

"Come by the fire and take a little brandy," he insisted. "Despite our lap robes it was a chilling ride. I've no wish for your first visit to France to be marred by a miserable English cold."

I did as I was bid, but I could not prevent my hand from shaking as I took the glass from him. He must have noticed, for he immediately removed it from my grasp and set it on the table and, taking both my hands in his, he rubbed them gently as though to warm them.

"Leonie," he began, using the French version of my name which he had adopted, "I did not realize until today, until we were alone together, just how very young and very vulnerable you really are. In your own circle of friends you have almost astonished me with your sophistication, but now I see you as you really are. Perhaps I have been selfish in marrying you, perhaps we should have waited, but never-theless we are now husband and wife; the church and the law say it is so. It may be an odd way to begin a marriage with a courtship, but that is what I propose. I have asked the landlord to prepare a separate chamber for me tonight, and so it will be until you feel ready and desirous of accepting me as your husband. I want you to do so only when you love me." He flushed suddenly. "That may be too much to expect—let me say when you feel some affection for me. I know that now you have none, but I hope with time I may gain it."

I smiled up at him in genuine relief.

"There, that's better," he went on. "Now drink this brandy. The ship has an excellent cook who prepares a superb sole with crab sauce and I've ordered an apricot tart to follow. It is preferable not to eat too heavily tonight for it may be a rough crossing tomorrow. The channel is unpredictable at the best of times but particularly so in winter. With a good night's rest, though, you'll survive tomorrow with flying colours, of that I've no doubt."

Etienne's prediction of the channel's roughness was borne out the following day. I had barely boarded his sumptuously outfitted yacht—renamed, I noticed, the *Leonie*—when the loss of solid ground beneath my feet drew all my attention to my queasy stomach. I immediately asked to be shown to my cabin, and almost as soon as we left the protection of the harbour I began to be sick. Etienne came to find me when I did not return above and refused to leave me alone, insisting that I return with him to the deck. I shook my head in horror, for the sea was now turbulent.

"Is this the young lady who was so impressed with controlling the power of horses the day I first met her? If you want to see real power, come and watch the power of the waves and the manner in which this magnificent rig handles them."

Against all my inclinations I made my way above with his help. There, though the waves were intimidating in their ferocity, seeing them at their worst rather than imagining them helped to allay my fears—that and the fact that

Etienne was so obviously untroubled by it all. In fact I felt he enjoyed it, and I began to see the beauty of it. He pointed out the seagulls following us through the storm. Occasionally we would sight another craft plowing through the turbulence and we would wave. Soon I was even able to partake of light refreshment, and by the time the coast of France loomed up ahead of us I had truly found my sea legs.

We rested that night in Calais before proceeding to Paris in a chaise kept by Etienne in France. He apparently came there often. He spoke the language like a native. My own attempts to speak it, learned at the hands of Miss Brewster, were deplorable, and I soon came to rely upon him to interpret for me.

Paris surprised me. I had expected disarray and dejection, for after all France had lost the wars with England, but around me in the Faubourg St. Honoré I saw nothing but elegance and gaiety. Our suite at the *Grand* on the Boulevard des Capucins was extensive and luxurious, and in Etienne I found I had a husband who, though certainly not of my choosing, was generous and thoughtful. Since he forced no intimacy upon me I was better able to endure our relationship, though it was by no means palatable knowing myself to be tied to him forever. Anything I desired was mine and I sought to alleviate my frustrations in an endless round of shopping; choosing perfume from Martin on the rue Royale, hats à la Clorinde from Madame Chaumeton, and dresses designed for me by Auguste Garneray. Etienne seemed to enjoy my indulgence and presented me with a magnificent emerald necklace, cool and clear against my white skin, and a chinchilla from the Reine d'Epagne of which there were only twenty in all of Europe. I became accustomed to being denied nothing and was surprised therefore, to have Etienne demur when I ordered a dress trimmed with roses. But he pointed out the beauty of the brocade, of a new *café au lait* colour woven with gold, from which any embellishment would detract. He ordered the most simple cut, and when the dress arrived and I put it on, the clean lines flaring slightly from my natural waistline with only a heavy rouleau of satin around the hem, I knew he was right. At his suggestion I had my hair styled in the middle with simple curls on each side of my face and surmounted by a fine gold diadem. Though I had always been a noted beauty, when I surveyed myself in the mirror I knew I had never been as beautiful as I was that night. When I went into the salon where he awaited me, I saw a light of fierce desire in his dark eyes which at once frightened and excited me. He crossed the room and I felt my heart beat faster than usual as he studied my face, then he bent down and lightly kissed my hand.

"You are a very beautiful woman," was all he said. "Come, for Fanny Cerrito is dancing tonight. I think you will enjoy it."

The Opera House was quite splendid after our London theatres. Etienne told me that the first opera performed in the first opera house on that site was the tragedy of *Orphée* and was given for the equally tragic marriage of Francois II and Mary Stuart. The light from the candles of hundreds of chandeliers illuminated the comings and goings of the elegant people in the gallery outside our boxes.

Fanny Cerrito, who had been publicly acclaimed in verse by Thomas Ingoldsby, was indeed a graceful dancer. Her bright smile was often directed to our box, but I failed to understand its attraction until at the time of intermission, when we were asked to join the party of the duc de Bertran, I overheard him ask Etienne whether he did not consider La Cerrito in particularly fine form that night, or whether he always considered her above criticism. Etienne tossed a noncommittal reply, but my curiosity was awakened. For my own part, though I was used to being stared at, I was quite unused to the openly seductive glances of the French men. I thought it would annoy Etienne, but he seemed to enjoy it and laughed when I mentioned the discomfort it caused me.

"Believe me, men in London think in exactly the same manner. It is just that Parisians are more open in their feelings, a trait of which I do not entirely disapprove."

When we returned to our box and the performance began again, I watched the dancer and was convinced that it was to Etienne that she directed her attentions. Somehow I felt annoyed when he bowed to her after she had completed a particularly admirable *pas de chat* and I pleaded a sudden headache and asked that we might leave. Though Etienne was solicitous, we did not leave with alacrity, and not before he turned to the stage with an apologetic shrug.

"Is it entirely necessary to apologize to the players if we leave early?" I asked frostily.

"It is when they are true *artistes*, as is Fanny," he replied in a level voice.

"Fanny! You appear to know her well."

"I have known her for a long time. She is a friend of mine." His tone of finality prevented further discussion on the subject, but I felt oddly chagrined.

With the Bourbon restoration, French nobility had returned to France and to Paris in full force. But despite their flaunted nobility, I noticed an underlying spirit of equality in the air. I felt that must account for the reason that Etienne was received everywhere. I was received only as his wife, not as the daughter of the Earl of Castleford, and I felt resentful. When I found myself addressed quite simply as Madame Lambert, I hastened to let it be known that although I had married a commoner I retained the title received at birth and preferred to be called Lady Leonora. Etienne heard my remark and smiled, and I felt suddenly pompous. More so when from then on he introduced me very exactly, very distinctly and with the least touch of irony as Lady Leonora Fordyce Lambert. In the drawing rooms of Paris it was he who was sought after and who was admired by the hostesses. At times I felt they almost resented my presence. Since I had trouble understanding the rapid flow of the Gallic tongue and felt out of my usual element, I grew tired of these visits. I noticed how often the name of Clavel-Grassin was mentioned and once asked Etienne what it referred to.

"Merely an acquaintance of mine, that is all," he responded in that voice which prevented further discussion.

One morning as we left the hotel for a walk in the Tuileries gardens I noticed a slight, familiar figure in the foyer and started at the sight. It was Francis. I remembered that I had mentioned our destination to him but I had no idea he would follow me. Since Etienne was engaged at the desk arranging for an express to be sent to London on some matter of business, Francis approached me and soulfully took my hand.

"How are you, Leonora? Are you alright? You must forgive me but I had to know. I couldn't stand London without you, and when cousin Perry said he was crossing to France I came with him."

His glance took in my new attire.

"You look different," he said almost accusingly.

I felt overjoyed at seeing his familiar face after all the strangers I had met but I realized the impropriety of his appearance in Paris at that time.

"Francis, you shouldn't—you really shouldn't," I protested.

He continued to hold my hand.

"I had to come, Leonora."

Sir Peregrine Waitley, Francis' cousin, sauntered up at the moment of Etienne's return and I introduced him to Etienne. If Etienne was surprised at finding Francis and his cousin in Paris he gave no sign of it, merely suggesting they accompany us to the Tuileries. Perry desisted—I suspected he had not come to Paris to admire its art treasures, at least not those of so inanimate a nature—but Francis accepted with alacrity and the three of us set forth.

Francis, with his great contempt for Etienne, was taken aback at his ready command of the French language, for Francis spoke that tongue as haltingly as I did myself. He was also astounded at his knowledge of Paris. Etienne showed us the *Allée des Orangers*, where orange trees in tubs, many of them of great age, were placed in the summer, and where the tumultuous crowd had waited for the sound of guns to announce the birth of a child to Napoleon and Marie Louise and then burst into shouts when the twenty-second gun made it known that child was a son. Etienne pointed out the window behind which resided the Duchesse d'Angouleme, the only surviving prisoner of the Temple, who kept beside her memorials of the last days of her parents, the tragic king and queen. Francis muttered to me,

"Wonder where he gets all this stuff. I feel as though I'm back with my tutor."

"Hush!" I whispered impatiently, for I was interested. Etienne must have detected Francis' lack of interest, for he soon suggested lunch on the left bank in the Latin Quarter.

Le Coq d' Or was crowded when we arrived but a table was miraculously set for us. The atmosphere was lively and soon we were devouring a repast of *turbot sauté a l'homme de confiance, vol au vent de poulet* and *parmentier*, the potatoes which had been brought into vogue by a French chemist of that name who had lived on them while imprisoned in Prussia and who returned to introduce them to French cuisine.

"Is there anything on which he is not informed?" Francis whispered caustically. But eventually the French wine improved his humour, and he became even more light-hearted when Etienne's attention was engaged in a long and heated discussion with students at the next table. From what I could understand they were comparing Bourbon and Buonapartist France, but with the rapid flow of the language and the many dialects I found it impossible to follow. I determined that before I returned to France I would gain a knowledge of the language which would allow my participation in such discussions, for it sounded more interesting than Francis' remarks which became more lugubrious as the carafes on our table emptied. Etienne seemed not to mind his attentions to me, even going so far as to invite him to accompany us to Versailles the following day.

When we arrived back in our suite I expected some question on Francis' sudden appearance, but none came. An express letter awaited him, and some business matter it contained seemed to cause him to consider a moment before turning to me.

"I think that we should return to London at the end of the week, if you have no objection."

"No, indeed," I said, drawing off my gloves. "If your affairs require your presence in London, by all means we should return, though I had thought that it was your intention that we should proceed from here to Italy."

"So it was," Etienne said, folding his letter. "Perhaps we can go there another time." Then he added with no attempt to hide the bitterness in his voice, "Italy, after all, is a land for lovers."

Chapter III

In London we settled into Etienne's four-storey house on Grosvenor Square. Though it was hardly more than a stone's throw from my father's house, I had not been inside it before it became my new home. It was one of the original terrace houses built by Sir Richard Grosvenor at the beginning of the previous century and had for a time been owned by the Duchess of Kendal, mistress of George I, bought with money she had gained from the South Sea Bubble scandal. Francis noted quite maliciously that it was apt for Etienne, who also profited from the misfortune of others, to have chosen to settle in that house.

But I liked it. The interior was spacious and, I had to admit, more tastefully decorated and furnished than our own house on Hill Street. The drawing room had been done by Adam in his favourite egg-shell blue panelling and it was there I suggested to Etienne that we place the largest of the Gobelin tapestries he had purchased while in France. He demurred, saying he would prefer to place in that space a likeness of me if I would consent to sit for Sir Thomas Lawrence, President of the Royal Academy.

"Going to exhibit another of his possessions," Francis sniffed when I began sitting for Lawrence. I felt there was some justice in his remark for the house was filled with priceless items, yet none of them was purely for show. Etienne had shown such taste and reason in their acquisition that I was sometimes given to question my own role among them.

Etienne's consideration and lack of demands upon me continued in London as they had in Paris, and I soon took up the strains of my old life much as before, though with increased opulence, and more often than not to his complete exclusion. Strangely, it was Cheddell, his secretary, and not Etienne himself, who resented my nonchalant behaviour towards my husband; but then Cheddell displayed toward Etienne the fierce loyalty of all his servants. He paid them handsomely for it I didn't doubt, especially after a particularly trying scene with his housekeeper, Mrs. Dunsmore. Though I took little interest in Etienne, I was determined to be mistress of his household and began by ordering the rearrangement of the furniture in the drawing room. When Mrs. Dunsmore protested, saying that it had been arranged according to Mr. Lambert's wishes, I became furious. I had been mistress in my father's house for a number of years, admittedly lackadaisically though it seemed to suit him well enough, and I let her know that in future I expected to be obeyed without question.

Later in the day I was of a mind to inform Etienne of the *contretemps* and went in the direction of his study. He was there with Cheddell, and I heard their male voices in the tones which bespoke their harmony with one another. I could imagine Cheddell's pale, earnest face as he hung on Etienne's words. Cheddell was the younger son of a reputable family known to my own. Etienne always spoke very highly of him, I suspected for my benefit because he knew I didn't like him. There could be no doubt that he served Etienne in an exemplary manner and had done so for nearly five years. I had been told he had refused more than one important government post.

Before I entered I heard him complaining to Etienne of my threatened dismissal of Dunsmore.

"Mrs. Dunsmore was very upset. She did not mean to be rude to Mrs.—I mean, Lady Leonora," Cheddell always seemed to have difficulty with my name, "but she felt the rearrangement of the large sofa so close to the doorway would impede those entering the room. I believe you tried it that way originally and found it to be so."

As I listened I had to admit that it was an inconvenient arrangement, but even when I had seen the difficulty I had refused to change it.

"I know, Alton," I heard Etienne soothe. "Mrs. Dunsmore spoke to me but I explained that Lady Leonora is mistress of this house and the servants must take their orders from her from now on. I'm sure I don't need to remind you of that should they speak to you. Now, what do you say to a visit to Lisbon. I have a delicate matter which must be negotiated with the minister of finance, and I don't wish to leave London myself just now. You are the only person I could entrust on such a mission. I need not tell you how much I rely on your good judgement."

Even though I could not see Cheddell's face, I guessed that a flush of pleasure mounted to his cheeks at Etienne's words. I had never known a dog to dote on his master as Cheddell doted on Etienne, though the praise, I suspected, was not undeserved. Etienne was always generous in praising those who deserved it.

The matter seemed settled and I saw no need of my

intervention, but as I walked away I overheard Etienne add,

"By the way, was that bank draft forwarded to Lord Castleford?"

"Yes, I attended to it myself yesterday," Cheddell answered.

I idly wondered why Etienne continued to send father money, for I knew his debts had been cleared at the time the marriage contract was signed. But it was of little concern to me, though there were times I remembered Phoebe's remarks and felt Papa had indeed used me as a pawn.

My friends had welcomed my return, and despite the unpopularity of my marriage our name was on every invitation list. I think they wanted to inspect Etienne and, though many were overtly supercilious, a surprising number of society matrons took a liking to him although he did not always return the compliment. When first we got back, Etienne accompanied me to balls and routs. He rarely danced, though, saying he preferred to leave me to younger partners. I noticed he soon grew bored with the social conversation which surrounded him, so much of which was pure gossip and in which he took scarcely any part, nor did he care for the card games in the adjoining rooms. He soon began to bring me to these engagements and then excuse himself, returning only to bring me home. Where he spent the intervening hours I could not say—he belonged to no club that I knew of—but I was too busily occupied with my own affairs to care much about it. As a young matron I had far greater freedom in my movements in society than I had been allowed in my single state. I was constantly surrounded by a bevy of admirers, none of whom I discouraged, though Francis was premier amongst them. Scarcely an issue of *Lady's Magazine* or *Ackermann's Repositary* failed to contain a complete description of what I wore, and the *Gazette* and *Morning Chronicle* were punctilious in detailing my activities with rarely any mention of Etienne.

Apart from seeing Francis almost nightly, I again took to driving with him in the park in the afternoon. I enjoyed his light, sometimes roguish banter, though his words of endearment sometimes caused me to question their propriety.

"Really, Francis, I am married now. You must not speak to me so."

"Pooh, all London knows it to be a marriage of convenience arranged by your Papa to get him out of a jam. Even Lambert's resigned to his position now. He lets you do as you wish. No other husband would stand for the way you flirt, I know I wouldn't. He's either very sure of his place in your affections or else he's married you for your connections, and from what I know of your lack of concern for him it must be the latter."

I started to protest but he argued.

"My feelings for you haven't changed, nor, from what I can see, have yours for me. Therefore if you still love me you cannot have convinced Lambert you love him. You're not that good an actress, Leonora."

It was true. I had myself sometimes wondered at Etienne's indulgence, but I had not before been aware that it was an open matter of discussion among my acquaintance. Francis examined my thoughtful face.

"Never mind," he said bitterly, looking down at the diamond on my hand and the sable-trim on the cuff of my *pelisse*, "You've done all right from it, though I dare say if you had married me we would have been happy without all the luxury."

I supposed he was right, though sometimes I found trying his persistent scorn of Etienne who invariably treated Francis with a courtesy of which he was totally undeserving. I was almost glad that Phoebe remained in Dorset, for I knew she would have given even less rein to a critical tongue than did her brother.

Etienne and I gave our first dinner at Grosvenor Square the day after my portrait was hung in the drawing room. Etienne studied it for a long time before turning to me,

"It is impossible to faithfully portray the original, but Lawrence has come as close as is feasible."

I smiled, but the intensity of his gaze, the desire I saw there, made me lower my eyes in embarrassment. I knew that one day I must allow him to become my husband in more than name—but not yet, not yet.

That dinner was the first of many which were to become the most sought-after engagements of the season. I had prepared my own list and casually, almost hesitatingly, asked Etienne if he wished to add any names, fearing he might choose some of his city acquaintances. When he returned it, it contained the name of that redoubtable statesman George Canning, and that of Sir Harvey Jerningham, an influential gentleman known to Papa, amongst others of note and repute.

"Are these friends of yours?" I questioned almost accusingly.

"You didn't take me to be completely friendless, did you?" he smiled.

"Of course not," I replied defensively, feeling however further baffled about his reasons for marrying me. If he had Canning and Jerningham among his acquaintance, what need had he for Papa's connections to advance him in society? Papa's friends were noble, but they were certainly not the brightest people in the world, most of their acumen being saved for games of chance with a notable lack of success. Besides, Etienne had shown a distinct disinterest in meeting people of my own acquaintance at the functions I attended. If he wanted to advance in society he was doing remarkably little to promote that cause. I was puzzled.

Jerningham, I discovered that first evening, was a particularly close friend of Etienne's and was also connected with his business dealings. He was a dashing figure, though older than Etienne I guessed, being closer in age to Papa. His brown hair was greying at the temples and he carried his beaked nose at a rather haughty angle though this did not prevent Etienne from treating him with an easy familiarity. I soon discovered he was a lady's man, for he never missed an opportunity of paying me extravagant compliments.

The acumen and wit of Etienne's friends and the beauty and style of mine made a stimulating combination. That and the luxury of our house and the ministrations of Benoit, who had studied with that master chef Carême, led to memorable entertainments at Grosvenor Square, evenings at which I much enjoyed presiding. In fact, as my presence there began to be accepted, though I knew the servants continued to look to Etienne for approval and it was always he who went down to compliment Benoit and joke with him on his constantly increasing family, I found I enjoyed entertaining at Grosvenor Square far more than at Hill Street. No matter the number of our guests, nor how unexpectedly they arrived, there was never a complaint from the kitchen, nor was there ever an insufficient number of dishes to go round. I was never troubled by tradesmen demanding to be paid, as had sometimes been the case at Hill Street. In fact I saw nothing of the household or my personal accounts. All were given to Cheddell and that was the last heard of them.

I observed my eighteenth birthday in May. It was to be our first ball at Grosvenor Square, and apart from the guest list Etienne told me to leave all else to him. Le Roy came from Paris to make my gown of nile green taffeta, and after much consideration I decided to wear only Mama's diamond pendant with it, which had been handed down through generations of my family. Though Etienne's emer-

alds were far more grand, I deemed it a fitting tribute to
Mama who had not lived to see me grow to womanhood. I
mentioned it to Etienne and he quite agreed.

A few days before the ball Francis called to suggest a
canter in the park since it was such a splendid day. I had
been bothered all morning with fittings and a visit from
Madame Garnier, a milliner of great repute and great expense whom Etienne had suggested I patronize; she had left
me with the distinct impression that she was looking me over
to see whether I was worthy to be her client. I agreed to
Francis' proposal with alacrity and rushed upstairs to
change. I burst into my room to find Etienne there. It was
the first time I had known him to enter my private apart-
ments. He must have realized the oddity of it also, for we
both flushed.

"Did you want something?" I asked, unable to keep from
my voice the annoyance I felt at his intrusion. That annoyance soon turned to curiosity as I looked down and saw
my diamond in his hand. He must have seen my glance for
he said, by way of explanation,

"I had your pendant cleaned and wished to put it away."

"You should have given it to my maid," I said and then
suddenly thought out loud, "But how did you get it?"

I kept my jewels in a locked box in a drawer in my dressing
table to which I alone kept the key.

Without replying he held up the heavy gold so that the
diamonds gleamed brilliantly,

"Don't you think it looks better now?"

It was true. It had not shone that way for years despite my
maid's brushing and polishing.

"It does indeed," I agreed, reaching for it. "How did they
do it?"

"I think they have a special kind of jeweller's rouge which
works miracles. Come, give me your box and I'll put it away
for you."

It struck me as odd that he wanted to do so, but I opened the drawer and got out the box which I began to unlock when he put his hand over mine.

"I'll put it away. Weren't you going somewhere? Why don't you run along."

There was no doubt he wished to be rid of me and I wanted to know why.

"What is it, Etienne? How did you get my pendant in the first place and why do you want to return it yourself?"

I had opened the box as I spoke and now stared down at another diamond pendant identical to the one he held in his hand but without its lustre and brilliance.

"Oh!" I cried in horror. "But how can it be?"

"It is paste, my love," he said, removing the pendant from the box and replacing it with the one in his hand. "I did not want you to know."

"But how—how can it be?" Then the truth jolted me. So, Papa had pawned even that but had replaced it with the replica of tin and glass, for since it had been Mama's I had always refused to part with it until he was threatened with prison. No wonder he had refused it then!

"Oh, Papa, how could he!" I cried out. "But how did you know?" Then I realized his practiced eye would easily tell glass from the brilliance of diamonds. Only I had been unaware of it.

"It doesn't matter," he said, slipping the replica in his pocket.

"Oh, thank you for finding it for me!" Impulsively I flung my arms around him and hugged. I felt his arms cling to me for an instant and his lips brushed my hair.

"Leonie, Leonie!" he whispered, "I would do anything for you, don't you know that by now?"

Immediately I stiffened, realizing the intimacy of our embrace, and just as quickly his arms dropped and he turned to go.

"I must not detain you. You were going somewhere, were you not?"

"Riding in the park with Francis."

"Then I certainly should not keep you," his voice was as expressionless as his face, though I detected a look of hurt in his eyes, as though I had suddenly berated him without cause.

"I suppose I don't have to go," I said lamely.

"It's a fine day. Why not enjoy it?" he declared unconvincingly as he turned to go, leaving me to dwell on Papa's duplicity and Etienne's generosity.

The morning of my birthday I came down close to noon, as was my custom, to find Etienne still at home. He was engrossed in the paper as I entered the morning room but immediately folded it and got up to kiss me on the cheek and to wish me a happy birthday.

"You're not going to the city this morning?" I asked in surprise and with some asperity for it was a cause of humiliation to me that he spent his time at a place of business rather than at a club.

"No." He offered no explanation, except to ask, "Have you breakfasted?"

"I had my usual chocolate and rolls in my room."

"Then come along. I've something to show you."

There was excitement in his voice and in the hand that gripped my arm pulling me over to the window. With puzzlement I looked out and then I gasped. There was the most elegant, silver-grey phaeton with smart black wheels, led by a perfectly matched, perfectly proportioned pair of greys.

"Oh! Is it really mine?"

"Happy birthday!" He smiled down at me.

"Then if it's mine I'm going to drive it immediately," I started to run outside.

"Not yet, Leonie. You may only drive it alone when you

convince me you are capable of doing so. You may have your first opportunity this morning."

Etienne was an admirable teacher, absolutely fearless even when I almost overturned us as we started off by taking a sharp curve at too fast a pace. He said not a word but dexterously took the reins from me and righted our course. He never admonished me for my mistakes but taught me by doing rather than telling. I discovered he was an admirable whip and admonished him for never driving in the park in the afternoon.

"If I want to drive a team I want an open country road. I see no sense in tooling around the crowded row showing off my skills or lack thereof for the benefit of others."

"But they would all admire you," I argued.

"What need have I of their admiration?" he responded.

It was true, I thought. He was sure of his own worth and seemed not to care what others thought of him. Yet I had been brought up to believe in the importance of public acceptance and found his manner of flouting society difficult to understand.

"If you choose to admire me, however," he went on with a slight smile, "I promise not to object."

Chapter IV

My birthday celebration was a success. Even the Countess of Newbury, who was noted for brilliance of her entertainments, had pronounced herself quite amused by the evening. Champagne had been brought from France. Benoit had outdone himself in the kitchen. Music was provided by the Philharmonic Society, and Louis Spohr himself sat at our grand pianoforte and played an overture which Beethoven had composed in my honour. Throughout the evening—in fact throughout the whole night, for many guests stayed to breakfast with us—I shone with a light only known on certain rare instances in life. It was all for me, the congratulations, the celebration, the glory—all was mine and I revelled in it. I went to bed that morning having come of age with a pomp and circumstance of which I felt thoroughly deserving and thoroughly satisfied. I awoke late, secure in the knowledge that when I descended, all the disturbance in the house would have been put to right and I had only to bask in my own glory. It simply didn't occur to me to think of Etienne's role in it all.

My driving lessons continued until Etienne finally pronounced me fit to drive my phaeton without his assistance. He insisted, however, that a groom accompany me at all times, riding postillion; nor would he allow me to select my own but chose a short, ugly little man, not at all the sort I wished. When I protested he merely said,

"Ennis is a good man. I can trust him to react with alacrity and with good common sense in any situation. As for his appearance, perhaps he is not the handsomest figure in the world, but believe me, with you at the reins no one will have eyes for your groom."

So Ennis stayed.

Etienne proved right, though. My first appearance in Hyde Park driving my phaeton and pair at the fashionable four o'clock hour created a minor sensation. I had commissioned Madame Garnier to make me a new Leghorn hat trimmed with silver and dark rust ostrich feathers for the occasion. That and the beauty of my horses and my ability to handle them in the crush of carriages at that hour caused many a glance of open admiration from the gentlemen and equally envious ones from their ladies.

"By God!" Francis said, drawing alongside. "I'll bet Lambert paid dearly for that pair."

"I have no idea," I shrugged. "Come on up with me Francis and let me show you their paces."

"And who's to take care of my rig?" he demanded.

"Ennis will," I replied, but on my motioning to the groom to get down and take the other chaise he adamantly refused.

"No, Lady Leonora, I can't do that. Mr. Lambert said I was not to leave you."

"But you are my groom and I insist on it. If I order you to do something you will do it." I flicked my whip angrily as I spoke.

"No, my ladyship, begging your pardon. Mr. Lambert

employs me and I follow his instructions," was his obdurate reply.

"We'll see about that."

But when I complained bitterly to Etienne on my return I became even more furious because he took Ennis's side.

"He was right, Leonie, those were and are my orders to him. He is there for your protection."

"But I thought you said I was mistress of the servants."

"Within the household it is so, but outside I must be the judge. I know London and I know what can happen."

At times I wondered whether I was even mistress in my own house. Though I was obeyed by the servants, it was never with the alacrity with which Etienne's slightest wish was answered or even foretold. In response, my own attitude toward them became more imperious and, though I knew they resented it, I knew Etienne unfailingly took my side.

"Whew!" Francis ejaculated the next day when he rode beside me having brought his own groom to walk his horses. "Where'd you ever learn to handle a whip like that?"

"Etienne taught me." I said nonchalantly, passing between two carriages with only inches to spare on either side.

"I didn't know he had much prowess with the ponies," he drawled with evident sarcasm. "I thought he confined his ability to the 'Change."

"Well, he's a fine whip," I replied firmly, "and he's a very good teacher. But go on, weren't you telling me about Dolly Meredith and the captain of the hussars who's been following her around."

I sighed with relief as Francis again took up the strain of his latest *on-dit*. For some reason I hated him to talk of Etienne to me; it always made me feel defensive and I didn't quite know why. I suppose I felt it was alright for me to denigrate him but I did not care to hear him maligned by others.

I and my equipage, with Francis seated beside me or riding at my side, soon became a familiar sight in the park, but I did not realize how conspicuous we had become until one afternoon when father was taking tea with me he suddenly exclaimed,

"I do wish you wouldn't see quite as much of young Oliphant as you do. I believe you see more of him now than you did before you were married. Everyone is talking. I wonder Lambert allows it."

"Etienne has no say in who I choose for my friends," I replied coolly.

"Well, there is such a thing as too much rein, and sometimes I think that is what he allows you." Then he added far too casually, "How is your marriage going by the way?"

"As well as might be expected,"

"And what, precisely, is that supposed to mean? He gives you everything, does he not?"

"Yes, I suppose he does."

"And you?" he asked again with the same studied casualness, "When are you going to give him a son? You've been married close to six months and I see no signs of your being in the family way."

My father's sudden interest in Etienne and the issue or lack thereof from our marriage surprised and annoyed me. I wondered what he would say if he knew I had not yet allowed my husband to share my bed. It was none of his business, I thought, angered at his probing.

"What concern is it of yours?" I responded, then I suddenly remembered that overheard remark of Etienne's on the subject of a bankdraft for father. "Is Etienne making you some kind of allowance?" I demanded.

Papa didn't reply, but his flushed cheeks confirmed my guess.

"And a child would secure that allowance, wouldn't it

Papa? It is not enough that you have sold me to the highest bidder with no regard for my personal feelings?"

I saw Papa look beyond me to the door and his eyes widen slightly until he composed his features into a wreath of greeting. I turned and one glance at Etienne's eyes told me he had at least overheard my last remark. He looked quickly away from me to greet Papa and when he looked back his eyes had the veiled expression which was to remain there in the days that followed.

From that time on his demeanour toward me changed in a way which was hard to pinpoint. He seemed more restrained in his admiration of my appearance and exploits, somehow quieter, more reflective than usual. For my part I found I missed his compliments and paradoxically went to more pains to please him, even refusing some of my invitations to spend those evenings at home with him. He made no comment when I stayed, accepting my presence or absence with at least outward diffidence.

It was after one of these evenings alone together—it had, in fact, been a pleasant evening, excellent duck for dinner served with a fine wine from Alsace—and after we had played chess (though he had finally bested me I had given him a greater fight than he had bargained for); as we were climbing the stairs towards bed, I abruptly made my decision, and I said in a low voice, perhaps not wishing to be heard,

"You may come to me tonight, if you wish."

He stopped and looked at me almost in disbelief.

"Do *you* wish it?" he asked roughly.

I could not bring myself to reply. The intensity of his tone and his gaze made me believe he would detect a lie if it were told. I lowered my eyes and nodded. I believe he took my response for shyness, for he took me in his arms, murmuring my name.

"Leonie, Leonie, how I've waited for you to say that."

Then he kissed me as he had never kissed me before, his lips meeting mine with such passion that all my former fears of lovemaking as Aunt Agatha had described it returned.

We reached my door and he was about to follow me inside, but I desisted.

"Wait, until I am prepared for you," I said hastily, but he kissed me again before he left.

I sat long before my mirror, brushing my hair, wondering why I had made such a rash decision. Was it because he had overheard my remark to Papa and had been hurt? But I had only told the truth—I had not wanted him. Still he was my husband and eventually I would be forced to acknowledge it in fact as well as in name. Tonight was as good as any, I supposed. I sighed. It had to be done but I vowed that I would not allow him to enjoy it. He could come to my bed but only on my terms, only when I allowed it. He might do whatever it was he had to do, but I would take no active part in it.

I heard him knock on the door and paused before bidding him enter. He came and sat beside me on the bed, taking my hands in his.

"Do you really want me?" he asked again. Again I nodded, fearing to speak, fearing truth would prevail and I would tell him how much I hated it.

Then he held me close to him, whispering my name softly, repeatedly, kissing me again with the passion he had shown earlier. But now his hands caressed my body in a more intimate way and I had to remind myself of my vow not to allow him to arouse me. It was only when I began to relax, against my better judgement, that he began to consummate our marriage. But then I intensified the pain I felt on losing my virginity far beyond its true extent and immediately he stopped.

"God knows I don't want to hurt you, Leonie."

"Go on," I said fiercely. "Finish what you have begun."

"Not yet," he murmured. "It's not that important. We can wait."

When next he made love to me I made no cry nor did I participate. True to my resolution, I held my body perfectly still as he completed his act, exulting in the knowledge of his dissatisfaction.

"It will be better later," he murmured, kissing me lightly. I said nothing, pretending to fall asleep, and not long after he got up and went to his room.

Nothing was said the next day, but soon after he asked if he might come to me again. I agreed, without enthusiasm, and when he came I lay as silent and still as before. Though he caressed me for a long time and though I felt strange emotions tingling through my body to the extremities of my fingertips and toes, and an even stranger churning, pulsating motion within, I steeled myself to lie still as soon as he began to make love to me. Again I succeeded and again I felt his disappointment. But I had cast myself in the role of Anaxerete, the cold-hearted Cyprian. Though I had no wish for Etienne to hang himself, as had her lover, nor had I any wish to be turned into a statue as she had for refusing her lover, still I was determined to play the role I had adopted. I had not wanted this marriage, I argued to myself. I did not love him, why should I pretend? If I had felt some passions within me as his hands moved deftly across those secret places of my body, it had not been love which aroused them, of that I was certain. I would allow him this intimacy to give him the child he wanted, but that was all.

But the next time he made love to me I found it increasingly difficult not to respond to him. I forced myself to be still but as I was beginning to wonder whether, in fact, I could resist matching his passion with the swell I felt gathering within threatening to overcome my sternest admonitions, suddenly he stopped and lay still for a moment before he got up and threw on his robe. I saw the outline of his face in the moonlight, stern and unrelenting.

"Where are you going?" I asked.

"Out," he said tersely, crossing the room.

"Out—at this hour? But where?"

"Somewhere—somewhere where there's warmth and human feeling," he flung at me as he slammed the door.

I heard him dress and stride downstairs and then I heard the front door slam shut.

I did not see him for two days.

I arose early the next day, determined to find out what had happened to him. I was sure that Cheddell knew of his whereabouts for I had seen him working in his study with a singular lack of concern, but I was loathe to ask him.

I went into the breakfast room and it was with great surprise and relief I saw Etienne's familiar, tall figure seated in his usual place at the head of the table. He was freshly shaved and wore clean linen, yet I knew he had not occupied his chamber for three nights. He looked up from the newspaper he was reading and wished me good morning in a tone of complete normalcy. My relief turned to anger.

"Where have you been?" I demanded. "You sent me not a word."

He raised an eyebrow. "I had no idea you had any interest in my whereabouts," he said, sipping his coffee and then reaching for a piece of toasted bread which he proceeded to butter with care. "The smoked haddock is excellent this morning. I highly recommend it."

"I only want coffee," I said haughtily, sitting down opposite him. I saw him about to reach for the newspaper again, and stung by his indifference I flung at him,

"I suppose you've been out with your Covent Garden hussies."

He stared at the paper for a moment with insouciance before turning to me.

"At least the hussies of Covent Garden have some feeling within them. Even those who are bought give return for their money. But of course, I forgot—I bought you also, didn't I? I have always tried to keep my personal life separated from my business affairs. In this case I didn't. It was a mistake but it is one which can be reconciled."

"And just how can it be reconciled?" I demanded. "We are married, are we not?"

"Even the bonds of matrimony, those crippling, silken cords, can be severed if one has the money and knows the right people."

"You can't mean a divorce!" My hands flew to my cheeks in horror.

He replied in a softer tone, "I really think it might make life more bearable for both of us."

"No!" I cried. "I will not hear of it. No Fordyce has ever been through the disgrace of such an action. I will never agree to it."

"I won't press the matter now," he said. "But I urge you to think on it."

"If it is because you wish to—to take your pleasure elsewhere, I assure you that you may. I don't care in the least."

"I'm quite sure you don't," was his laconic reply.

"I am perfectly willing to give you the heir you want. I shall then have fulfilled my part of the bargain."

"I assure you I have no wish for any child born of a nuptial couch such as I experienced with you on those few occasions you allowed me into your cloistered, hallowed chamber. I could have no love for any infant that would result from such a sorry mating. For my part I found it more obscene than any Roman orgy, and I have no desire and no intention of ever repeating it."

"But how do you plan to beget an heir for your fortune?" I demanded, stung by his scorn.

"Not in that manner, I assure you. I would prefer to leave

my fortune to orphanages and hospitals where it may serve a useful purpose rather than to some child of duty born, begat by an unwilling wife and a foolish husband."

"Why did you marry me, if it was not for an heir?" I challenged.

He paused, deep in thought for a moment, before answering.

"I did not expect to find myself saying with Epictitus, 'A worthless girl has enslaved me whom no enemy ever did,' yet that is about what happened. You see, I saw you at the Drury Lane theatre long before I met you. I had gone for the play and now I cannot even remember what it was that took me there. I only know I saw you in a box with a group of your friends and I thought of nothing else after that. I made it my business to find out who you were but I made no effort to meet you. I had more sense then. I thought it would be quite as impossible as it has turned out to be. But then your father came to me for help. I knew him for a reprobate. I never waste money pulling such people from their own foolish quagmires, but I admit I went to him only because I hoped to see you. And when I did, everything I had felt the first time returned. Call it foolishness, call it stupidity; I have pitied other men for less. You were right when you said I bought you, but I bought you hoping that it would not always be so, hoping that you would come to care for me. That was my greatest stupidity, but at least I now clearly see and acknowledge it and it may not be too late. I offer you your freedom and in doing so I assure you I will take all the blame. I have no intention of naming that simpering fop who follows you like a comet-tail. I doubt he would ever have the audacity to allow his feeling full rein for fear of creasing his neckcloth. You are an admirably matched pair."

"I will not consider divorce," I reiterated, overcome by learning now of his true reason for marrying me, and flushing at his reference to Francis. "I cannot allow my name to be dragged through the courts and Parliament even as an innocent party."

"Ah, yes, your precious name. I forgot about that—that and the necessity of keeping up appearances. Neither have ever been very important to me."

"Of course not," my voice was sharp as a whip, stung as I was by his present indifference. "You never had anything to protect."

As soon as the words left my lips I wished I had not uttered them. I saw his cheek flush and his eyes grow dark as craters on the moon.

"No, you're right." He folded his serviette in a deliberate manner. "I have nothing to protect, nothing at all. It is not a matter which must be decided this morning, but I suggest you think on it carefully. I assure you I shall be generous in settling an allowance upon you as well as your illustrious father."

A retort rose to my lips, but before I could say anything more he bade me goodday and was gone, the revelations of the morning leaving me more disconsolate than I would have believed possible.

Chapter V

Though Etienne continued to be polite and considerate toward me after that morning encounter, no longer was there the slightest overt expression of admiration or affection from him and, unaccountably, now that it was not there, I missed it. We entertained a great deal in the weeks that followed at my instigation, for unless guests were invited, more often than not he would go off on his own leaving me to my own devices whether I had an engagement or not. Our lives became more separate than ever but strangely it pleased me less. We seldom dined alone anymore, for when Etienne was at home he always had friends or business associates with him. Quite often Jerningham was at our table and on those occasions I made a marked effort to attract his attention. It was not difficult for he was fond of pretty women and I knew he was attracted to me. That I openly encouraged him and that he responded with pleasure did not escape Etienne's attention. It was my intention and I was pleased because, for the most part, Etienne seemed to give not one jot for anything else I did.

After our quarrel I had deliberately invited Francis into

our house, often allowing him to spend entire afternoons with me and making sure that he would be there and very definitely visible at an hour when Etienne usually returned. But his only response had been a pleasant, even friendly greeting for Francis and then withdrawal to allow us to continue our *tête-a-tête*.

"I can't understand him," Francis shook his head. "Any other husband would be beside himself with rage at a young wife carrying on with her former lover, but he seems almost to encourage it."

"To call yourself my former lover implies more than ever existed between us," I responded sharply. "You should not even think of yourself in those terms."

"If you mean we have not actually made love, I see no reason why we shouldn't," was his frank reply. "Goodness knows I've wanted to often enough. You allow me so many liberties already I don't see why we should not indeed become lovers. You know how I feel toward you and I know your feelings for me are unchanged."

But my feelings for Francis were changed. I don't know when or how it happened, but when he suggested that we should become lovers, a relationship on which I had often dwelt ardently, I found I was actually repulsed by the idea.

"How could you suggest such a thing, Francis Oliphant," I jumped up. "And under my own roof. I am shocked. I begin to suspect you have no respect for me at all. I'll thank you to leave and not return again unless you are invited by my husband."

Francis looked at me in disbelief.

"Good God, Leonora, you're not going to give me the bit of the dutiful, faithful wife horrified at the advances from her former—" he must have noticed the dangerous light in my eye for he concluded carefully "her former admirer, are you? You know you don't give a fig for that husband of yours and no more does he for you from his attitude. He may have done once, but not anymore."

Francis' outspoken statement of the truth, that I had had Etienne's love and had lost it, made me angrier than ever and I stamped my foot and ordered him from my sight that very moment. He left in a huff of discontent, shaking his head.

"I don't understand you, Leonora, I really don't."

Nor did I understand myself. I only knew that now that I no longer had Etienne's attention I wanted it more than ever. Yet no matter how well I dressed, or how satisfied I was with my own image in the looking glass, I could never produce that light of admiration in his eyes and I missed it. I spent even larger sums at the dressmaker and the mantuamaker. I had Madame Garnier make me several hats, each one more elaborate than the last, and I sent to France for velvets and laces. I bought expensive jewellery; anything which caught my eye which I thought would attract Etienne I wore, only to throw it aside when it aroused not the slightest comment. If I deliberately brought something to his attention, he would nod and say "Very nice" in a tone which he might have used to admire a new picture on the wall or a cushion on the sofa. Altogether it infuriated me. Even the huge sums of money I was spending aroused no comment. My bills were paid without a raised eyebrow or a single caution against my heedless extravagance. Even I was shocked one month when I totalled the amount I had spent and found it to be more than nine thousand pounds, yet there was not a word of rebuke.

The balls, the assemblies, the routs, all that had formerly been so amusing, my bevy of admirers, the envious glances aroused by my jewels and furs, the flirtations, all of it now bored me. Etienne graced none of these affairs, nor did he any longer conduct me to them. He delegated this function to Unwin, a young assistant of Cheddell's. When I complained he merely shrugged.

"You don't have to attend if you don't wish. You know that I care for none of it. However, if you do wish to be with your friends I suggest either that they call and accompany you or allow Unwin to escort you. I would hardly suggest you go abroad at night merely with your groom, though it is your decision. You are of age."

I was provoked beyond endurance. He did not attempt to hide his complete indifference for me and my welfare.

"Unwin can hardly provide much protection," I snapped.

"He acquitted himself very favourably at Waterloo. I have no reason to believe he would do less for you than he did for his country."

"There is little you would know of Waterloo. You were not there. You have never served your country."

"No, I was not at Waterloo. You are quite right. Nevertheless you may take my word for it, Unwin was and he acted very bravely."

Again he retired behind his wall of indifference, a wall which was becoming more impregnable as time passed.

One night I was almost expiring from boredom at the Meredith's rout. The crush was formidable and Dolly was at her most exuberant, an air of hers which invariably irritated me. There was absolutely no one there who interested me and I was about to call my carriage when I ran into Perry Waitley. I had not seen him since Paris and the sight of a new face pleased me.

"You're looking very elegant, Leonora. Where are you off to?" he asked in response to my greeting.

"It's all too boring here, Perry, and too hot by half. I've decided to go home."

"Don't blame you," he agreed. "I'm off too, but it's too early to go home. I'm going to Lorimer's establishment on Curzon Street."

"What's the attraction there?" I asked without much enthusiasm.

"Oh, a hand of whist in pleasant company, or some speculation at hazard. Jolly good food too. Why don't you come? You might enjoy it, at least I assure you the company will be more select than here. Lorimer doesn't let just anybody in."

I had no interest in gambling. I had seen what it had done to Papa. But that evening I had a desire for a change—I didn't care what. I had never tried my hand at either game he mentioned. It might be fun. At least it would ensure I was not in bed before midnight, something I could scarcely endure.

I need not have worried. It was almost four by the time I put my head on my pillow and I had had a splendid time. Lorimer had welcomed me effusively and had personally conducted me round his lavish premises showing me how each game was played—hazard, faro, piquet, whist—and he proudly told me that if I did not find my preferred form of speculation he would personally see that it was instituted before my return. He was an amusing man, short, dark inclined to be swarthy, probably of my father's age but not altogether unattractive. He paid great attention to me, escorting me to late supper where an impressive array of dishes was offered. I saw many of my friends among his chosen guests, but it was Perry who encouraged me to make my first bet. As I laid that first guinea on the queen of hearts at the faro table and the dealer dealt the coup, my queen falling on his right hand and my own guinea being joined by one which I had done so little to earn, I chortled with delight. Mr. Lorimer at my side whispered,

"You see how easy it is, Lady Leonora."

I did. I could do nothing wrong that evening, even when I moved to hazard, a game seldom played by ladies, grasping the die and casting my main with the best. If that number did not turn up as I had forecast, more often than not it was a nick, a number by which the caster also won, and when odds were called I won, either in the role of caster or setter. The gentlemen there began following me in my line of betting and Mr. Lorimer, who at last saw me to my carriage, said that though he was delighted to have me grace his establishment, if my luck continued I would make of him a ruined man.

"Such beauty and such chance, what a devastating combination to a man in my profession," he murmured as he bent over and kissed my hand, holding it a trifle longer than necessary. "Nevertheless, I earnestly hope you will come back."

"Perhaps," I said airily.

I was, in fact, there again the following night, but instead of winning I went down—a mere hundred guineas, hardly enough to deter me. It was enough, however, to make me empathise with Papa as the die rolled and I felt an involuntary tightening of the muscles of my stomach. The stake meant little to me, but it became important to win for the sake of winning. Even when, without my at first realizing it, the stake increased and still I lost, still I played. This turn in my fortunes continued so that a few nights later I found myself unable to settle my losses. Mr. Lorimer was quite apologetic as he asked for my note.

"A mere formality, Lady Leonora, but in this business I must keep track of my gains as well as my losses. I am sure you understand."

I nodded briefly as I scribbled an IOU.

"Present this to my husband's secretary, Mr. Cheddell, and you will be paid."

To me that was the end of the business. I hardly found gambling as attractive when I lost. I supposed I was not a true gambler in the sense that Papa was. I would probably not have returned to Curzon Street had it not been for

Etienne. He met me in the hall the following afternoon as I returned from driving in the park.

"There is a matter I wish to discuss with you if you have a moment," he began. From the straight set of his mouth I suspected trouble as I followed him into his study but somehow I didn't care. At least I had broken through his indifference.

He reached across his desk and handed me the note I had written Lorimer the previous night.

"Is this really yours?" he asked.

"Of course," I averred, giving it a cursory glance.

"Then I will pay this one, but it will be the last gambling debt of yours I will pay."

I looked at him in astonishment. The amount was far less than my dressmaker's bills, or the cost of one hat from Madame Garnier. I wondered why he drew the line at this. In answer to this unspoken query he went on,

"If it becomes known that you gamble, half the sharks in London will be on your trail. I have no intention of them gaining my fortune through you. I have seen that happen to too many men and so, I should have thought, have you. But perhaps that is your intent, to ruin me financially. I regret, however, that it will not work. I intend to let it be known that I will not cover for your future gambling losses. For your part do not expect me to be duped by presenting them to me in the form of personal or household accounts. Believe me, I know the difference."

"Are you ordering me not to frequent Lorimer's?" I tossed my head in disdain, though secretly I was glad of his albeit disapproving interest.

"You may go where you wish. I neither tell you where to go nor what to do. I thought you must have realized that by now. I am, however, telling you that if you suffer losses you must be willing to pay them yourself."

"But I have no money in my own right, you know that—apart from my allowance, of course."

"Are you finding it difficult to exist on a thousand pounds a quarter as pocket money?" he asked blandly. "If so, it can be raised, within reason of course. If separation between us comes to suit you, rest assured I shall make a settlement upon you in which you or some legal representative can have every say."

I decided not to pursue his last remark.

"My allowance is a generous one, I am aware of that. But if I go over that limit, I wonder how you suggest that I pay my own losses?"

"You could sell your jewellery, I suppose," he said in a disinterested tone, turning to the stack of papers in the midst of his desk as though the matter were closed. "Some women, I understand, settle these matters in other ways."

"That is absolutely disgusting," I objected.

"You are quite right, it is disgusting, yet it is done."

"And is that how you propose I should settle my debts," I pressed.

"If you choose to contract those debts, it is for you to decide. I suggest nothing."

"No gentleman would refuse to settle a debt of honour," I flung at him.

"You seem to overlook two things. Firstly the debt, should it arise, would be yours, not mine. Secondly, I have never at any time taken upon myself that appallingly thin cloak of an English gentleman and all the meaningless *fal de ral* which accompanies it. I would prefer, for instance, to pay my tailor or bootmaker or cabinetmaker, any man who has expended his materials and labour on my behalf, before I would consider paying a debt incurred in the frantic attempt to drive boredom from one's doors. Yet I have seen men, even men in the flower of their youth, commit suicide or fight meaningless duels over such frivolities. If to be a gentleman means to embrace such foolishness, I want no part of it. I seek only to act honestly and with reason in my dealings with all men—and women, too. It is for that reason I am talking to you now. I hope you can understand."

For a moment I thought I saw a softening in his dark eyes as he looked up at me, but immediately he turned away again as though he sensed I had noticed it and felt vulnerable, adding coldly,

"I have nothing more to say on the matter. For my part it is closed."

I ignored an inexplicable impulse to run to him and throw my arms around him. As though to squelch that desire, I turned to leave, but not before uttering,

"I have no intention of allowing you to rule on my activities."

"No more shall I, though I would suggest that if you continue to gamble you decide not to lose."

That night I returned to Lorimer's to be greeted warmly, my debt having been paid as promised. I gambled extravagantly and with abandon. Even Perry, who was with me at the faro table, cautioned,

"Steady on, old girl, don't want to lose all Lambert's blunt in one night."

By the time I left I was down close to five thousand pounds and I wrote my IOU with a flourish.

Etienne made no comment to me in the days that followed and I decided he had retreated from his intractable position. On my next visit to Curzon Street, however, Lorimer called me aside and showed me my IOU to which was attached a terse note from Etienne refusing to pay it.

"I spoke to Mr. Cheddell," Lorimer explained apologetically, "but he says there is nothing he can do. Mr. Lambert is adamant in his refusal to pay and suggested I speak to you about settling the matter."

I saw Lorimer's eyes run assessingly over me and replied

with as much dignity as I could muster at that moment. "You will be paid."

He smiled in a more intimate manner than before.

"I'm sure I shall, one way or another."

That night I played not for the fun of the game but to win, for the money. Yet when I left in the early hours of the morning I was forced to leave another note for close to three thousand pounds.

"I hope to see you again soon, Lady Leonora," Lorimer stood over me as I wrote. "Perhaps you would care to call to discuss the matter. I am at leisure in the afternoons. We could be alone."

"I would not care to call on you then or any other time. You will be paid—tomorrow."

In truth I had no idea how to raise the sum if Etienne would not pay it and, despite my fatigue, I went down to confront him at the breakfast table.

"How could you humiliate me so!" I raged, forgetting all my carefully planned speeches at the sight of his bland face.

"Humiliate you, how so?" he asked, as though in genuine puzzlement.

"Your refusal to pay my note to Lorimer."

"Oh, that. But I told you I would not pay any such debts. Don't you yet know me well enough to take me at my word?"

"It was disgusting and humiliating. I have told him he will be paid today."

"Then I suggest you arrange it without delay. It was something over four thousand was it not? Your allowance is due shortly. I can advance it if you wish."

"It is closer to eight thousand," I said, gulping slightly.

"Ah, eight thousand pounds, that is different. Lorimer might not consider your favours worth such a sum."

"You beast, I hate you!"

"I am well aware of that," he replied evenly.

"I must have that money today. I promised it."

"Then I know that if you gave him your word as a lady, you will comply. But I warn you not to use my name in finding the sum. I told you, I shall pay any expenses of yours except those incurred in such foolish waste."

"But what shall I do?"

"I suggest you go through your jewellery and then become acquainted with London's pawnbrokers—they're an odd breed, but not without their own fascination."

"But you can scarcely expect someone like me to go to such a place as a pawnbrokers!" I said in horror.

"Someone like you?" He raised his eyebrows in question.

"A lady, a lady of noble birth," I said firmly.

"I dare say you will find plenty of your noble friends from Curzon Street there. You will feel quite at home."

"Well, I refuse to go. If you will force me to do such a humiliating thing, then I shall ask Cheddell to take care of it for me."

"Then perhaps I must remind you that Cheddell works for me. I have expressly forbidden him to take part in this matter. It is your affair. You got into it despite my warning. Now it is for you to get out of it. If you learn a little about life in the doing it will not come amiss."

It was with great humiliation that I made my way later in the day, after some cautious enquiries, to a dark shop in Cheapside where I parted with my emeralds for the sum of eight thousand pounds, well aware that they had cost over four times that sum. Despite the mortification of the moment, I had an odd sense of pride. It was the first matter I had ever handled on my own without any help from others. I think it was then, as I wrote my note to Lorimer enclosing the sum owed and vowed to myself to visit neither establishment again, that I first came of age.

Chapter VI

A quiet truce ensued between us. Etienne did not ask whether my debt was settled nor did I volunteer any information. With the onset of the summer months London society began to thin out, and I considered repairing to one of the estates Etienne held or even going down to Briarsmere. But somehow the thought of going anywhere on my own was unappealing. Boredom was staved off, however, by the advent of the Countess of Newbury's masked ball, the last event of the season and one which promised to be the most exciting. Everyone was keeping secret the identity of the costumes to be worn, but speculation ran rampant and provided many a piquant guessing game.

"I suspect you will go as Cleopatra," Jerningham said to me one evening after he had dined at our table. His remark surprised me since I thought he had no interest in the ball. Although he was on the most sought-after guest lists, he rarely attended any purely social functions, unless it were something likely to advance his fortune. Etienne was the one who did that, and though at first I had considered that the basis of their friendship, I saw he relied upon Etienne rather than Etienne being the one at pains to keep that friendship. Jerningham was a widower, his wife who had been some years his senior having passed away—some said from boredom, others from being forced to entertain her husband's paramours. Despite these rumours he was sought after by London hostesses but he rarely graced their drawing rooms. I suspected he preferred to take his pleasures in a more raffish element of society.

"Surely you are not attending?" I replied, neither acknowledging nor denying his guess. In truth I could not decide on my costume, though the thought of going as Cleopatra had crossed my mind.

"Why not," he replied. "It's just the sort of thing which might amuse me, somewhere I can go completely incognito. It is such a help in discarding one's inhibitions."

I laughed outright. "There is nothing inhibited about you."

"It wasn't myself I was referring to." He looked at me speculatively. "I would like to see you with your guard down."

"What guard?" I challenged.

"Oh, you have a guard around yourself all the time. I see it constantly, even when you flirt with me, perhaps then most of all. It makes me wonder what the you underneath is like."

He eyed me lazily as he spoke, and without quite knowing why I found myself blushing. My discomfort was enough to persuade me to discontinue a conversation which I felt was becoming subject to misinterpretation, but I noticed Etienne's eyes drift enquiringly from me to my companion before returning to his own conversation. It was enough to make me continue the game a little longer.

"And what should I look for at Lady Newbury's ball. Will you go as Nero, complete with fiddle, or Sir Gawain, or perhaps the green knight himself?" I teased.

"Oh, dear me, no. Lovelace would be more to my taste, though I think I might make a dashing Casanova, don't you? But I won't press you any more on your costume. I think no matter how good your disguise I shall recognize you. I have memorized that splendid shape of yours. I think of it often, especially when I am alone at night."

I was now sure that I should discontinue the trend our conversation had taken, and I offered to refill his coffee cup in such frozen tones that though he smiled with malicious satisfaction, he did, in fact, begin to talk of running into Papa at White's and of how well he had found him.

It was not until a few days before the event that I decided what I would wear. I had been hesitating between Helen of Troy and Queen Elizabeth, but I knew there would probably be more than one of each of them represented. Then I wandered into Etienne's library and picked up a book on Joan of Arc. I'd never thought much about her before, except that she'd been burned at the stake, a particularly revolting end, and by the English, too. But I read on and was enthralled. That a girl, a girl of my years, could have the fortitude to lead an army in defence of her king. How noble! How admirable! By the time I closed the book I had decided that I admired her more than any woman and I determined that for one night at least I would go in her guise.

The crush at Lady Newbury's was beyond belief, but it was a fine evening and the French doors to the garden were open to allow for fresh air and a gradual exodus from the crowded ballroom onto the terrace and the walks beyond. The exterior grounds were well lit and presented the appearance of a miniature Vauxhall, though the twinkling lamps did not extend to the outermost walks.

The sumptuous, often bizarre costumes, and the masks

which covered the guests' faces almost completely obscuring them, gave an air of fantasy and mystery to the evening and there was a general atmosphere of merriment and carefree gaiety. It was true that, for the most part and despite attempts at disguise, the voices gave away the identities of the illustrious throng, so that there were soon cries of "Not you as Alfred, burning cakes and all, oh dear, no!" and "I might have known you would be Juno, it is only too apt," to poor Miss Talmadge who stood close to six feet in height.

I spoke little beyond a few murmured assents and denials, enjoying my anonymity, until I found myself grasped round the waist and whirled out onto the dance floor by a dashing Henry the Eighth who informed me triumphantly,

"I told you I would discover you immediately. I recognized that tiny waist and the sumptuous form above immediately." He caressed that waist freely as he spoke and I warned him sharply.

"Really, Sir Harvey, behave yourself. This is no Cyprians' ball!"

"Frankly I find it hard to tell where it differs from one— just look around you."

It was true. The dancers were behaving in a more abandoned manner than I had ever observed in a London ballroom.

"I assure you," Jerningham continued unperturbed, "they are even freer with their embraces on the terrace and beyond."

"I thank you for your warning, then," I replied haughtily. "I shall confine my activities to within."

"Dear me, don't tell me you're the type of woman who conducts all her flirting before her husband and is a perfect prude when alone."

I flushed at his perspicacity without reply.

"I don't approve of teases, and I don't put up with them. If women tease me I make it my business to gain what their eyes have promised, preferably with, but if necessary without their consent."

"I promised you nothing," I objected, "and you can demand nothing from me."

I attempted to leave him on the dance floor but his grip upon my waist tightened.

"We shall see," he said, smiling, and began to chat innocently of our joint acquaintance while I made a resolve not to approach the much-married monarch again that evening.

My hand was claimed almost immediately by a Robin Hood who spoke English so atrociously, and with such a heavy French accent, that I took it for a disguise until all my efforts to catch him off guard failed and I decided he must be a visitor to our shores.

"Please excuse the Eengleesh," he apologized after having got hopelessly tangled in a description of a visit to the Tower.

"But you speak very well," I lied, adding quite superfluously, "Are you from France?"

"*Justement!*" he cried triumphantly. "How you know?"

"Oh, I've spent a great deal of time there," I replied airily. "I know Paris almost as well as I know London."

"You know perhaps then Saint-Germain-des-Prés?"

"Of course," I said quickly but having no idea where it was, "and I am quite enchanted with that area of Paris."

"*C'est formidable*. I feel like to talk to a woman of my country. But of course, you are our Pucelle, you are a Frenchwoman."

"Tonight at least," I agreed.

"*Que vous êtes charmante*. La Pucelle d'Orleans my partnair . . ."

"An English Joan of Arc who has a French Robin Hood as her escort."

We laughed.

"*C'est drôle, n'est-ce-pas?* You French *combattante*, me *Anglais—comment dit-on en Anglais—proscrit, voleur?*"

"Outlaw. Robin Hood took from the rich and gave to the poor. He wasn't a robber."

"Perhaps many in my country think otherwise after what happen."

"The revolution! That was terrible but it was completely different. Robin Hood is a romantic figure in our history."

"But those he take from, they think him *romantique?*"

"I doubt that they did," I laughed, "but don't destroy one of my romantic heros."

"*Vous êtes romantique, alors?*"

"A romantic, yes I am," I said decidedly.

"*Ce n'est pas*—excuse I forget to speak your language—it is *très difficile. Mais, alors, romantique* I think not English trait."

"I think we English are every bit as romantic as you French. We just don't talk about it as much."

"*Peut-être, peut-être, mademoiselle—c'est mademoiselle, j'éspère.*"

"At such an affair as this, monsieur, I am the Maid of Orleans and you are Robin Hood, that is all."

"Then we must enjoy."

His efforts with the English tongue seemed to have exhausted his vocabulary for he said little else, but he led me in the waltz in such a graceful and masterful fashion, weaving through the crowded dance floor with such ease that I decided that though Englishmen might be every bit as romantic as Frenchmen, perhaps Frenchmen were the better dancers of the two. As we left the floor he asked whether he might waltz with me again and I readily agreed.

All around me identities were being disclosed as one after another commented on the cleverness of the disguises. I had no need to be told that the pale, fair Endymion was Francis, and in case I had not already guessed he came up to inform me he was Keats' hero.

"I wish Phoebe had been here tonight. She would have enjoyed it."

"Oh, she is in London?" I asked in surprise.

"No, but she comes soon."

"Oh, good," I said with genuine pleasure. "But where will she stay?"

"With my aunt, though I fear her stay may not be long. Perry told me he plans to go to Norfolk soon, and if he goes, his mother will surely go too—she doesn't let him out of her sight for long—and then Phoebe will have to decide whether she wants to rusticate in Norfolk or Dorset once again. I'm sure I can't put her up in my lodgings."

"But why does she not stay with me in the first place?" I was suddenly excited by the idea of having my best friend as a house guest. "It would be perfectly proper. I am a matron now and could chaperone her."

"Pooh, you a chaperone, Leonora! Mama would never allow it."

"I shall write her anyway," I said tossing my head, "and I'll thank you to keep out of it."

"I shall," he promised, "for with Phoebe esconced at Grosvenor Square I'll have a good reason to call on you every day, which suits me ideally, husband be hanged."

I noticed my French Robin Hood at hand to claim the next waltz. From the sharp look he threw at Francis, I wondered whether he had discovered I was Etienne's wife and perhaps counted him among his acquaintances.

"Do you know many people in London?" I asked casually.

"*Non, chère mademoiselle,*or is it madame?"

"I have told you, I am Joan, you are Robin, that is where it begins and ends."

"And if the heart break?"

"The heart does not break in a single evening."

"*Malheureusement, c'est possible.*" He was suddenly silent and looked at me so intently that I feared he would turn into another Jerningham and I began to prattle about the variety of costumes, identifying some of their owners to him.

"Helen of Troy over there is Lady Delaney, wife of an Irish baronet. I doubt even in her youth that she launched a thousand ships, nor was she ever carried away by Paris except in her fondest dreams. But on this night of the year she can pretend it was so, and as you see she is."

An exceedingly young fop was gazing transfixedly at Helen's almost totally exposed bosom.

"*Peut-être ce soir* Paris will—how you say?" My companion grinned.

"Helen is far too heavy to be carried off," I snorted.

"I think it not necessary to carry—perhaps she follow."

I laughed. "Perhaps."

"*Et lui, Henri huitième, n'est-ce pas?* You know?"

Jerningham's eyes were following our progress round the floor.

"I know him," I said abruptly.

"You no like?" he asked.

"Not particularly."

"He, I think, like you."

I shrugged and pointed out to him a Romany waltzing wildly with a Queen of Sheba, wondering out loud how the people they represented would feel to suddenly find themselves in one another's company.

"Change sometimes good. Perhaps they like."

"Perhaps."

It was stuffy and hot now, especially after the elation of the waltz; and while my French acquaintance went to find some cool lemonade I wandered onto the terrace to await his return. It was a fine evening and I descended the terrace steps to enjoy the air but keeping within easy view of the doorway so that I could see Robin Hood on his return. He was right, change was good. I had found him refreshing after my other partners.

"The king demands a kiss or it will be your head!" a voice from behind ordered. I whirled around to find myself face to face with Henry the Eighth, and moments later I was within his grasp and pulled into the seclusion of the rhodedendrons.

"Let me go this instant," I hissed, not wishing to scream and cause a fracas.

"Let go of my prize when at last it falls into my hands? I should say not."

"Let go of me," I repeated through clenched teeth, pushing against him with all my might. "You had better do as I say or I shall be forced to report your behaviour to Etienne."

"I don't believe he cares a hang, my dear. But if you intend to babble to him you might explain how you came to be here with me in the first place."

"You forcibly pulled me here."

"Forcibly!" He laughed. "That may be your description of how it occurred. Lambert knows me well enough to know I rarely use force—persuasion perhaps, but not force. I detest violence."

"Then let go of me this instant," I begged. "I promise to forget the entire incident."

"But the king demanded a kiss of his subject. He has not yet received it."

"No more will he." I struggled, but pitting my strength against his superior height and weight was as unavailing as the beating wings of a moth against a lighted window pane. I was no match for him and he took his kiss hungrily, almost viciously. As soon as his moist, clinging lips left mine I ordered,

"Now you've had your way, let go of me. You'll never touch me again I can assure you of that."

"Had my way?" he questioned in mock surprise. "I've had nothing. It is you who have encouraged me. Your eyes have made all the advances I need to be convinced of your willingness. I trust you were not teasing for that would be unkind. I've promised you to myself. I always keep promises I make to myself."

"Your audacity confounds me, sir. Let go of me this instant or it will be the worse for you."

"And who will make it the worse?" he laughed. "Only another kiss will release you now."

I could not tell whether I was more startled or relieved by the cool voice behind me.

"Pardon, monsieur, mais je crois que madame ne veut pas vous embrasser."

"Who the devil do you think you are, Frenchie. Be off—" His grip around me had tightened but suddenly I felt it broken and a yelp of pain escaped from his lips.

"Damn you!" he swore. "I'll have your hide for that."

But before he could say anything else Robin Hood had pulled me aside and with a lightning blow hit Jerningham so hard that he fell like a ninepin. When he tried to get up the Frenchman hit him again and I saw blood pouring from his nose.

"Ça va?" Robin Hood seemed undaunted by his efforts.

"Ça va, thanks to you. But if I were you I think you should leave. Sir Harvey Jerningham is not a man who likes to be crossed, let alone knocked down and injured. He'll want your blood in return," I warned.

"Mine he can have, but not that of la Pucelle. Now, do you

wish to take your lemonade here or inside?" he asked as calmly as though nothing had occurred.

"I wish to leave," I said, still shaken by the scene. I held out my hand, "But first I must thank you."

"Perhaps we meet again."

"Perhaps, London is a small place. I am sure I shall recognize you."

"I shall not forget you."

He bowed to me and I turned and pushed my way through the costumed figures, now becoming rather the worse for wear, suddenly distasteful and grotesque.

Chapter VII

"Would you care to go out for a drive? It is a sultry evening but there may be a breeze."

I looked up from the book which lay on my lap in a desultory fashion. I had taken to reading of the Middle Ages since becoming enamoured of Joan of Arc. This was another book of that period, *Ivanhoe*, with which I had sought diversion after dinner. Since the episode at Lady Newbury's I had preferred to stay at home rather than risk a recurrence of such unpleasantness. I was hardly depriving myself, for London society was remarkably thin and at its least stimulating. I would have left town had it not been that I had already invited Phoebe and she was even then persuading her mother to allow the visit.

Etienne stood expectantly at the door of my sitting room, waiting for a response. I had not realized that he was still at home.

"I'd love to go," I said, closing the book hastily and getting up.

"Which way would you prefer?" he asked, after helping

me into his chaise and then climbing up beside me and taking the reins.

I had never been out in the evening simply to drive, but he was right, it was a great deal cooler outside, especially as we moved at a smart pace towards the river.

"Anywhere, just anywhere." I sat back to enjoy the novelty.

He turned in the direction of Chelsea and I felt the balmy breeze against my face and took off my hat and let it ruffle my hair, feeling like a country girl. The first stars appeared in the evening sky, strong and unfailing, always there even when they were not to be seen. Everything in life changed so, it was comforting to have something constant. I felt happier than I had in weeks. We spoke little. When we did it was merely desultory words made in passing in keeping with the laziness of the evening. We drove by the river and I could see the lights of Vauxhall reflecting across the water. I thought of the frenetic gaiety which would now be engulfing its pleasure seekers and, for the first time in my life, I had no desire to join them. The sudden realization took me by surprise and I must have shown it for Etienne asked,

"Why did you smile just then?"

"For the first time I realized I felt happy, yet I could not understand why."

"When you feel happiness, never question it. Just accept it gratefully and be glad."

"And you?" I asked. "You show so little of what you feel. How do you react to happiness?"

"In truth I am not sure," he replied slowly. "I haven't known a great deal of it. If you must have an answer I presume it would be as I am reacting now, for I feel happy at this moment, though perhaps contented is a better word."

It was the first of many drives we took through the warm August evenings, forming a pattern of restful, undemanding companionship which I enjoyed more than any companionship I had previously known. Had I been forced to explain the reasons I could not, for nothing of great moment occurred, no titillating pieces of gossip or clever aphorisms passed between us. Yet I basked in the stability and firmness which emanated from him and found a responsive chord in me.

Sometimes we returned to sit on the terrace and sip sherry over a game of chess. Despite my outward lassitude I felt a sharpened mental capacity and my game improved. Etienne rarely invited anyone to dine. I was particularly grateful that Jerningham did not call and hoped that he had left town for the summer and that by next season all could be forgotten.

It was Papa who reminded me of him one afternoon when he took tea at Grosvenor Square as was his custom.

"I ran into Jerningham at White's yesterday and he asked after you. Says you never go out any more. Not the only one who's mentioned it to me." He stirred his tea carefully, concentrating on the flow of the warm, brown liquid.

"I've stayed home lately. It's been warm and lazy. I'm just rather tired of partying."

"You—tired of partying! Don't tell me that, Leonora!" He looked at me closely. "Not in the family way are you?"

"No, Papa," I said firmly. From the way he continued stirring his tea, deliberately, ponderously, as though the whole point of taking tea was its circular rotation rather than its consumption, I knew he had something he wished to say. Yet for some reason he was loathe to begin.

I considered whether I should help him or let him come to the point by himself. The continued clink of the spoon against the side of his cup decided me.

"Come, Papa, out with it, what is it you wish to tell me?"

"What makes you think I have something to tell you?"

"Oh, Papa, we know each other too well for such games. It is far simpler to come directly to the point to begin with. What is the matter? Are you down again?"

He nodded.

"Heavily?"

He nodded again.

"Papa, why will you do it—" I began in annoyance. Then I stopped, remembering my own experience at the tables. It was a fever which overtook him. I had felt it at Lorimer's. Perhaps I would have succumbed to it, as Papa had, except for Etienne's intransigent stand. For the first time I appreciated his refusal to pay for my gambling.

"How much are you down, Papa?"

"Thirty thousand pounds."

I stared at him in disbelief. How was it possible? Not a year had passed since Etienne had cleared all his obligations.

"Thirty thousand pounds!" I repeated slowly. "How long has it taken to accumulate such a debt?"

"One evening."

"One evening! But how is that possible? With whom did you play?"

Papa squirmed in his chair.

"Jerningham."

"Jerningham! Papa, surely not. I thought he never gambled except on a sure thing—" I realized he must have thought Papa a sure thing, yet why? His financial state was no secret. He may have learned of his allowance from Etienne, but would he wish to rob someone unless . . . I remembered his voice that evening saying, "I've promised you to myself. I never break a promise I make to myself." Was he thinking to use Papa to get at me? If so, he was in for a sore disappointment.

"Look, Leonora," Papa stopped stirring his tea and set aside his cup, "Jerningham says he will give the note to you for your asking. You need do nothing, only go to him and ask for it. He believes he has annoyed you in some way and he wishes to make amends."

"Then why does he simply not send the note to me?" I demanded.

"He wishes to apologize in person."

"Then let him bring it here."

"To your husband's house? That would never do. He asked that you call on him." I heard the note of pleading in Papa's voice but my heart hardened against it.

"I love you, Papa, but I cannot continually come to your rescue. I simply will not visit that man."

"It is such a little thing he asks," he pleaded. "Only to go, to receive his apology, to get my note. What does it cost you, Leonora, yet what will it cost me if you do not go."

"I cannot, Papa, that is all. The money to pay him must be raised in some other manner. There is still Mama's pendant. You may have it."

He shook his head.

"My child, I did not tell you before, I was ashamed to own it, but the pendant you hold is not your Mama's. It is merely paste. I was forced to pawn it long ago, but I hoped you would not find out about it. I kept hoping I would have enough to buy it back."

"I know, Papa. It doesn't matter." I reassured him, and in answer to his questioning look, "Etienne must have known it also, for he restored the original to me on my birthday. Don't ask me how or where he found it. He did not tell me, and I should probably never have known of it had I not found him replacing it in my room. You may have it now."

Yet still Papa shook his head.

"No, I fear it won't do, Leonora, it simply won't fetch thirty thousand. I doubt I would get half that. When it is known you need money, true worth is never given."

I knew this to be only too true, having discovered it for myself. My emeralds had been worth far more than Mama's diamond, yet I had been lucky to gain eight thousand for them. The only other thing I had of sufficient value was my engagement ring, but I could hardly give that away.

"The fact of the matter is that if you don't ask for the note I must sell Briarsmere."

He was right, it would have to be that. But to have to part with Briarsmere for one night's play with that—that monster. What foolishness!

A brilliant idea suddenly occurred to me.

"If Briarsmere has to be sold, Papa, you must offer it to Etienne. He will buy it, I am sure of it, and it will remain in the family."

Papa flicked at an invisible speck on his immaculate sleeve as he often did when loathe to speak.

"I can't, Leonora."

"Why not?"

"Well, you see, when he—when you married and my obligations were settled, I gave him my pledge that I would never again gamble for such stakes. He is bound to conjecture why I must sell Briarsmere."

"Then why did you do it?" I asked in exasperation.

"I still can't quite understand how it happened. But, anyway, before I knew it there I was signing the note."

"Papa, Papa, even so, Etienne must be told."

"He must not, Leonora." Papa's voice was sharp. He had never spoken to me in such a tone. "He must never know. When a gentleman gives his word on something it is just that—his word. I could never face him again if he knew I had not kept my promise."

"But you—" He had not kept his promise, but what use to remind him of it. His face was tense with deep set lines around his eyes. For the first time I saw him no longer as a handsome, dashing man but as an old and rather foolish one. Papa, old—I had never thought it could be. A surge of sympathy overcame my frustrations. Whatever it was, was done. Recriminations would settle nothing.

"Yet surely not Briarsmere," I said half to myself.

"What else is there?"

"There must be something."

He must have suspected I was wavering for he leaned over and patted my hand.

"It would be so simple for you, Leonora, just to ask. That is all that he wants. But of course, if you cannot do this for me . . ." his voice trailed off and he shrugged helplessly.

"Oh, Papa!" I got up and paced the floor. I could not bear to go near Jerningham. I had no reason to trust him, yet, if it were true, if he did only wish to apologize . . . if I did not go I would never know. Papa would sell Briarsmere and I would not know, I would always wonder. I thought of Joan of Arc, she had dared everything. In comparison this was so little.

"Will you accompany me?" I asked at last.

"I regret that I cannot. It would be embarrassing for me to be present at such an interview as well as for Jerningham. I'm sure you can understand that what he wants to say would be between the two of you. My position there as his friend and your father would be impossible. But if you say you will go then I will call for you and bring you home."

"At what hour?"

"Whenever you say."

"Very well. Then tell him I will call at three tomorrow and I want you to call for me at three fifteen and not a moment later. Do you promise?"

"Of course, my dear, anything." He got up and came over as though to hug me and suddenly I remembered Phoebe saying, "He uses you." It was true. I had let it happen again, but it would be the last time.

That evening every instinct told me, Papa's pledge notwithstanding, to tell Etienne of the visit as we played chess on the terrace. I played very badly, and when I lost my queen on the seventh move, Etienne took the pieces and put them back in the box.

"You're not in the mood for play. Is anything wrong?"

I looked at the concern in his eyes, then I thought of all he had already done for Papa and of the low opinion in which he held him. To confess this latest episode would further debase him when perhaps there was no need that Etienne need ever know of it.

"Oh, it's nothing. I just have a little headache, that is all. I played very stupidly just now."

"Why don't you go upstairs and rest. I think it is probably this sultry weather which is affecting you."

"No doubt."

As I left, on an impulse I lent down and kissed his cheek. I know he had not expected it and I saw questions forming, questions I didn't want to have to answer, and I hurriedly bade him goodnight and retired.

The following afternoon I sent Ennis on an errand, for I had no wish that he accompany me when I called on Jerningham. He was too closely allied with Etienne and was likely to let him know that I had visited his friend on my own. One of the young grooms readied my phaeton and drove with me on a journey of only minutes, which was at once an eternity yet an eternity over all too soon. I threw the reins to him, telling him my father would bring me home, and then climbed the front steps. I wondered if Joan of Arc's heart at Orleans had pounded as mine did when I lifted the brass knocker at the front door. I felt the colour flood to my cheeks as I asked the young footman who answered whether his master were at home, hoping his answer would be no and that I might walk home without the interview I dreaded. I was expected, however, for he immediately showed me back to a sitting room in the rear of the house overlooking a rose garden.

Despite the fact that it was a warm summer day, a fire burned in the hearth. I found myself glad of it, for the fear which had been rising within me since the previous day and which I had so desperately refused to acknowledge now overcame me and I felt numb. I was holding my hands out to the flames when Jerningham entered.

"Not cold, my dear Lady Leonora? But let it be my duty to change all that."

His opening sally did nothing to alleviate my fear.

"I am delighted to have you at last as a guest in my house. I have so often wished you would come to see me. Allow me to pour you a glass of wine."

I had, in truth, no wish to prolong my stay a minute longer than necessary, yet civility demanded that I observe the social graces and we sat together chatting aimlessly of the weather and his roses.

"It is my hobby. I take delight in nurturing tender shoots into full flower. The delicate pink buds over there I have produced by crossing a hybrid with my favourite tea rose. I have called it the Lady Leonora. I hope you do not object?"

Jerningham was playing with me, I knew, and he showed no sign of coming to the point of my visit so that I was forced to broach the subject myself.

"I believe you know why I am here, Sir Harvey." My cool tones belied by inner confusion.

He raised his eyebrows. "I presumed it was because you wanted to see me."

"I came because you asked it. You hold a note of my father's which you must be aware he is scarcely able to pay without giving up the only thing remaining in the family, Briarsmere. He said you were willing to give me the note if I called upon you."

"Ah, the note," he murmured as though he had quite forgotten it. "And I thought it was for me that you came."

"You know very well it was for the note." There was a hint

of savagery in my voice at this cat and mouse game which I would feign have concealed. "You spoke of it to my father. He told me you wished to apologize to me for your conduct at Lady Newbury's ball."

"Apologize for my conduct! My dear lady, what an odd idea. Had it not been for that bumbling fool of a Frenchman perhaps something might have resulted from that evening, though nothing for which an apology would be due or would be sought, of that I can assure you. As it was the whole thing completely frustrated me. I have desired you and wanted to see you more than ever, yet you have gone into seclusion and made it impossible for me even to talk to you."

The interview was not progressing at all as I wished or as Papa had predicted. I looked at the clock on the mantle: it was almost a quarter after the hour. Thank goodness Papa would soon be here. But I must get the note before he came or all would be for naught.

"Sir Harvey, may I at least see Papa's note which you hold and which he told me you would give me for the asking," I pursued boldly.

"Of course, dear Leonora." He went over to a small table by the window and opened a drawer to pull forth a folded piece of paper which he handed to me.

"Here, it is yours."

I looked down and immediately recognized Papa's scrawled hand and the figures thirty thousand. Then I looked back at Jerningham and smiled at him for the first time that afternoon and held out my hand.

"I simply don't know how to thank you for your kindness and generosity."

"Oh, but my dear—I think you do, though." He took the proferred hand in his and pulled me to him.

"Sir Harvey!" I protested, but before another word could be said he covered my lips with his own. I detested their touch, heavy and moist, and his hands exploring my body. When he released me I could not conceal my disgust.

"I think now it is quite time I left," I averred.

"Time to leave, Leonora, when I have given you your father's note for thirty thousand pounds and you have given me nothing in return? Surely you don't think that feeble kiss was worth the sum—why it wasn't worth three." He laughed unpleasantly.

"If you think I came here to trade with you, you are mistaken. I came as a lady to ask a gentleman to carry out a promise given freely."

"I believe you flatter yourself as well as me in using those terms."

"If my husband should ever learn of your conduct it would be worse for you, I can assure you."

"Lambert!" he shouted with laughter. "I don't think he gives a hang for you. He has his own interests and he lets you do as you wish with whomsoever you wish. I've watched you these past months. I know. And if you favour him with those same mealy-mouthed kisses it's no wonder he seeks comfort elsewhere. But I don't give up so easily. I believe there is more to you than that and I intend to find out. Besides, as I told you, I have promised you to myself. It is a promise I intend to keep."

I felt trapped. It was almost half past three and no sign of Papa. Surely he could not have deserted me. I had sent my own equipage away but I determined to walk home if I could safely leave the house.

"My father will call for me momentarily," I warned. "I suggest you not do anything for which you will be sorry later."

Again he shouted with laughter. "Your father! That's rich. Believe me, little dove, he will never set foot again in this house after last night. He was too badly trounced and he doesn't hold his wine as he used to. It's a shame. But of course, he has you to help him through his difficulties. It was why you married Lambert in the first place, wasn't it? All London knows that."

"Perhaps you should dwell a little on your friendship with my husband and how much you may be jeopardizing it," I hinted darkly, alarmed now that he might be right about Papa. He was unconscionably late. Perhaps he would not come.

"You dismissed your carriage. I saw it from my room upstairs. Who knows you are here besides your father? He won't tell. Don't tell me you announced to your husband that you were calling on me this afternoon."

Even I, desperate as I was, knew he would never swallow such a lie.

"Come, my little dove, I must not frighten you this first time."

He took my hands and pulled me over to the sofa and sat beside me.

"It will be enjoyable, even for you. But don't withstand my every move. Let me teach you how we may enjoy one another."

I hated him. I hated his confidence. I hated the way he was savouring these moments. How could I have been so foolish as to get myself into this trap from which I could see no reasonable escape? Even though I would prove obdurate he was not above rape, I thought bitterly, and stupidly I had allowed Papa to lead me into this incredible predicament. My heart sunk in despair at Papa's treachery, but no sooner had it done so than it jumped in jubilance as I heard the door behind me flung open. Dear Papa, he must forgive the bitterness I felt for him. I saw Jerningham's jaw drop and a look of horror cross his face. I rose quickly to join Papa, only it wasn't Papa who stood in the open doorway. No, it was not Papa but Etienne!

"Lambert!" Jerningham tried desperately to compose his features. "Your wife called to look at my roses. She is thinking of raising them in Grosvenor Square."

"So I see," said Etienne evenly. Then he turned to me, "Perhaps if you have learned all there is on the subject for one afternoon I can escort you home. I believe you returned your carriage so you are in need of a ride."

My cheeks were scarlet. Every line of my body bespoke guilt. So that was how he had known I was here. No matter, thank God he had come.

"I trust you have no wrong impressions," Jerningham continued, "I assure you it was all quite innocent."

"I'm quite sure it was. Lady Leonora is free to see you whenever she wishes. For my part, however, I prefer to discontinue our relationship both personal and professional. In the morning I shall have my solicitors draw up papers severing all our business transactions."

"No, Lambert, I beg you not to be hasty. Nothing has happened I assure you. Tell him, Leonora," he appealed to me.

"There is nothing either of you can say which would make the slightest difference. I dislike people who give me cause to distrust them whatever the reason."

"But, Lambert, no one understands finances as you do. No one can advise me as you do."

"You should have thought of that before you made this assignation."

"But you have always allowed your wife complete freedom."

"So it has been, and so it will continue to be. I shall not interfere in the future, I assure you. However, all transactions between you and myself are at an end."

"I never want to see him again," I said to Etienne, finding my tongue at last.

"That is quite up to you. Come, it is time to return home."

I looked down at the crumpled note in my hand, the cause of all the trouble. Impetuously I flung it into the open fire and watched it burn. Jerningham saw it, Etienne too, but neither made a comment. Etienne probably thought it was a note of assignation, I realized bitterly.

"I am quite ready to leave," I said abruptly, yet I dreaded being alone with him. What could I say? Papa had been wrong, but he was my father. I could not disclose what he had told me, for to do so would reveal he had broken his word as a gentleman. Only he could do that. Much as I wished to, I could not. Yet I could think of nothing else which could explain my visit to Jerningham on my own.

All was silence in the carriage. Etienne's face was expressionless. Even if I set aside all loyalty to Papa and to the code of honour which was mine as well as his, would he believe me? I no longer had Papa's note to prove that it was so. Etienne would detest Papa even more after he knew, yet I could think of nothing else. It must be.

I cleared my throat. "I think I should explain why I was—"

"Spare me, please. 'Never apologize, never explain,' is a truism I learned early in life and which has served me well. I suggest you adopt it. It is the preferable course in the long run, I assure you." He stopped and added with utter contempt. "I thought you learned your lesson about Jerningham at Lady Newbury's ball."

"How did you know about that?" I gasped.

I remembered then the French Robin Hood. Had Etienne met him, had he told him of the incident?

He turned to look at me squarely and then I knew, even before he drawled,

"London is a small place. But I thought you knew that."

Chapter VIII

I did not come down to dinner that night. The headache I had feigned the previous evening became a grim reality. I wondered for the hundredth time whether to tell Etienne of Papa's duplicity; each time I remembered his caustic "Never apologize, never explain." Well, I wouldn't, I resolved. Then again I was overcome with remorse. Why should this have happened now, now when there had been peace and contentment between us.

I spared few thoughts for Jerningham, except for his remarks about Etienne seeking his comforts elsewhere. Had he a mistress, I wondered. It was a common happening in my circles, but one which I found perversely lowering. Was it to her he had gone when he had left my room that night? Had he sought solace with her on those evenings when he refused to stay at my social engagements? I had never bothered to ask. Now that I desperately wanted to, I could not ask.

I tossed and turned in bed thinking of Papa. I should have let him sell Briarsmere, I thought savagely. Perhaps he would have learned his lesson then. The thought of Briarsmere now made me long for the green and calm of Dorset. but much as I longed to flee London I could not. Phoebe had written to me that she had at last gained her parents permission to come and stay with me. After all the pains she had taken and her obvious excitement at the visit I could not disappoint her. She would never forgive me if I left London now.

Not the least recurrent thought that night was that I had flirted outrageously with my own husband at the masked ball. I tried to remember all that had passed between us. I remembered bluffing about my superior knowledge of France and felt foolish. He must have been laughing at me, I thought furiously. Then I remembered how he had waltzed with me, holding me close to him, leading me dexterously through the crowd. I had always thought he hated dancing. but then I had never urged him to dance with me. Never before had I seen him so relaxed and gay as he had been that night.

I slipped at last into a troubled sleep and woke late, still in low spirits and heavy-eyed. When my maid brought my morning chocolate she conveyed the news that Madame Garnier was below waiting to see me. I had no idea why she had come. I could think of nothing I had ordered from her recently. Anyway I knew she would not ever demean herself to deliver a bonnet. She enjoyed a large staff of milliners and from the exorbitance of her prices and the names of her clientele, her business was a prosperous one. For all that, I knew she wasted little of her time on purely social calls. With some curiosity I asked that she be shown up.

Madame Garnier was no longer in her first blush of youth, but she was, nevertheless, strikingly attractive after the continental fashion. Her dark hair was piled high atop her head with soft curls framing her black, expressive eyes and delicately arched brows. Her hat, I noticed, was deceptively simple, yet I recognized the creative genius behind the folds of the yellow watered taffeta ribbon and the slight touch of blue in the straw which precisely matched the blue of her exquisitely cut cambric walking dress.

"Do sit down, Madame Garnier." I motioned her to a seat opposite me. "To what do I owe the pleasure of this visit?"

"Lady Leonora," she began and immediately I sensed a hesitance in her voice. "Your husband asked that I call upon you."

"My husband?" I responded quickly in complete puzzlement. "Was it about a new bonnet?"

"No, your ladyship, nothing like that. It is just that—well, there are certain things Monsieur Lambert wished me to explain to you."

Though she looked at me directly as she spoke, I noticed a hint of embarrassment in her eyes which mystified me.

"Things you were to explain to me?" I repeated, unable to keep disparagement entirely from my voice.

"Yes, Lady Leonora."

"What things precisely?" I asked coldly.

She spoke more boldly now. "What I am about to say may embarrass you. Nevertheless, Monsieur Lambert has asked that I explain it to you and I will do so. I would refuse him nothing."

Now I was not only mystified as to the cause of her visit but I had a growing suspicion that she knew a great deal more of Etienne than I had ever supposed.

"What is it you wish to tell me, or have been told to tell me?" I was avidly interested, but I preserved my bored tones, determined she should not forget her inferior status. I refused to look at her and deliberately turned my attention to the newspaper lying in my lap, stirring my hot chocolate while I glanced at it. In truth I read nothing. My attention was entirely focused on my visitor but I had no intention of allowing her the satisfaction of knowing it. Her next words, however, jolted me and I was forced to drop all pretence of disinterest.

"Monsieur Lambert has asked me to explain to you how it is possible to make love and yet prevent conceiving a child."

"What!" I cried. I could not believe I heard her aright, yet the steadfastness of her gaze convinced me it was so.

"How dare you speak to me on such a matter!" I choked. "I will have you thrown out this very minute. How could you expect I would sit here and listen to anything so disgusting."

I reached for the bell rope but not before her hand darted out and firmly grasped my wrist.

"I advise you against that, your ladyship. Monsieur Lambert has asked that I do this and I intend to do whatever is necessary to assure that it is done, no matter how distasteful it is for you. I do not enquire into his reasons for asking it of me, but I can assure you whatever he wants will be done."

"I have no doubt that you have been acceding to all his wishes," I flung at her angrily.

"If you are suggesting that I am his mistress, that is not so, Lady Leonora. I only wish it were. He has been good to me, very good indeed, and he has demanded nothing of me. I was the daughter of French émigrés, abandoned by them here and forced to make my living as best I could. It was Monsieur Lambert who became acquainted with my plight and who helped me to achieve independence. He lent me money to start my establishment, he gave me advice on how to run my business, and he sent me my clients. It was he who established my reputation as London's foremost milliner. In return I have been able to do little except provide him with a sympathetic ear from time to time. But now he has asked something of me and I have no intention of leaving until it is done."

She had continued to hold my wrist as she spoke but now I moved my arm impatiently, saying,

"Very well, get along with it and begone."

She sat down again opposite me and produced from her reticule an assortment of small sponges and a vial containing a golden liquid which, when she uncorked it, I recognized to be brandy. She then explained to me in detail, in clear and unembarrassed tones, the method of soaking a small sponge thoroughly in brandy and inserting it deeply into the woman's body prior to the act of lovemaking in order to prevent undesired conception.

I listened to her measured tones, torn between horror and disgust. That Etienne should wish me to know of such a thing—me, his wife, a peer's daughter—and that it should be explained to me by a woman with a disreputable past who, if not his mistress, clearly had designs to be, was simply intolerable. All this went through my mind, but I listened without interrupting until she concluded. Then I snapped in cold fury,

"If you are quite finished with your loathsome description, madame, you may leave, preferably by the back stairs. I can quite understand how a woman of your calling, by your own admission a woman of the streets, would need to know of such things. Why my husband should wish me to learn of them is beyond my comprehension."

I saw the flash of anger in her eyes and I was glad that at least one of my sallies had registered, but her voice continued calm.

"No more do I, Lady Leonora. I know that if he were my husband, my dearest wish would be to present him with the children I know he desires and longs for. But you are his wife, not I. It is your affair. I have done as he asked, that is all."

She shrugged as she spoke and then closed her reticule and rose to go, leaving her disgusting assortment of sponges and the vial on the table. I felt like throwing them at her.

"I bid you good morning."

I made no attempt to return her parting salutation, but as she reached the door I could not prevent myself calling out to her,

"Are you in love with my husband, Madame Garnier?"

She turned her dark eyes on me steadily.

"I have been in love with him ever since I first met him. Again, good morning to you."

As the door closed behind her I got up and violently swept from the table the assortment she had left. The brandy spilt on the carpet, filling the room with its pungent fumes. I flung myself on my bed and burst out crying.

I stayed in my room until well into the afternoon, unable and unwilling to consider all the implications of Madame Garnier's visit. My anger against Etienne mounted as the hours passed. Only when I heard his steady, measured step on the stair and the door to his room next to mine opened did I get up and, without a second thought for my dishevelled appearance or my eyes, swollen and unsightly, I made for the door which connected our rooms.

His room was large and airy, somehow brighter than mine, perhaps it was because of the absence of hangings around the large mahogany bed which dominated its center. I noticed his clothes set ready for dinner, the silver-backed brushes devoid of monogram which reposed on the high mahogany chest, and an open book which lay in front of the silver-framed miniature of a woman on the table beside the bed. It was a room which precisely reflected his plain but elegant taste, but though my eyes had flitted across it as I entered, it was on the room's occupant, who now stood at the dressing table removing his neckcloth, that they were concentrated.

"Leonie!" he gasped. For the first time I realized what a spectacle I must have presented, but I was past caring about that.

"My name is Leonora, not Leonie," I tried unsuccessfully

to control my anger. "Perhaps you should remember that in future."

"I beg your pardon, but then perhaps I should have said Lady Leonora, or Lady Leonora Fordyce."

"That's hardly necessary, though I'll not deny my pride in my family connections."

"Unlike my own, you imply. At least my connections stayed out of debt."

I was stung by his remark, particularly in view of the latest *contretemps* in which Papa had embroiled me.

"If you refer to my father, then I should point out assuredly there is no question as to who he is. As for my mother, she was as far removed from being a servant as is possible."

His dark eyes which had been filled with compassion on first seeing me were now cold and hard.

"If you had but one iota of my mother's courage and integrity I would value you a thousand times more than I do at this moment."

"And that woman you sent to me, that Frenchwoman whom you requested I patronize, I suppose you value her."

"Madame Garnier?"

"Yes, Madame Garnier. She is just the sort of low creature with whom I would expect to find you involved."

"She is a friend of mine. I value that friendship."

"How dare you send her to me. How dare you ask her to speak to me on such an immoral matter. How dare you!" I would cheerfully have struck him as much for his cool, disdainful attitude as anything else.

"If you will act in a promiscuous manner you must know what other promiscuous women of your class already know. I thought you differed from them but yesterday I discovered that you are just like all the rest, all modesty before marriage and anything but after."

"She disgusted me," I railed. "I would have had her

thrown out but she insisted she would tell me everything. I believe she would do anything for you."

"She is very loyal. If you had allowed yourself the opportunity, you would have discovered that she is a compassionate woman."

"Is she your mistress?"

The question, suddenly blurted out, came as much of a surprise to me as it did to him. Though I had thought of nothing else since her visit I had not intended to breathe a word of my suspicions. He seemed to take it in stride though, answering slowly,

"I cannot see that it can make any difference to you whether she is or is not. But if you must have an answer it is no, Madame Garnier is not my mistress."

For some reason I breathed a sigh of relief which momentarily caused me to forget my reasons for confronting him, until he asked quite seriously whether I had fully understood all she had told me.

"It was totally loathsome."

"Loathsome you may think it, but you have not suffered the pangs of childbirth which, I can assure you, can be much more loathsome. It can be ugly even when the child being born is desired, but when the child is unwanted it is pure agony."

"But ladies are not supposed to know of such things," I said hotly.

"That is remarkably stupid. All women should know of them and should be able to make their own free choice. All I did was to put that weapon in your hands. Use it or not as you wish. But I should warn you that I have no wish to be foisted with another man's child to bring up as my own. While you confined your activities to the lukewarm passions of Francis Oliphant I saw little to worry about, but now you have moved your sights to Jerningham and I suspect you have already discovered that men of his ilk are not to be encouraged and then admonished for their advances with a tap of the fan or a coy glance. They will expect more and if, my dear, you don't give it, as likely as not they will take it."

"But I have no interest in Jerningham. I told you that."

"If not him it will be someone else. Once a woman has begun that game it does not stop with the first lover. At least now I can content myself with knowing that you are armed to prevent tragedy to yourself and others. Quite selfishly I want you to know that I have no intention of bestowing my name on another man's child."

"Yet that name was not even given to you by your father. It is your mother's name," I scorned. My barb caused him to pause momentarily, and he directed a glance at the silver-framed miniature.

"It is, and it is a name of which I am proud. She gave her life in giving me birth, I cannot ever forget that. She was a brave and courageous woman. A woman who has neither of these qualities, nor kindness or compassion besides, would do well not to speak ill of her."

"I will speak of whom I please," I blustered.

He seized me by the shoulders.

"Not in my presence," he retaliated.

In that moment of intense hostility between us, I felt the hatred in my heart suddenly turn to raw desire such as I had never experienced before. I had raised my arm to strike him as he seized me but, almost without volition, instead I put both arms round his neck and pulled his lips down on mine. I felt him draw back for an instant, but only an instant, then his arms closed around me and his lips, which had hesitated at first, took possession of mine with a desire and demand which forced everything from my mind. I belonged more completely to him at that moment than I had belonged to anyone else in my life. When he at last released me, I felt him look down at me, but I could not bring myself to meet his eyes.

He was the first to speak, and his tones were those of a stranger, but a cool, harsh stranger.

"If you fear I may withdraw my support of your father because of your sentiments on my parentage, believe me that is not the case. I have long been aware of your feelings on that subject which you have expressed quite freely to others. It is a pity they should have been so tardy in being aired between us. In any case, I made an agreement with Castleford. I honour my agreements even when they turn sour on me."

I wanted to tell him he was wrong, nothing had been further from my mind when I kissed him, but I remembered again—never apologize, never explain. Well, I had no intention of apologizing. As for explaining, I couldn't, for I really did not know why I had kissed him except that at that moment I had desired him more than I had ever felt possible.

Chapter IX

Phoebe arrived within the week. Such a joy it was to see her, her dark curls flying as she ran up the steps at Grosvenor Square, her arms extended in greeting.

"Phoebe, Phoebe!" I flung my arms around her, laughing and crying at the same time. "How happy I am that you are here. You've no idea how I've been counting the hours, the minutes till your arrival. How lovely you look, so well, so happy." Much as I would, I could not keep the wistful note from my voice.

I sat with her as she changed and brushed her hair, chatting as we had always done, yet I felt there was something unsaid on her part and I knew there was on mine.

"How is your—your Mr. Lambert?" she asked at last.

"He is well," I replied quietly

"Is he here now—in London, that is?"

I saw her face cloud as I replied affirmatively.

"Oh, Phoebe, don't worry." I wondered whether to tell her of any of our difficulties but it was all so complicated. Though Etienne and I had been living quite separate lives since the Jerningham episode, I had asked him to treat Phoebe with civility while she was with us. He had assured me, quite coldly, that he would do no less for any house guest.

"I doubt that we will see a great deal of him, and I know you do not care for him, but that is of no great moment. I'm afraid he finds most of my friends far too frivolous. We will have fun together, though, for we are quite free to go to parties as we please—and just think, now I can chaperone you! Remember how we used to run and hide from poor Miss Brewster and how she always threatened to tell our parents but never did. Poor dear, our fathers would certainly have removed us from her school had she done so and I suspect we realized that that bound her to secrecy, for we never mended our ways. I hope you will not treat me so, Phoebe," I ended with mock seriousness.

But instead of replying to this sally, Phoebe was pensive.

"You don't want to talk of him, do you Leonora?"

"No." I bowed my head.

"You poor dear, you poor, poor dear." She took me in her arms and embraced me. "How could your Papa have done such a thing to you. I have thought of you so often. It was one reason I was not sorry to be buried in Dorset these past months and why I hesitated before I asked Mama to allow me to stay with you: I feared I could not be civil to the man you were forced to marry. Mama has no great opinion of him either, that was why it was so hard to get her permission once I had overcome my own scruples. I think she felt sorry for you, though, so she at last consented."

"But Phoebe, he is not as bad as all that." I found myself forced to take his part, remembering that our difficulties had not totally stemmed from his misdoing.

"That is so like you, Leonora, to leap to his defence. Dear, generous Leonora, you have not changed a bit. You always protected your Papa, now you do the same for Lambert."

I was not at all sure she was right, but she went on,

"Never fear, I shall try my best to be civil to the man while I am under his roof."

Phoebe's manner of being civil amounted to a cold, studied aloofness toward Etienne which, despite the fact that I had been furious with him ever since Madame Garnier's visit, I found embarrassing, especially since he treated her with the greatest courtesy. He made a point to dine with us when we were at home, though for the most part, once the round of London's assemblies and balls began again, he left us to our own devices. Although I found the round of these entertainments certainly more enjoyable with Phoebe for company, somehow they no longer held the same fascination they had once exerted over me.

"But does Lambert never accompany you to balls?" Phoebe asked as I was accepting an invitation to Sir Humphrey and Lady Claremont's.

"In the beginning he did on occasion, but no longer." I continued to write.

"I really think he should do so, at least sometimes. Does he not dance?"

I remembered the French Robin Hood. "He dances very well."

"Then he should certainly take us to the Claremonts. People will talk if he never goes anywhere with you."

"They already do talk, but I don't care and I'm sure he never has."

"Nevertheless, I think that at least once during my visit he should accompany us. Mama is bound to ask me, and if I am forced to say we were always accompanied by Francis or that doltish Mr. Unwin she will find it very odd."

"But your mother does not care for Etienne," I pointed out. "You told me so yourself."

"Nevertheless, he is my host. She would expect it. I intend to ask him to do so tonight."

"But, Phoebe," I protested, "we do very well on our own."

I found her sudden insistence on his presence difficult to understand though I had noticed an almost imperceptible change in her manner to him, a slight softening, which had made our meals together more tolerable.

She was not to be dissuaded from her notion that he should accompany us to the Claremonts, and that evening at dinner she accosted him on the subject.

"Miss Oliphant, you flatter me," Etienne replied in what I considered exaggerated surprise. "I did not believe you cared enough for my presence to wish me to be at your side at the Claremonts when undoubtedly you both will be surrounded by a swarm of admirers."

It was Phoebe who flushed furiously at this, and Etienne added in a gentler tone,

"I believe there is little my presence there could add to the glory of the occasion. I know that neither of you will want for partners."

"It is not that," Phoebe said weakly. "We would—like you to come."

I don't know whose surprise was greatest at this admission on Phoebe's part, Etienne's or mine. He glanced over at me briefly before saying quite sincerely,

"In that case I shall most certainly accompany you, though I reserve the right to refuse to dance."

"But you are not so—serious that you cannot benefit from the joys of dancing," Phoebe protested.

"Not so old, I think you were about to say. No, I am not so old, neither am I so serious that I have forgone dancing entirely. It is simply that I find little pleasure in it as a rule when it is undertaken in crowded ballrooms more for the purpose of being seen than for the enjoyment of the dance itself. Now dancing in the country is another matter. There it is so often such a natural expression of joy at the occasion or at one's partner that it is difficult not to take pleasure in it. I must admit to having found the waltz quite possessing on occasion."

Again he glanced at me briefly with this closing remark and unaccountably I felt my cheeks redden. I realized it was so seldom that Etienne talked of himself that now I found myself resenting the fact that it had been Phoebe who had made him do so.

"Will you come then, if we promise not to make you dance against your wishes?" There was no mistaking the cajolery of her voice and manner. Surely Etienne would not be deceived by it after her insulting behaviour in the past.

"It is impossible to refuse an invitation put to me in such plaintive tones by so charming a guest."

I looked up sharply as he smiled at Phoebe and she in turn smiled back at him. To see them one would think them bosom friends, even—no it was silly to even think that. Phoebe really despised him and I suspected now she only wanted him to go to embarrass him. I almost felt like warning him, but the remembrance of the manner in which he had smiled at her stopped me. It was an age since he had smiled at me like that, but then I would not stoop to employing feminine arts to induce it as Phoebe had just done.

Not only did Phoebe succeed in getting Etienne to attend the Claremonts' ball, but she also succeeded in gaining a dance with him. I had not realized it until I almost bumped into them while I was waltzing with Freddie Blake, who was a tolerable dancer but a terrible bore. It quite put me out of humour, especially when Etienne made no attempt to demand my hand for the next waltz. By midnight the crush became quite unbearable and when Etienne said he would leave and return for us at any time we cared to designate, it was Phoebe who caught hold of his arm and agreed to accompany him, leaving me to follow convinced that it was somehow one of the evenings I had least enjoyed. This conviction continued through Phoebe's voiced elation all the way home.

Thereafter it was Phoebe who constantly insisted that Etienne accompany us, and though she was not always successful, I noticed that on those occasions when he refused to come she would more often than not develop a sudden headache or case of fatigue. Then we all would remain at home and play three-handed piquet, or whist if Francis were at hand—in which case Phoebe and Etienne would be teamed against Francis and myself. I fancy they had more fun critiquing the game together afterwards than they did in playing it. In either case it was I who felt like the outsider.

If Phoebe had some dastardly scheme in mind in her change in attitude to Etienne, I could not fathom it. She rarely spoke of him to me when we were alone, but I could not overlook the softening of her manner whenever he appeared. For his part, his manner of open courtesy had changed to easy friendship which resulted in an easing of tension in the household and a thawing of the hostilities which had existed between us. Of this I was glad and I hoped that once Phoebe left we could take up our life as it had been before that disastrous Jerningham episode. I would tell Etienne the truth about that. Papa must fend for himself. Strangely enough, I began to long for Phoebe's departure almost as much as I had longed for her arrival, perhaps more so.

Each afternoon Phoebe and I would drive in the park. She was delighted with my phaeton and with my skill in handling the team.

"Where on earth did you learn to feather the reins in that manner?" she asked, her voice tinged with envy.

"Etienne taught me."

"But I have never seen him out here. Why does he not drive us?"

"He just doesn't care for driving in the park at this hour. He scorns almost anything which is counted fashionable when it is merely done for that reason. I think he prefers clear roads and unheeded progress which, as you can see this afternoon, is an impossibility."

We were, in fact, quite hemmed in, but as usual Phoebe was enjoying the fun of greeting people in other carriages and being surrounded by a swarm of young gentlemen on horseback. I am sure she would normally have thought that to drive at any other hour was pure insanity; now, however, I suspected she would make it a point to either get Etienne to drive us at this hour or else change our habits to drive with him when it was less crowded. Somehow the thought annoyed me. Possibly I feared she might succeed where I had failed.

That afternoon as we were entering the square a dog darted out towards us. I swerved to avoid having him end his days beneath the wheels of my carriage when, at the same moment, a phaeton driven by a young swell at far too fast a pace rounded the corner in the opposite direction, frightening my already disgruntled team and causing them to shy violently. It was as much as I could do to keep the reins and bring them to a halt, but before I had done so Phoebe had been tossed from the seat beside me to the street below. Immediately I jumped down, as did Ennis and the young gentleman who was full of contrition at the mishap he had caused.

"Phoebe, say something. Are you hurt?" I cried out, bending over her.

She was pale and shaken but she sat up, much to the relief of the young man who hastily introduced himself as Mr. Harry Foxcroft from Heath Park in Surrey. He was so obviously overcome with regret that I could scarcely berate him for his recklessness.

"It's just my shoulder hurts," Phoebe murmured. "Please take me home."

Nothing would do but for Mr. Foxcroft to lift her up and drive her to our house in the square, leaving me to follow. Ennis had already run ahead and notified Etienne of the mishap and he came out on the steps as soon as we arrived. He immediately took in the gravity of the situation, sent Ennis for Dr. Hamilton, bade Mr. Foxcroft wait in the salon where he instructed the footman to wait on him, and carried Phoebe up to her room. By the time I arrived at Phoebe's side, after making sure Mr. Foxcroft was soothing his jangled nerves with a glass of claret, she was lying on her bed, holding fast to Etienne's hand and crying with pain.

"Keep that arm quite still," he told her gently. "Dr. Hamilton will be here soon and he will have you right in a jiffy. If your shoulder should prove to be broken there is nothing to do except keep it immobile for a period of time."

"Do you think it is broken?" she asked through her tears.

"I don't know, but from the pain you described to me I fear it is possible. I know you will be brave even so."

I saw him attempt to loosen his hand from hers, but she pleaded,

"Don't leave me, please don't go. I shall be afraid if you are not here."

Her speech astounded me. Was this the daring Phoebe I had known in school who had thought nothing of climbing out of a second storey window to attend some fair which had been forbidden to us, who had raced me across the Dorset fields heedless of the menacing stares of the Hereford bulls, who had sprained her ankle in a fall from her horse yet gone on to hunt all day without complaint?

"You have nothing to fear. You are young and healthy and should it prove that your shoulder is broken it will soon knit quickly and easily. Wait till you're my age to make it a more serious challenge!" He laughed, I sensed to cover his embarrassment at her manner of clinging to him.

"I doubt there is much more than ten years between us," she said stoutly.

"Never mind that," he said. "Leonora is here and she will do whatever is necessary until the doctor arrives."

"You'll be all right, Phoebe, we'll take good care of you," I said briskly, but if she heard me she made no acknowledgement, continuing to cling to Etienne as though her life were held in his grasp.

Dr. Hamilton had not been home to answer Ennis's summons, but his assistant, Mr. Tucker, was there and it was he who soon entered, conscious of the importance of his mission and intent on serving well one of whom he obviously had heard much.

"Ah, Mr. Lambert," he bowed, "I am Mr. Tucker, Dr. Hamilton's assistant. Dr. Hamilton, I regret to say, was away from home when your man called, but I made it my business to come here as fast as possible to give immediate aid. Let me see now, what have we here?"

"It is the left shoulder," Etienne said briefly and, seeing Mr. Tucker about to commence another speech, he cut him off. "Perhaps you could examine it immediately."

"Ah, yes, of course. If Mrs. Lambert will allow, I must, I am afraid, ask her to sit up."

There was a momentary pause during which Etienne succeeded in loosening his hand from Phoebe's hold.

"Mr. Tucker, it is Miss Oliphant, a friend of my wife's and our houseguest, who has suffered the accident."

Mr. Tucker flushed and turned to me quickly.

"Please excuse me, Mrs. Lambert—"

But again Etienne cut him off with, "My wife's name is Lady Fordyce Lambert," which did nothing to lessen his discomfort. I motioned Etienne to leave the room, angry at the whole occurrence and at the way he now used my title to divide us. It was true I had chosen to use it for that purpose in the beginning; now he was determined I should not forget it.

I helped Phoebe to sit up and loosened the fastening of her dress to allow Mr. Tucker to examine her shoulder. Despite his gauche manner, he was surprisingly gentle and skillful, and soon had the shoulder set and bound. I noticed that Phoebe cried little at what must have been the most painful part of the whole business, the setting, but then, I realized, Etienne wasn't there.

She was soon asleep with the draught Mr. Tucker left for her after assuring me that Dr. Hamilton would call to make sure that everything was satisfactory, and I was able to report to a discomfitted Mr. Foxcroft, who was being laboriously engaged in conversation by Etienne, that from all indications she would do very well.

"Thank God!" he cried in relief. "I should never have forgiven myself if she had suffered any permanent injury on my account. There can be no doubt that she has suffered. I only hope that with time she will pardon the foolishness on my part which caused it to happen. One so fair should never have to know such anguish."

The tide of Mr. Foxcroft's feelings seemed to have no ebb. I found his effusions difficult to take seriously but it was, I discovered, his style to emote. Etienne at last interrupted him to thank him for his concern in a tone which even that distraught young gentleman could not overlook.

"Have I your permission to call to enquire after Miss Oliphant?" he asked before he left.

"It is hardly for me to grant it," I thought Etienne's tone was cold, even hostile. "Miss Oliphant is a friend of my wife's."

He turned to me hopefully.

"I am sure Miss Oliphant will appreciate your concern,

Mr. Foxcroft. I do not know how long it will be before she comes downstairs, but be assured I shall convey your wishes for her speedy recovery."

I had thought, not without some satisfaction, that her injury would cause Phoebe to remain in her room for some period of time, but I was surprised and not altogether pleased when, the day following the accident, she insisted she was well enough to dine with us below.

During her convalescence Etienne did everything for her comfort, making sure that her food was prepared in bite size portions, arranging for books and flowers to be delivered to her. But when she felt unable to attend the opening night of *The Barber of Seville* and he arranged for Rossini and his wife, doubtless at a handsome fee, to come and sing and play for us, I felt his boundless consideration had gone too far. And I was annoyed at the way Phoebe was revelling in the role of the invalid.

"Surely you are well enough to be out and about now," I said with asperity some time after the accident.

And Phoebe, whom I'd never known to have a sick day in her life, replied with a wan smile,

"These things take time to heal. As Lambert says, nature must take its course."

Nature might take its course, I thought savagely, but there was no harm in prodding it along a bit, and I was glad when Francis, who called often and dined with us frequently, one day told her he felt forced to write to their Mama to inform her of Phoebe's lack of progress.

"Don't do that," Phoebe said hastily. "You know Mama. She will be up here in an instant and then force me to go home, and I don't want to leave London now."

It was enough to make me consider writing to Lady Oliphant myself if Francis did not.

Mr. Foxcroft called almost as often as did Francis and sometimes stayed to dine with us, but more often than not, despite his strong predilection for Phoebe, it was I who was forced to entertain him while all of Phoebe's attention was given to Etienne.

My annoyance climaxed one morning when I descended at my usual hour, close to noon, to find Phoebe was not at home. On enquiry I found she had breakfasted with Etienne and they had both left the house together.

She did not return until late in the afternoon, her face flushed and happy and, completely forgetting her injury, using both arms with apparent ease.

"Oh, Leonora, it was so exciting! I wish you had been there. Etienne took me to the Bank of England and the Royal Exchange, and there was such a scramble and scatter everywhere. I didn't understand a thing at first until he explained what was happening. Then he took me to his offices. You never told me he had such a beautiful place. The paintings alone must be worth a fortune! If I were you I would insist on having them here, especially the Rembrandt. I told him so, but he thought you might not care for it. And the desk he has was once used by Louis XIV—only think! It shines so beautifully. And he has his own rooms there. He said he often used to stay there and I don't wonder, everything is so masculine and so elegant. Cheddell was there, of course, and the three of us dined at Lloyd's Coffee House. Etienne knew just everyone there but he insisted we have a private room because I was with them, though people kept coming to speak to him. It was so exciting."

"I thought you had sworn never to set foot in the city or have anything to do with Cits," I said severely. "What would your Mama say?" I was furious that she had been privy to a part of Etienne's life unknown to me, albeit by my desire, and her use of his Christian name had not escaped my attention.

"Oh, Mama," she tossed her head in disdain. "She is so stuffy. I shall certainly go again if Etienne asks me."

I was now determined that Phoebe's visit should come to an end and seriously contemplated writing to her Mama with a hint of Phoebe's latest excursion which I knew would bring her posthaste to London to save her daughter from the lowliness of City life. But before I had time to do so an event occurred which I had not envisioned and which put an end not only to Phoebe's stay in Grosvenor Square but to my own life there also.

A party of us had gone to Vauxhall for the evening. Etienne was there, and Foxcroft and some of his friends, as well as Francis, Phoebe and myself. I knew that Phoebe had been there countless times before, but she insisted on seeing everything, the statues, the fountains, the Grand Walk and the fragrant bowers, and nothing would do but Etienne must show her.

After dinner she took his arm in a proprietary fashion and said he had promised to show her Ramo Sammee, the Indian Sword-Swallower.

"I would like to see him also," I said firmly.

"But you promised this dance to me," Francis protested. "Besides he is not due to begin for at least half an hour."

I had, and short of a sprained ankle I could think of no reason for refusing him, though on the dance floor I made so many foolish mistakes that it was Francis who at last suggested we leave the set and go in search of his sister. But though the crowd had begun gathering for the performance and others of our party were there, there was no sign of Phoebe and Etienne. We were returning to our box through one of the dark walks, thinking perhaps they were still there, when I spied what I was sure was the shimmering green of Phoebe's dress in an alcove off the walk.

"There they are!" I said in triumph, but no sooner had I

spoken than I wished my feet had never been led in that direction, for I saw Phoebe close against Etienne's chest, her arms locked around his neck, his face pressed against hers.

"Oh!" I cried, and Francis who had also caught sight of them took my arm and pulled me away.

"Wasn't them," he said briefly when we were safely removed from the spot.

"You know very well it was, Francis Oliphant. Don't attempt to deceive me about your sister's conduct. She has been behaving in an outrageously flirtatious manner toward Etienne, in case you hadn't noticed it before. Don't try and deceive me now as she has deceived me all this time."

"But I thought you were glad they were getting along together," he said. "Besides, it's as much his doing as my sister's."

"Take me home this instant," I demanded.

"Don't do that. It was nothing. You know how things are at Vauxhall. Don't be such a prude. You know you've allowed more than one kiss to be stolen here—it's expected, but it isn't taken seriously."

"I know nothing of the kind. If you will not take me home, I will leave on my own."

Francis did so, but not before making excuses to the others that I had a headache. I could scarcely conceal my fury when Phoebe and Etienne followed me home soon after, enquiring solicitously after my health.

That night as I tossed and turned in bed I was determined that Phoebe should leave, and by dawn a solution had occurred to me, albeit a drastic one.

I rose early, though I had hardly slept, and joined Etienne at the breakfast table.

"You are quite recovered then?" he enquired. Then, looking at me more closely, "But you are very pale. Why up so early? Are you sure you would not like to rest today?"

"I am quite sure." My lips tightened before I added, "I am going away, Etienne."

"Going away?"

"Yes, I am going to leave London."

"Oh, for any particular reason?"

I looked at him steadily. "Because I am finding it quite insufferable."

"I have often found it so this past year," he agreed coolly.

"Then you will not object to my leaving?"

"Not at all. You know you may always do as you wish." Then he added, almost as an afterthought, "Might I ask where you intend to go?"

I had thought of going to Dorset, but I had no wish to be near Phoebe. My reason for quitting London was to force her to leave and I was sure she would return there. Nor had I any wish to be with Papa. He had, after all, precipitated my rift with Etienne. Despite his pledge as a gentleman, a pledge never again to gamble deeply, a pledge he had not kept, I might have disclosed Papa's culpability in the Jerningham matter had it been a means of setting matters aright. No longer, however, was I tempted to do so. Not now. Etienne had betrayed me. Whatever he believed was the reason for my visit to Jerningham was no longer of any importance.

I knew Etienne possessed several estates, Lansbury Park in Gloucestershire being the largest and most splendid, but I set aside all thought of going there.

I wanted to hurt him, and I said the one place by which I was sure I could succeed.

"Pelham Manor."

I had not been wrong. The coolness in his eyes turned to wrath.

"Why on earth would you wish to go there?"

"Just a fancy of mine, if you have no objection. I have

never seen Yorkshire. I hear it is very quaint and very rural. It seems just what I need at the moment."

He was silent for a moment, before saying slowly,

"If this sudden decision of yours has anything to do with last night, perhaps I should explain that—"

But I cut him off abruptly.

"It was you who told me, 'never apologize, never explain.' Please don't! Besides, your conduct is of no interest to me."

"I had never supposed it was." The bitterness in his voice cut even through the anger in my heart, and I sought some amelioration, but he was already rising from the table.

"Very well, then, go to Pelham by all means. I doubt you'll last there a week. It is hardly your setting."

"It will be more to my liking than is Grosvenor Square at this moment," I snapped.

"We shall see."

"We shall, indeed."

PART II
PELHAM MANOR, YORKSHIRE

Chapter I

I left the soft, rolling hills of the south to travel to the vast, unkempt and, to me, foreign and forbidding Yorkshire landscape. Cheddell accompanied me, but we talked little. My heart grew heavier as the miles passed but I was determined not to reveal my misgivings to him.

My first sight of Pelham Manor, an H-shaped building of greystone with a sharply sloping tiled roof, equally grey, small-paned lattice windows, surrounded by a break of silver birch trees attempting to hide the bleak moorland beyond, did nothing to improve my spirits.

Cheddell had to climb down from the carriage to help the coachman open the five-barred gate which led to the driveway. Both the gate and the driveway appeared not to have been used for years.

Pelham's only occupant, apart from two elderly and extremely deaf servants, was Mrs. Thistlwaite, a woman who belied her name by being exceedingly round in face and figure, rosy-cheeked, and with such a pleasant smile that my arrival was not quite as bleak as it might otherwise have been.

"Mrs. Lambert, what a delightful surprise. How I have wanted to meet you ever since Mr. Lambert wrote to tell me he was married. I never expected it this way, so suddenly, for his note announcing your arrival came only yesterday and I've barely had time to get in provisions, let alone get the house ready for you."

She looked questioningly and not altogether happily at Cheddell until she learned that he was Etienne's secretary who had accompanied me on the journey.

"Well, menfolk are good for something, I suppose," she sniffed.

Cheddell further annoyed her by explaining stiffly that I was to be addressed as Lady Fordyce Lambert rather than Mrs. Lambert, but she never understood this and, to my relief, called me Mrs. Lambert, as did everyone else in Yorkshire. It was ironic, though, that only after leaving Etienne did I become his wife, in name at least.

Mrs. Thistlwaite had been housekeeper for the Salters who had owned Pelham before Etienne purchased it. He had kept her on and she had remained virtually as mistress of the manor, though she seemed not to have taken advantage of her position as she might, for she had continued to use the small housekeeper's sitting room at the back of the house, leaving the rest of the rooms in dustcovers, some of which she hastily removed on our arrival.

I was glad when Cheddell made no plans for an immediate return to London, for one look at the dismal front parlour with its threadbare furnishings and sparse comfort, its windows giving onto derelict barns and rugged, barren land, made me glad of his urbane presence. It was only after I learned he had been instructed by Etienne to delay his return, so sure had Etienne been that I, also, would decide to return south after seeing Pelham, that I insisted he leave without further delay. It was as much to prevent my succumbing to the temptation to leave and to thwart Etienne as anything, for when he was gone I missed him.

After his departure I wandered disconsolately from room to room but there was nothing—nothing to see, nothing to do, no one to talk to except Mrs. Thistlwaite, or Thistle as she preferred to be called, and she was kindness itself. But I was lonely.

I rode into the nearby village of Sembourne, with its narrow main street skirted by low, whitewashed cottages huddling close to one another as though for protection from the surrounding moor. At the end of the street stood the church, squat and sentinel-like, with only the tower, I judged, part of the original structure. Surrounding it was the churchyard. Beyond was a low grey building which did not invite investigation, and beyond that farms and moorland. I saw no one on my ride, though it was early afternoon, except rosy-cheeked children in clean pinafores who looked at me curiously as I passed but made no effort to return my greeting. I fancied their mothers were behind the lace curtains which occasionally moved. Once I thought I saw a face, but when next I looked it was gone. I returned more depressed than ever.

That night I thought I would have to write to Etienne and admit defeat. He was right. I could not last a week in this place. But the next morning I determinedly dismissed the idea of leaving. I would stay—at least until winter came. Instead of writing to Etienne I wrote to Papa and suggested he come for a visit.

The next day the vicar, Mr. Rankin, called. He was a tall, thin, aesthetic-looking man with sparse, light hair given to falling this way and that beneath his Rehobeth hat and the most determined chin I had ever seen. When I discovered he originally hailed from Dorset I greeted him with open arms, bestowing a welcome upon him which I might have given to a long lost uncle. I chatted away of the house, its furnishings, the village and its inhabitants, the wasted farmland, the weather, anything and everything I could think of. When he at last rose to go I begged him to stay and dine with me.

"I can't, Mrs. Lambert. I'm so very sorry, but Dulcie expects me home, you see, and if I'm not there she will worry."

"Your wife?"

"My daughter. She has cared for me these last five years since Mrs. Rankin died, God rest her soul. She is not much above your age, I'll be bound, and would be delighted to meet you if you would care to dine with us one day." He looked doubtfully at my London clothes. I think those and my magpie talk did not altogether meet with his approval.

"Of course I would love to dine with you." My delight in making an acquaintance of my own age was apparent.

"Would tomorrow be too soon?" he asked dubiously.

"Not in the least."

The vicarage, I discovered the next day, was the low, rambling grey house which I had seen on my ride but had not then considered even of passing interest. Now it became the dearest place to me, with its old brick walkway and its mass of dahlias and chrysanthemums which, I later learned, were the work of Dulcie's nurturing hands.

Dulcie Rankin was, I discovered, just one year older than me. She was somewhat taller, brown-haired with the clearest brown eyes, pleasant rather than beautiful, neat rather than stylish, but altogether the nicest person I had met in an age and a most charming companion. She welcomed me warmly and we were soon ensconced, side by side, talking of everything and nothing. I found everything about her pleasing, not the least being that she seemed to have an immediate caring for me which I found irresistible. Though I had had many friends in the past, none of them, even Phoebe, had ever shown the outward manifestation of tenderness for my well-being which Dulcie exhibited. It was odd, I thought, to come all the way to Yorkshire to find it, first from Mrs. Thistlwaite and now from Dulcie.

At dinner over the plain fare of roast mutton and Yorkshire pudding, which I ate with unaccustomed relish, I spoke again of the terrible condition of the Pelham lands.

"Could no one be found to tend them?" I asked.

There was silence for a moment until Mr. Rankin replied,

"It's not so much the difficulty of finding anyone. Goodness knows there are men by the score without work. Rather it seems a lack of interest on the part of the present owner, your husband, in upgrading the property; indeed, I may say, even in keeping it in the condition it was when he acquired it some eight years ago."

Dulcie interjected quickly, fearing, I think, that, her father's words might have upset me:

"That is but one reason we are all so delighted you have come at last, for now, perhaps, something will be done. Of course, that is not the only reason for our pleasure. I have long wished for someone like yourself to be a close neighbour."

In truth I had given no thought to upgrading Pelham's land or house or anything else, but now, suddenly, the idea seemed appealing. It would give me something to do for the next few months until, after a reasonable absence, I returned to London.

"Could I find men to work the land then and prepare it for planting?"

"Indeed you can," Mr. Rankin assured me, "as long as they haven't been given notions by that rabble-rouser Jeremy Salter."

"Father!" Dulcie snapped in annoyance.

"Who, pray, is Jeremy Salter?" Though I guessed Dulcie did not wish to speak of him, my curiosity got the better of me.

"Jeremy Salter is the youngest son of the family which used to own Pelham. When old Mr. Salter died eight years ago, he left all he possessed to his wife. She sold everything, making some allowance to the boys, and then returned south to Hampshire where she had been born. Jeremy Salter was the only one to remain in Yorkshire. He kept the small northwest corner of the property as his share and he farms that. I must admit he is doing a creditable job despite his political leanings."

"And those are?"

"Oh," Mr. Rankin hesitated, "giving men ideas above their station, telling them the land owes them a living, that sort of thing."

"Then why did he do nothing to see that Pelham was kept productive?" I asked.

"He took care of his own corner of the place well enough, but personally I think he took a delight in the rest of it disintegrating, even the tenants' farms, and I'd not be surprised to find him responsible for the vast amount of poaching that goes on there."

"It was not out of spite, Father," Dulcie put in hotly. "He was upset with his mother for selling the place. He thought it should have been kept in the family. As for the poaching, nothing has ever been proven against him."

"That's as may be, but it doesn't excuse his giving the labourers ideas—riding around with them, holding meetings, haranguing them. Everyone in the riding knows of it, though he's managed to stay clear of the law somehow."

It was apparent that Dulcie and her father did not see eye to eye in the matter of Mr. Jeremy Salter.

"Is there no one I could get to act as bailiff in helping clear the lands?" I asked once more.

"Yes, I think there is. Jeff Hodges has recently returned to this parish after farming for some years in Norfolk somewhere near Coke's estate. It was there he got imbued with Coke's ideas. I know, for he's talked to me endlessly on the subject, but you see I understand little of it. My ministry is to people, not to the land. Anyway his wife died and after that the place had unpleasant memories for him and back he came. Now I think he's sorry. I know he's looking for a challenge to take his mind off things. Pelham would be just that. I think he'd be your man."

"He sounds just right."

Hodges was a man of middling years, open countenance and a pleasant, easy manner. He listened to my proposition of restoring Pelham's lands to productivity without fidgeting, in fact with keen attention, then he paused before replying,

"I'll do it. I'll help you all I can, but only if you'll allow me to institute the new farming methods I learned in Norfolk. Only then will I consider the work worthwhile."

"By all means," I said, "but I know nothing of it. It will all be up to you."

"But you should, Mrs. Lambert. If I work for you, you should know and agree with what I am doing, otherwise I would not wish to do it."

"Very well, then," I replied reluctantly, though I had no wish to be involved.

He returned loaded with literature on farming. I sighed as I looked at the dry, uninviting bundle he gave me but promised him I would read as much as I could.

"In the meantime take on as many men as you see fit and get them started on clearing the debris. And call on the tenants and check into their wants," I told him.

"It will be costly, Mrs. Lambert, especially when we start buying the machinery I recommend."

"It doesn't signify."

No more did it, for though I had had no word from Etienne since my arrival in Yorkshire, the bank at Harrogate had been prompt in notifying me that five thousand pounds had been placed there at my disposal and I had only to notify them when I required more. I could think of nothing in Yorkshire that would require such a sum, but my eye fell on the drabness of the window coverings and the worn seat cushions, and when Hodges left I called in Thistle.

"Thistle, we are going to refurbish this house from top to bottom, starting with this front parlour. I want you to find good painters, cleaners and upholsterers and give me your ideas on materials to use. The furniture for the most part is satisfactory, but it is in sore need of refurbishment. Those curtains are past everything, and as for this carpeting, I cannot believe it is fit for use in a pig stye."

So the days passed in a hum of activity, a coming and going. Smells of fresh paint mingled with those of newly-baked brown bread. Upholsterers fell over mops and pails. Window cleaners hastened with their task before newly-made bright chintz curtains were hung, the oak of the furniture was polished to a mellow glow before new seats and backings of rich yellows and bronzes were affixed to stand out boldly against the clarity of the newly-painted walls. In the midst of it all were Thistle and I, dustcaps covering our heads, answering a thousand questions and helping with a myriad of tasks. I had given up my London finery for the stout, low shoes and light, loose worsted dresses worn by Dulcie. I ate more than usual and physically I did a great deal more than I had ever done in my life, but when I retired I fell asleep with a feeling of pleasant relaxation I had not known since I was a child.

I took to going to bed early and rising early, and before retiring and in the early mornings I read the material Hodges had left me. Far from being dull I found the story of the accomplishments of men like Coke, Turnip Towns-hend, Bakewell and Young exciting. They were men who had seen a need and had set out to fulfill it no matter the cost. Why could it not be done here? The need was self-evident.

So engrossed was I in the subject that when Papa wrote saying that he could on no account leave London and that I should immediately leave the wilds of Yorkshire for civilization, I did not bother to reply.

Hodges came and we discussed the merits of root crops and mulching, of shorthorn cattle and cheviot sheep, and of employing new machinery to aid in sowing and threshing, none of which I had heard of, let alone had any ideas on, prior to arriving in Yorkshire. I instructed him to buy the machinery as soon as possible for the four-coultered ploughs and the seed drills would be needed immediately. I think my excitement matched his as he set out for Manchester.

I dined often with the Rankins but, because of the havoc at Pelham, they rarely joined me at table there, putting this off until the house was in order. But they often rode out in the afternoon to admire and comment on the activity within and without.

On those evenings when I dined at home, more often than not I ate with Thistle in her back sitting room, the only room untouched by the turmoil, and the comfort of her presence grew.

"I suppose you knew the Salters well," I said one day as we sat by the fire after dinner, myself attempting a knitting pattern she had shown me earlier, with dire results.

"Indeed I did. I have worked for them for most of my life, that is until Mr. Lambert bought the place. Even then I didn't realize it was he—only that some gentleman from London had acquired it. I thought I would have to leave. It was only when he wrote asking me to stay, telling me to make it my home, that I knew he was the purchaser. He still writes once or twice a year, but he's yet to come up here. Perhaps now you're here he will."

I had no wish to pursue that topic, but there was another which interested me.

"Did you know his mother?" I asked with studied disinterest.

"Oh, my dear, yes. She was employed here for almost three years."

"Oh!" I could not restrain my surprise. I knew Pelham had some special meaning to Etienne but I didn't realize it was the estate where his mother had worked. No wonder he had purchased it once he had the money to do so. It must have been satisfying to him to own the house where his mother had once been employed as a servant. No wonder, too, he had not wished me to come to a place where his mother had served the gentry. It must have galled him when I decided on Pelham.

"I suppose she worked for you," I said, concentrating on a stitch which had completely escaped from my needle.

"Dear me, no. She was employed by Mrs. Salter as a companion and governess for her children. Mr. Salter was so much older, you know, and Miss Lambert was such a charming person, everyone loved her."

"But I thought she was a servant." I made no further pretence of coping with my knitting, much preferring Thistle's story.

"No, indeed, Miss Lambert was a lady, the youngest daughter of the Lamberts over at Herenton. They wanted her to marry that old skinflint who owned property to the north of them, a more plain, ill-humoured gentleman it would be hard to find. Anyway, she refused. Said she'd rather work as a governess than be mistress of his estate. So she found this position with Mrs. Salter, not that it was an easy one with three boys already and then Mr. Jeremy came along, and Mrs. Salter always wanting her to do this and that. But she was good-humoured and pretty as the day is long and every ounce of her was courage."

"But who—what happened?"

"Oh, the baby, you mean. They went away, all of them, and when they came back she was with child. She didn't speak of it but I knew. I could tell by her eyes. She told no one of it, went on with her duties as before and when her weight began to show she wore loose fitting gowns and joked about eating too well. Mrs. Salter never knew, but I did. I could hear her crying at night when she thought everyone was asleep. One night she came to me in pain. The baby was due and she begged my help. I brought her down here and pleaded with her to allow me to call the midwife but she wouldn't hear of it. The baby came at last, a fine boy, but the afterbirth wouldn't loosen. She lost a lot of blood and against her wishes I got the midwife, but it was too late. I saw to the burial and the baptism. There was a lot of talk, you can imagine. She wanted the name Etienne St. Clair, and so it was, but as far as I know she never told anyone who the father was. Mrs. Salter would have nothing to do with the child, or the funeral either for that matter. She said she was furious after all she had done for the girl, said she was tainted and had her just rewards, and not the least of her sins was that she left the boys to Mrs. Salter, for she was never again able to get anyone to stay with her. Mrs. Salter was all for putting the baby on the parish, but I wouldn't have that. I took him over to the Lamberts and forced them to take him. They were none too happy about it, I can assure you, but there was nothing else I could do. I couldn't keep him. I had no money for his care and he couldn't live here with me. Mrs. Salter wanted him gone, said he reminded her of his mother and she'd rather forget her. The Lamberts sent him away somewhere but when he was about ten he came back. He was strong and you could see he was going to be handsome even then, straight teeth and good bones, and those dark eyes, like hers yet different. He came to see me often. He'd rattle away in French to make me laugh. I think I was the only one who gave him any affection and how he craved it, poor little soul. Mrs. Salter wouldn't speak to him and the Lamberts were awfully strict. They soon packed him off again to the Bluecoat School in London. He hated it. He wrote to tell me he was leaving, then I heard nothing more of him till he bought Pelham."

So that was it, I thought, that was why he hated Pelham. I wondered why he'd bothered to buy it. Revenge, perhaps, for his mother's death; he certainly didn't want the place. "If you had an ounce of her courage," I remembered him once saying. How had she endured that life as Mrs. Salter's companion and governess to those boys, and that terrible ending. Looking around Thistle's cheerful little room which had seen Etienne's entrance into the world, I shuddered.

Chapter II

After Hodges' return from Lancashire, we waited expectantly for the arrival of the first machinery. It came at last, a four-coultered plough and a seed drill, made after Tull's design, with more promised the following month. The men gathered round silently and watched as the unwieldy monsters were hauled into the old barn, but without sharing, at least outwardly, the excitement and curiosity felt by Hodges and myself.

"They're beauties, Mrs. Lambert." Hodges caressed the plough's blades. "Feel it. That's workmanship, that is! They're getting better and better at it. Pretty soon you'll see everything done by machinery, and done better, mark my words."

"I can hardly wait to see them working."

"The north field is just about cleared and should be fit for turning over. Don't see why we couldn't have a try at ploughing it tomorrow."

"I'll be there to watch," I promised.

That night I fell asleep as usual but, unlike other nights, I was awakened by a noise. I listened. It seemed to come from the direction of the barn. I remembered the machinery and rose hastily and dressed, praying it was not a fire. I wondered whether to alert the others but realized how stupid I would feel if it turned out to be nothing more than an animal that had got loose. It was only a step to the barn and I could discover the trouble. Should there be nothing, there was no need to sound an alarm and frighten them, and truly I could smell no smoke. I tied a scarf over my head and hurried down.

I ran towards the barn, its familiar shape looming up in the moonlight with no sign of smoke though I thought I saw flashes of light within. My heart was already pounding as I swung open the heavy door. It pounded even more at the sight of a crowd of men, some of whom I recognized as Pelham workers, gathered around the new pieces of machinery. They did not hear me enter, for all their attention was on a young man in their midst, of slight build, brown haired, bronze skinned, but with the most dynamic voice I have ever heard. I became as enthralled as the men with his cadences, though his subject, the evils of machinery, pleased me less. When he concluded with a ringing cry to "destroy this evil in our midst," I stepped forward.

"I think I have some say in what happens to this machinery."

I heard mumbling cries of "It's Mrs. Lambert," "It's the mistress," and I saw one of my men lolling on the plough and ordered him off. He looked sullen but did as he was bid.

"This machinery is mine, chosen and bought by me."

"It's your husband's blunt that bought it, not yours," I heard a man in the crowd call out, followed by several cries of "Aye!"

"That is quite true, nevertheless it is through me that machinery was bought with that money, it is through me that that money is being used to improve the land, and it is through me that you were employed here for that purpose.

It may be my husband's money but I have the use of it. I want to use it to good purpose."

The young man in their midst had been watching me with a look of derision as I spoke.

"Mrs. Lambert—or is it Lady Lambert, or Lady Fordyce Lambert that you like to be called, in London anyway—perhaps having lived so little in Yorkshire you are unaware of our lack of esteem for the gentry in this part of the world."

"Yet you yourself, sir, by your voice and air, are part of the gentry whom you so freely degrade, but you have not seen fit to identify yourself to me."

"As you rightly guess, I was so born, madam, but I now identify myself only as a Yorkshireman and as such I deplore what is happening in this county. It is, I believe, happening in other parts of the country, but it is here in Yorkshire that my friends and I see it, and it is here we must fight it with whatever means are available to us."

"It is to this machinery that you refer?"

"It is. You, and people like you, are taking the very livelihood from our men—men with wives and families, forced on the parish, their very bread taken from their mouths by the gentry, and what are they doing about it, inventing and making more infernal machines to add to man's burden rather than alleviate his problem. And that problem is bread, madam, bread. But perhaps you prefer cake."

"There is no need for sarcasm, Mr. Salter," I cut him off sharply. I don't know whether it was my remark or the fact that I knew his identity which threw him off stride for a moment, but he caught himself up.

"We Yorkshiremen are men of the soil. This is our soil. We want no foreigners standing upon it, taking bread from our mouths with this—this damnable rubbish." He kicked the drill as he spoke. "It is for your benefit, not ours."

"Let us not kick at the object which may be the means of feeding all of us eventually, Mr. Salter."

"To feed you, you mean," he said savagely. "None of this is designed with us in mind."

"There, I believe, you are wrong. It is designed to feed us, all of us."

"It is designed to make money, and if you don't know it, it is well your husband knows it. Has he not equipped his cotton mills with weaving machines?"

Since I knew nothing of Etienne's activities, and since this was the first time I knew he owned any cotton mills, I could scarcely argue the point.

"My husband's endeavours are his affair, Mr. Salter. I cannot speak for his intentions, only for my own. On that matter I can say that in bringing this machinery to Pelham I have nothing but the good of the estate and the community as a whole in mind."

"And how many Yorkshiremen will you put out of work with this? I speak to you as one of them, but I doubt any of it would signify much to a southerner like you, and a member of the nobility to boot."

"I admit to being Dorset born and to having spent a great deal of my time in London, but that does not mean I have no Yorkshire connections. My husband was born here."

"Yes, he was born here all right, on the wrong side of the blanket, a bastard who has risen to take our land from us."

I had no thought to do it, my action took me as much by surprise as it did Salter, but hearing Etienne called aloud a name which I had at times given him in the privacy of my own mind made me realize the terrible injustice of it all. What had he to do with his own coming into the world? Why should he be forever stigmatized by it? He was more a gentleman in mind and manner than many I knew who had been conceived between lawful sheets. All of this went into the blow I dealt Salter, so that even when my hand fell to my side I could clearly see the mark I had left on his face, red and ugly against the bronze of his skin.

"I will not have my husband spoken of in such a fashion." My voice was clear and cold despite the shaking anger I felt inside.

As unexpected as the blow I had dealt him was his apology.

"I spoke out of turn, forgive me." He seemed, momentarily, to have forgotten the men and the purpose of being there. But then, almost visibly, he pulled himself up.

"But you cannot deny that this machinery will keep men from working, men to whom you have given hope by coming here and opening up this dormant land."

I turned to the crowd which had been watching with fascination the *contretemps* between the two of us in their midst.

"I have given you work. I have given work to many in this village. What you have done in return has given me pleasure. You have worked hard and well. My intention in buying this machinery is not to put you out of work, rather it is to make work better for you. It will take skill rather than mere brawn to make these machines do what is now being done by men. Machines will do nothing in and of themselves, they will only do what men make them do, and men must be trained for this purpose. While these machines will do away with some jobs now done by many of you, there are those jobs for which no machine has yet been invented— caring for animals, reclaiming the land fronting on the moors. Machines are no good there, and it is there that those of you not employed on the machines and their concomitant tasks will be working. In buying these machines I have no intention of taking away honest labour, I only wish to ease it. I want to move ahead into this nineteenth century and I would like all of you to move with me. It is your decision. I am well aware that the law is in your hands tonight. I ask you to remember, though, that it is easy to make another machine. All it needs is *blunt* as you call it. A man, however, is not so easily replaced."

Without another word to Salter I turned towards the door. The men cleared a path through their midst and I walked through them, my head held high. As I neared the door a young man with a shock of sandy hair crossed my path.

"Rich bitch, what would you know of how the poor live!"

The remark was flung at me through clenched teeth and was swiftly followed by a mouthful of spittle which landed on the skirt of my blue kerseymere dress. I stopped abruptly and we faced one another as though in battle. I feared the men would side with him, for there was a murmur of assent around me and I knew I was completely alone.

"I am from a noble family," I said clearly, "but I assure you I am not rich. All that I have is from my husband. I know the power which wealth brings only by proxy."

He continued to stand in front of me, fists clenched. I felt helpless. Then I heard a movement behind me and someone stepped by and pushed the young belligerant roughly aside. It was Salter. He knelt down and with his sleeve wiped the spot on my skirt where the spittle stood out, bright, glistening and distasteful, in the light of the torches.

"I'm very sorry, Mrs. Lambert," was all he said.

Still holding my head high, I nodded, and walked past his kneeling figure to gain the barn door and thence, with a deliberately unhurried step, the door of the house. Once inside, however, I shut it firmly and leaned against it, my body throbbing with fear. How had I dared to speak so to such a mob? The fellow had been right, I knew nothing of the troubles of the poor. I had had nothing to do with them. Only now did it occur to me, having met some of them, that there were people in England totally different from me yet belonging equally to this land. Only now did I begin to see people as individuals in their own right, regardless of their station in life. Etienne knew, I thought. He could speak to anyone with understanding, be he a peer of the realm or a groom, but he had lived a different life from mine. I had never envied his lot until that moment.

I went upstairs and changed my dress, uncertain whether to raise Thistle and the servants. If the men fired the barn, the house could easily catch; not the greystone walls perhaps but the trees surrounding it with their dry autumn foliage would light quickly. I sat by the window, watching, waiting.

I don't know how long I sat there, one hour or five. I saw the signs of a lightening sky in the east and the moon was on the wane. At last I heard a murmur rising from the barn. I stood up, yet away from the window. Then I saw shadows filing by, in twos and threes, but I saw no smoke. Thank God, I thought, they had not fired the barn. At last came a figure on his own. I saw him stop and look up in the direction of my bedroom window. I don't know whether he saw me or not but I fancied he smiled. I am quite sure that he waved his arm before he turned and vanished into the night. I knew it was Jeremy Salter.

I said nothing of the incident to Hodges, to Dulcie or Mr. Rankin, to Thistle, particularly not to Captain Redmond who commanded the ninth militia at Knaresbridge, not to anyone. I ordered Hodges to train as many men as possible to use the machinery, and once it was operating to set men to clearing rough land near the moor for potato planting and set others to work putting the tenants' houses in order. I also asked him to buy additional sheep, a hardy breed, to keep on the land too rough for planting. He complained of the expense, but I argued that the end worth of our productivity would justify it. He did as he was bid, grumbling, but secretly glad to have so many tasks to oversee.

I began to accompany Dulcie on her Sembourne rounds when she called on Squire and Mrs. Rokeby who, in their own pompous fashion, ruled over the village, or Mrs. Dorling, the widow of a wealthy Yorkshireman who had settled in her native village and who, feeling her own life was past, lived on the lives of others. I was also with Dulcie when she visited the small, white cottages of scarcely more than one room, but that one clean and neat, to deliver her baskets of food and knitted goods. With time the cottagers, at first reticent, began to receive me with as much trust and respect as they accorded Dulcie. I saw for myself the loathesome conditions under which they were forced to live; not just the difficulty of keeping a family in food and clothing, but the monotonous regularity with which women produced children to act as a further drain on their meagre resources. I knew of a solution to their difficulties but I had not the courage of a Salter to get up and speak openly on a forbidden subject. I feared the men's reaction and that of the women also. I was sure they wished freedom from their burden but I was sure they regarded it as an act of God to breed like animals. Yet I knew it need not be.

Gradually I began to know Pelham's tenants: Duggan, who regularly beat his wife and provided her with a continuing chain of offspring, Stott, who was known as Scartop because of an accident he had suffered while ploughing, and Clayton who worked day and night and cursed having to rest on the sabbath. As I began to know them, so they began to know and trust me and gradually I became the one they came to with their difficulties. Mrs. Duggan arrived one morning, bruised, bleeding and crying of her husband's treatment of her. It was to her I confided the secret of controlling birth to which she listened wide-eyed, astonished and alarmed. Later I sought out her husband and assured him that I would see to it that he was no longer served at the *Red Lion* in the village if he did not mend his ways. He grumbled but, watching my men mend the roof on his barn, agreed as how he might have a little too much ale from time to time—not that he was ever drunk mind you, but perhaps there were occasions he acted a little hastily—and that he would watch for it in the future.

When Stott brought back a sheep from market and discovered it had foot rot which threatened his whole flock and would, if unchecked, contaminate all others in the neighbourhood, it was I who insisted they all be killed and I who replaced them. And when the Clayton's eldest boy, who was obviously meant for something other than farming, talked whenever we met of his dreams for the future, it was I who arranged for him to go to school in York and for his place on the farm to be taken by one of my own men. It was true that I had the money to do these things, but I had never spent it in such a manner before. I now found it very satisfying.

By the end of November the redecoration of Pelham Manor was completed and it was, I decided, my turn to entertain before the winter set in in earnest. I was proud of the changes I had made in the house and the way the land was assuming a new identity under the watchful eye of Hodges. Dulcie helped me with the invitations.

"I'll write one to Mr. Salter," I said as we sat together in the now comfortable parlour.

"Have you met him?" she asked, her voice masked to hide a too evident curiosity.

To admit to our meeting would arouse too many questions.

"I think I know him by sight," I said, still writing.

"He doesn't go out much socially," she said, but before she could pursue a subject which I felt was close to her own heart but might arouse awkward questions, I said, "Perhaps you could address a card to the Lamberts. Do you know who still resides at Herenton?"

"Old Mr. Lambert and his daughter."

"My husband's grandfather and aunt?" My curiosity was piqued.

"Yes." She was quieter than usual in her response and I felt she wanted to talk as little of the Lamberts as much as she had wanted to talk of Jeremy Salter.

"Then they shall be invited."

"They rarely go far," she hesitated. "Herenton is some distance from here."

"To be sure it is. Perhaps I'd better write them a letter and suggest they stay overnight in that case."

The kitchen was a hive of activity for the event. Extra maids were taken on from the village, cooks, and bottle washers. There was a pig for roasting, fish from Carnaby Bay, kidney for pies, jams, jellies, sweetmeats, fruit tarts, and Thistle presided over it all. I was proud of what I had accomplished and wished Etienne could be there to see it. I thought of writing to ask him to come but the thought died aborning. He had never come back to Yorkshire; my presence there now would provide little added inducement.

I could not decide what to wear. My London clothes were too fine, my Yorkshire ones too utilitarian. In the end I settled on the most simple of my London clothes, a brown silk frock, plainly cut and without adornment except for two bands of darker brown satin around the hem and matching silk slippers. Yet even this was too much, as I could tell by Mrs. Dorling's opening remark as she eyed me from head to toe,

"Oh, so that is how they dress in London now, is it?"

The guests arrived: the squire and his wife, Captain Redmond who came with Merston, the lawyer from Knaresbridge and his wife and son, several wealthy farmers who endeared themselves to me by admiring the changes in the land and by taking time to go to the barn to examine drills and threshers, and finally Jeremy Salter who greeted me as though for the first time, and who caused Dulcie to spill a glass of ratafia in her pleasure at seeing him. But there was no sign of the Lamberts, for whom I waited all afternoon in vain.

The party was a success. All ate well from the sumptuous buffet, all admired the house and its refurbishment, and all spoke highly of the improvement of Pelham. I was gratified. It was Mrs. Rokeby, however, who first spoke of the Lamberts.

"I'm so sorry not to see them here today. I remember dear *Miss* Lambert well when she worked for the Salters." She made it impossible to overlook the unmarried status of Etienne's mother.

Mrs. Dorling quickly joined in, "A dear creature they say she was—until that unfortunate event."

"I hardly feel that the birth of my husband can be classified as an unfortunate event," I replied evenly, "though it was a tragedy for his mother."

I was aware of Jeremy Salter listening to our conversation though he was half turned away from us.

"Of course not," Mrs. Dorling continued unphased. "And you cannot be blamed that your father allowed you to marry someone of, let us say, uncertain origin. I see that your husband is not here with you but undoubtedly he will come." I heard the lingering question in her voice.

"Undoubtedly," I responded as I turned, anxious to get away from her spiteful comments. I found Jeremy Salter at my side,

"Will he come?" he asked.

"Who?"

"Your husband."

"I expect so."

"Oh, I was hoping—but I have no right to say what I was hoping, or all the things that have been on my mind since last I saw you."

There was no mistaking his look. I had seen it many times before and I knew its meaning—another conquest—but this time I knew it was different. He was no young London beau, and even had I felt so inclined, he was no man to be played with. I saw Dulcie's eyes on us. She knows, I thought, and suddenly hated him for the rift I felt he would make between us.

"Just so, Mr. Salter, you have no right," I said briskly.

"How can he bear to let you out of his sight for so long?"

"He trusts me."

"Should he?" he asked softly. "I thought—I heard—it was said—oh, I know I shouldn't repeat gossip but I must ask. I was told yours was a marriage of convenience, rather than a love match."

"I have no intention of answering such an impudent question," I replied haughtily. "Now if you will excuse me."

He was embarrassed, and I made no attempt to alleviate his misery, nor would I talk to him for the rest of the day. Yet his remark rankled long after the evening was past, long after Thistle and I had held our post mortem on the guests and the fare, long after I had received congratulations from neighbours on the splendid occasion. Why, I wondered, did his remark have the power to hurt me so. It was open knowledge in London. I had never gone to any pains to deny it. Why should it disturb me so now, here in Yorkshire, when Etienne and I were separated, at my instigation, by two hundred miles rather than the few feet which separated our rooms? It was then I owned to myself the truth I had never allowed myself to acknowledge before. I loved him.

Chapter III

As December arrived, winter in Yorkshire began in earnest. The days were crisp and each morning as I woke I saw the thick frost coating the birch trees outside. I watched the squirrels collect hazel nuts and hoard their treasures away for the days ahead, and I in turn alerted Thistle to make sure we had a good supply of wood and coal.

But one day midway through the month dawned brighter and clearer than the rest. The sun shone as though determined to ward off winter, at least for that day, and I got my horse and started out across the heather-covered moors north of Pelham. The wind blew in my face making my cheeks tingle, and I felt free and glad to be alive on what would probably be my last long ride of that year. I wondered what I would do in the new year. All of my interests now seemed to be in Yorkshire—all except one, and that was the one I was never allowed to forget nor ever wanted to forget. The subject of my thoughts was brought more than ever alive to me by a signpost I could not remember having seen before, showing Herenton only eleven miles to the north.

The Lamberts had never replied to my invitation; now the idea occurred to me to go and find out why. The morning was fine and I could ride that distance in less than an hour. Even allowing for my call, which might be quite lengthy, I could still be home in plenty of time for dinner. I turned towards the north and was off at a gallop.

I arrived in Herenton without mishap, though I was dishevelled and both my horse and myself were tired. It was a village in the midst of the moors, much as Sembourne; the same white houses huddled close together, the same perpendicular style church, yet there was something cold about it, something uninviting. I remembered my first view of Sembourne. Hadn't I felt much the same? It was merely because it was unfamiliar. I shook myself mentally to escape the pall which came over me.

It was not difficult to find the Lambert's residence. There was only one house of any size or distinction, and it faced the village squarely on an elevation which set it apart. It was built of the local stone I had seen so often, but here it had been used in a more imposing manner, extra large blocks having been found for the walls and set lengthwise giving the house an impregnable air. As I struck the brass knocker shaped to the likeness of a lion's head, I was aware of how it must have looked to a small boy unsure of his welcome, for my own feelings at that moment must have reflected something of what Etienne had felt. •

An expression of surprise, even alarm, on the face of the elderly servant after hearing my name did nothing to alleviate my anxiety, nor did the anteroom into which I was ushered while he announced my arrival. It was a small, dark room furnished with dreary stuffed armchairs covered with a host of antimacassars, equally dreary window hangings and a picture on the wall of The Burning Bush, all of which I had ample time to examine before I was shown into a parlour of much larger dimensions, though scarcely more cheerful. A lady, a white cap covering her dark hair, sat near the window busily engaged in crocheting what promised to be yet another antimacassar and from which she barely raised her head as I was announced. The room's chief occupant, on whom my eyes were quickly fixed, was a white-haired gentleman seated in a large wing-backed armchair by a smouldering fire. He rose to greet me and I discovered he was exceptionally tall and, despite his years, he held himself remarkably straight. His countenance was hawk-like, a large nose surmounted by piercing dark eyes with no trace of a smile on his pursed lips in answer to my greeting. If anything, his expression grew more pained as I spoke.

"You must be Etienne's grandfather."

"I am Sheldon Lambert," he said stiffly and, in answer to my questioning glance in the direction of the seated lady, he waved a hand. "This is my daughter."

"Your elder daughter?"

"I have only one daughter."

"I know that is the case now, but that was not always so. My husband's mother was your younger daughter, I believe."

He had kept his eyes fixed on me since my arrival, but now he turned them to the fire.

"Her name is never mentioned in this house. It is as well, for we should not speak ill of the dead."

The interview was worse than any I had envisioned. He had not yet invited me to be seated and already we were in open hostility.

"You cannot expect me to share your sentiments, of course. I value my husband too highly." My voice snapped like the lash of a whip, forcing his eyes back to me.

"Your father is the Earl of Castleford, is he not?"

I nodded.

"And he allowed you to marry—Etienne Lambert?"

"Your grandson, you mean?"

"I'm not sure that is the title to which the law entitles him."

"I believe it is one which is his due by a higher law." I saw no softening on his part, no sign of cordiality but I continued, "May we not be seated?"

He nodded without grace and I caught another quick glance from Miss Lambert before she once again became engrossed in her handwork.

"And how did you know of your grandson's marriage, Mr. Lambert?" I asked, ignoring his disclaimer.

"He wrote to me of it."

"Yet I saw no reply from you."

"That is because I sent none."

"Just as you sent no response to my invitation to visit Pelham last month. I regret you did not come. I believe you would have enjoyed it."

"How can you know anything of what I would or would not enjoy?"

"I spoke more from courtesy than conviction. You are quite right, I cannot know with any degree of certainty your likes and dislikes, nor will you allow me to know them as long as you keep yourself distant from me," I replied, determined not to be bested.

"My dear young lady—"

"Mrs. Lambert."

"My dear Mrs. Lambert, then." His hostility in using his name in any connection with Etienne was obvious. "I see no reason just because you have come to Yorkshire on some whim or other for any need of an acquaintance between us. My grandson, as you choose to call him, spent little enough of his time here."

"Was that through any fault of his own? Can a child decide where he will or will not live?"

I saw a flush of anger creep into his cheeks.

"You are an outspoken young woman, even impudent I might say."

"I see no need to mince my words, sir, nor, I believe, do you."

We eyed one another like sparring partners in a match, taking each other's measure, and at last it was he who went on as though he felt some explanation was due.

"I sent him to school, a good school, the Bluecoat School."

"A charity school."

"Nevertheless, a good school. He chose not to stay there—ran off to the Americas or some such place without a word. He came into this world unwanted. I did what I could for him though I owed him nothing."

"Including never letting him forget he was unwanted, I have no doubt."

"I could scarcely pretend he was of legitimate birth."

"Scarcely." Sarcasm edged my voice like brimstone. "I dare say you could not show affection for him either. How many letters did you write to him in school?"

He flushed again.

"That is hardly the matter at hand. If he intended to leave the school to which I had sent him, it was for him to write to me and explain his reasons. I received not a word."

"Yet he wrote of it to Thistle."

"Thistle?"

"Mrs. Thistlwaite, the housekeeper at Pelham."

"Oh, that woman! Why would he write to her?"

"She saw him into the world. She found him a home," my eyes travelled around the oppressive room, "of sorts. She looked after his welfare. She gave him love. But you, you gave him nothing. Certainly nothing of yourself."

"He has my name, does he not?"

"But it was not you who gave it to him. It was your daughter, your younger daughter. It was her name, too. But I forgot. She is not to be spoken of, is she?"

I could see I had thoroughly infuriated him now and,

realizing the futility of my mission and the change in the weather outside, I rose abruptly.

"It was good to meet you, Mr. Lambert, but I see we have very little in common, as you have so rightly pointed out. I feel more than ever for Etienne now after meeting you, for I understand what he must have suffered in this house as a small, unwanted child. I bid you goodday, sir."

My abrupt departure had startled Mr. Lambert. Perhaps he enjoyed the battle of wits. He started to rise.

"Please do not trouble yourself, sir, I can see myself out."

I looked in the direction of the window at Miss Lambert's figure, bent more assiduously than ever over her work.

"Goodday to you also, Miss Lambert."

She looked up quickly, and I thought I saw pity in her eyes but I could not be sure, so quickly were they returned to her work.

As I strode towards the door Mr. Lambert's voice stopped me momentarily,

"Etienne—I know he is rich now, but how is he? Is he well?"

"He is quite able to take care of himself now. You need worry yourself no further about him."

The way home was difficult beyond all measure. I took the path I had followed that morning, but so incensed was I in thinking of that house and its occupants that I paid little heed to the way. Both myself and my horse lacked adequate rest and after I had gone some miles I realized that I had been offered no refreshments and I was now exceedingly hungry. The bleak scene ahead reminded me that there was little likelihood of either inn or farmhouse between there and Pelham. I would have to make up for it when I got home. But time passed and I failed to find the signpost which had sent me on my fruitless mission earlier in the day.

It was the changed direction of the wind, still blowing in my face despite the fact that I was going in the opposite direction to this morning, which made me aware of the changing weather conditions; that and the darkening sky. There was little of beauty about the moors now. They surrounded me on all sides, sombre, grey and forlorn, endless nothingness.

I tried to forget tales I had heard of wolves and bears which had once roamed freely. It was said they were still there—not many, but I had heard the oft-repeated story of the boy who had not come home and whose body had been found a week later out here, mutilated beyond recognition. I urged my horse on. He stumbled at a confluence of streams that I could not remember having crossed before. I remembered Thistle talking of Robin Hood and his men having a meeting place where two streams met, a dismal spot if that were it. Thoughts of Robin Hood made me long for Etienne. If he were there beside me we might be just as lost, yet it would be so different. But I had no one to rely on except myself. I would come through it, I determined, even though I knew night was falling and I had no idea where I was. The gorse bushes assumed strange shapes which loomed up at me. There was a gnawing voice inside which kept telling me it was the end. If it were, I wondered how others would feel and, for the first time since I had arrived in Yorkshire, I allowed myself to think of Phoebe. If anything happened to me she would be sorry, no doubt, yet I knew it would mean Etienne would be free and I knew she wanted him. With that knowledge came strength. She could not have him while I was alive, and I would live. Lost in these thoughts I was at first unaware of my horse's stumbling gait, but when I dismounted to see whether he had caught a stone in his hoof, I found with horror that the shoe on his left foreleg was missing. It must have happened crossing the stream. Poor creature, but it couldn't have happened at a worse time.

I began walking, bridle in hand, in a direction which

nothing but instinct told me was the way home. In the failing light I could see no familiar sign. The cold wind was now joined by a steady rain which kept up a ceaseless patter on the bracken, and as I trudged through it my clothing became drenched. I felt like Mary of Modena, the Queen of Tears, for I knew my strength was failing and I cried in the knowledge I might never see Etienne, Dulcie, Pelham, Thistle, anyone or anything that was dear to me ever again.

I had once read that people lost in the desert dying of thirst often imagine they see water where there is none. Now, in the distance across the moors I thought I saw a small light. I wondered if it were the same phenomenon and whether others lost on the moor in the past had seen that same light and had imagined shelter as I did now. I blinked through my tears but the light did not go away. I had no recourse but to investigate.

How long it was before I came to a low, well-built farmhouse I cannot say, for, finding an end in view paradoxically made the way seem longer rather than shorter as I stumbled and ran. Though I had taken the house to be in the midst of the moors, even in the darkness I could tell that the land around it was cultivated. All this occurred to me only in passing. My main thought was that it was shelter. I had found shelter on that cold, friendless night. I would not die, at least not for the moment.

My knock was answered by a manservant who, if he was put out by the sight I presented, must have been used to handling every kind of emergency. He saw me into the parlour, a low-ceilinged, warm, friendly room, though lacking any frills or decoration, and promised to inform his master and to take care of my horse. I could hear men's voices coming from the rear of the house, but all that concerned me was the fire burning in the hearth. I knelt before it and put my head in my hands and thus I remained until I heard the door open. Even then I did not hurry to sit up, thinking it was the manservant again, but when I did I saw I was mistaken. Standing in the middle of the room, a startled expression on his face, was Jeremy Salter.

"You!" I exclaimed. "I never thought to find you here, though I was never so pleased to see anyone in all my life. But how do you come to be here?"

"I live here," he said simply. "And may I say that I was never so happy to have anyone call upon me before."

He knelt beside me and took my hands in his.

"But you are frozen. What has happened?"

I explained that I had been to Herenton and had lost my way on the moors.

"Herenton! But that must be twenty miles from here. Why there?"

"The Lamberts live there and since it was fine earlier I thought to visit them. They are my husband's relatives—but, of course, you know. It was all a mistake, the journey, the visit. I should never have gone, but I am safe now."

"Don't talk any more. I will have my man bring you something dry to put on and some hot broth to drink. Meanwhile I will try to close the meeting I have here and will return to you soon. I shall make no mention of your presence, never fear."

"But it is no secret," I protested. "I was lost, that is all."

"I don't believe you know the Yorkshire tongue."

By the time he returned I was warmed within and without. I knew I must present a pretty spectacle, swathed in his house robe, but if it was displeasing he gave no sign of it, seeming only to delight in my presence. We sat by the fire talking as though we had known each other for years. He told me of his Yorkshire life, his childhood at Pelham and his political activism since that time. His obvious sincerity for his cause impressed me, yet it was he, I discovered, who had succeeded in saving my farm equipment from the men that night.

"Are you sorry now?" I smiled.

"No," he said. "Then I did not want them to harm it because it was yours. Now also I would protect it for that reason, but I am also watching to see what will result from its use."

"You promise to keep an open mind, then?"

"Sometimes you make it difficult for me to do so."

"Why?" I wrinkled my forehead in puzzlement.

He looked down at his hands.

"Because I am so biased in your favour."

It was a topic I did not wish to continue. Instead I told him of my visit to the Lamberts and of the humiliation I had suffered at their hands and how I felt Etienne must have suffered under their roof.

"You are a loyal wife," he said at last.

"My husband would be surprised to hear you say so," I replied almost to myself.

He looked at me sharply, as though there were a thousand questions he wished to put to me but did not dare.

"I don't know why you came to Yorkshire on your own," he ventured, "but I know that I, for one, will always be eternally grateful that you did. I have never known a woman of such courage."

The look which accompanied these words made me acutely conscious of our intimacy. I was alone with him, under his roof, at night, and in a state of undress. What a moment before had seemed perfectly natural now seemed highly improper.

"I must get home," I said abruptly. "It cannot be that far now, for this house was originally part of Pelham, was it not? If you can lend me a horse I can find my way. My own is lame."

He agreed that I must go but would only hear of it if I allowed him to drive me in his gig. Furthermore he insisted I take a glass of spirits to ward off the chilling wind and rain.

I put on my damp clothes again and swathed a shawl belonging to one of the servants around my shoulders before climbing into the gig.

As we were about to leave I heard horse's hooves and saw a rider loom up out of the darkness.

"Mr. Salter!" a male voice called out. "What are you going out for on a night like this when you are already at home and need not stir abroad. I came back for there was an important matter I wished to discuss with you."

I recognized the voice as that of the father of Betsy Hawly, a village girl I employed from time to time, and as he came closer I knew he recognized me in the light of the lantern Salter had been holding.

"Another time," he muttered and rode away into the sodden night.

"Damn him!" I heard Salter curse under his breath, though outwardly he gave no sign that he was disconcerted and nothing was said of the matter on our way home.

All at Pelham were too happy at my safe return to ask many questions about my absence. My story of being lost on the moor and my horse's loss of a shoe seemed sufficient. But I became increasingly aware that I was the subject of village gossip and that the gossip included Jeremy Salter. The stares I received and the hastily quieted tongues on my approach did not unduly concern me, but I was upset by the reticence now shown toward me by Dulcie. I had come to rely on her friendship and her new coldness hurt me more than anything. I knew she loved Jeremy Salter over her father's objections. I felt I should say something, yet I was loathe to talk to anyone of that Herenton visit. The Lamberts had been despicable to Etienne. I could not talk of that day without mentioning them. Perhaps I should have told Dulcie of finding refuge with Salter that night, but I was not sure she would understand it was nothing more than that. Perhaps it would only lend credence to the village gossip.

Perhaps she, too, would think I had had an assignation with him. If she thought such a thing I preferred not to hear it.

Salter did little to ease the burden. His obvious predilection for me was apparent and my very indifference to it seemed to heighten it. Whenever he dined at Pelham I made sure that Dulcie and her father were of the party and always arranged the table so that Dulcie sat beside him. Yet inevitably I noticed she lost her tongue. All of her sweet, natural air left her and she became silent and stiff in his presence. It was love, I supposed, which affected her so. I wondered it had never done so to me, but then I realized I had never acknowledged that love until ten score miles separated us. I wondered if I would act so if Etienne were to arrive one day. How he would laugh if he knew, I thought bitterly.

Chapter IV

At Christmas I gave a party for the Pelham tenants. Thistle prepared an enormous bowl of punch together with a feast under which our large oak table groaned in stolid contentment, as did the guests after partaking of its contents.

I gave in to an impulse and wrote to Etienne, inviting him for the occasion. In reply I had a brief note wishing me the joys of the season, indicating that Cheddell had deposited another five thousand pounds to my Yorkshire account and that he was sending me a Christmas present and, by way of afterthought, that his affairs in London required his presence there.

The present came. It was a pair of Meissen porcelain figures, a drummer and fifer, exquisite in detail and colouring. Beautiful to look at, but utterly useless.

This is how Etienne sees me, I thought, beautiful and useless. I remembered Salter's words—I have never known a woman of such courage—and wished Etienne could say that to me at least once.

The first months of the new year passed slowly. A heavy

mantle of snow had enveloped the landscape since Christmas, forcing us to seek our entertainment inside. I read a great deal and studied French but rarely stirred farther than church for Sunday service or to the parsonage to have dinner with the Rankins. Occasionally enough of us were present to make up a table of loo or speculation, and much ponderous play resulted when a shilling was at stake.

By late February nothing was left of the snow except the worsened condition of the roads, but by the time March came and planting was taking place we had become used to the bumps and holes and accepted them as the norm. I loved being out again. I loved being active. I felt more capable and sure of myself than at any other time in my life; this was manifested in the decisions I made daily and the satisfaction I felt at the end of the day. I thought scarcely at all of my London life. Papa and I had exchanged letters at Christmas, just as Etienne and I had done, with no greater intimacy. I began to believe that all that part of my life was closed, that I would start anew here at Pelham, on my own.

I had not anticipated, therefore, seeing Etienne's travelling chaise before the door as I rode back one fine April afternoon from the parsonage.

I dismounted hastily and threw my reins to the groom and ran up the steps two at a time.

"Etienne!" I called.

He was in the hall, hugging Thistle with all his might, his tall frame bent over her short, stocky figure almost lifting her feet from the floor.

"Mr. Lambert! Mr. Lambert! How's a body to stand it!" she cautioned as he put her down. "Why didn't you tell us you were coming?"

He turned as I called his name again, but his greeting of me was much more restrained than it had been of Thistle. In fact he shook hands and it was only when I held up my face that he bussed my cheek. I saw his eyes run over my plain cambric dress and my hair tied back without curl or style.

Thistle thought it was her presence which acted as a deterrent and she immediately turned to leave.

"I expect you want some good Yorkshire ale after your journey, don't you?" I asked.

"Aye, that I do," he replied, adopting a Yorkshire dialect.

Thistle promised to bring it to us in the parlour, and while we waited I showed Etienne some of the redecoration that had been done.

"You've done wonders," he asserted. "I always remembered this as such a sombre room, but look at it now!"

The afternoon breeze wafted through the open window to gently flare the bright chintz curtains, and the shadows danced on the brightly polished oak floors and casements, reflecting some of the joy I felt at his being there.

We sat long in the parlour talking, mainly about London and its amusements. He told me of plays that had been presented, operas that had been performed, important visitors, fashion, in fact trivia he had rarely discussed when I was in London. I wondered if he did it now for my benefit because I had been away so long.

"I always thought you hated operas and plays. You never seemed to want to attend."

"I go only when there is some attraction, some new idea or some old idea put in a new way, some singer of unusual talent—in other words I go only for the spectacle itself. If it does not meet my expectations, then usually I leave."

"You must leave early often," I commented, thinking of his discriminating taste.

"I'm afraid often I do, though lately I—" his voice trailed off as though there were something more he wished to say but he was not sure that that was the time to say it.

We looked at one another and I am sure he was about to

begin when Thistle popped her head around the door to announce,

"I've readied your room, Mr. Lambert, and dinner will be ready in a half hour."

"There was no need to go to a lot of trouble on my behalf. I can stay only one night at most. I had meant to be on my way before this, for I only stopped here after attending to a business matter in Lancashire. I decided to return by the York road."

"Mrs. Lambert and I won't hear anything of that," Thistle declared. "There's much to see and people have been asking about you ever since Mrs. Lambert arrived. If you left without seeing them it would be the devil to pay. You tell him, Mrs. Lambert."

More than a week later he was still at Pelham. At times it seemed he was the one who had been there six months and I the new arrival. He won the hearts of Hodges and the men by understanding the intricacies of the seed drill and plough and insisting on trying everything out, even the thresher, though there was nothing to thresh. We rode through the fields, examining the first signs of the corn, and he dismounted to pick me the first stichwort of the year.

"Make a wish," he said as he handed me the starry white bloom.

"I will," I promised.

He came with me to All Saints for morning prayer on Sunday and charmed Mr. Rankin by agreeing with the ideas expressed in his sermon, quite unusual for the time, that the church should serve the people rather than the people serving the church. He mentioned many Anglican ministers he knew, some of whom were also known to Mr. Rankin, who was so delighted that he invited us to dine with him that very afternoon. Dulcie stood in awe of him and received him with shyness not usual to her until he complimented her on the fine Yorkshire fare, especially the lightness of the Yorkshire pudding. I knew she always oversaw its making personally and that he could have praised nothing else which would have pleased her as much. In the village he bought hounds-tooth sweets from Mrs. Mayberry because, he said, they made him feel like a boy again, and proceeded to eat all of them as we walked down the street greeting other villagers. Mrs. Dorling was captivated by his tales of France when she and the Rokebys dined with us at Pelham.

Only with Jeremy Salter was there any tension. I had thought they would like one another—both were men of strength and independence—but from the first they eyed one another with disfavour. On Etienne's part I suspected it was because Salter was a member of the family which had treated his mother so harshly. As for Salter, I could only suppose Etienne's power and wealth were not to his liking. When Etienne spoke favourably of the farm machinery, Salter was quick to observe,

"I might expect that from a man who uses infernal weaving and spinning machines in his cotton mills."

And Etienne was just as quick to reply,

"Not to anyone's detriment. I suggest you come down to Manchester some time and see for yourself. I know how keenly you feel on the subject of mechanization but I think if you will examine the way it has been handled there you will see it can be done without detriment to the working man. No children are employed by me, but, by the same token, the children of the families who work for me are well provided for. I urge you to come and look."

I had not spoken to Etienne of Salter and I wondered how he knew of his leanings, but I discovered there was little Etienne did not know about all of Sembourne by the time he had been there for three days. Within a week he was greeted as a fellow countryman, just as though he had lived in Yorkshire all his life. But then he insisted he must return to London.

"I have a dinner planned for the first week in May," he told me. I had no wish for him to leave so soon nor, I felt had he, for the regret in his voice was obvious. "I have invited leaders of both the Whigs and the Tories, and their wives, to dine at Grosvenor Square. So often they do not freely intermingle socially and I thought it would prove an intriguing evening. Since it has been set for almost a month now, I dare not renege."

I knew I did not want to be separated from him. That was what prompted me to ask,

"Would you not like a hostess for your dinner?"

Yet he did not accept immediately.

"Had you planned to return to London now?"

"Not really. I think Yorkshire has made a country girl of me."

"You have never looked better," he agreed, eyeing my reddened cheeks and windblown hair.

"Nevertheless, a few days in town would provide a change."

"By all means, come if you wish. Stay at Grosvenor Square for a week or so."

It was not said in the manner I would have liked. He might have spoken so to a distant aunt or cousin. Nevertheless I went.

The Great North Road bore us south, Etienne telling me tales of Dick Turpin along the way.

"You like outlaws," I said, thinking of Robin Hood.

"I like those who dare."

"You like those who dare and succeed."

"Only because we don't often hear of the others."

We travelled with all speed, yet stopping frequently to admire the scenery at Grantham, the cheese at Stilton, and the repasts at the *George* in Woburn.

On arrival, it was apparent that London was in the throes of the season. I had never before realized what a bustle and commotion there was about it all, or how foolish much of it was. I busied myself with preparations for the dinner, though Cheddell, who had greeted my return with the greatest surprise, had done much already.

Etienne arranged for Le Roy, who was then in London, to call. But apart from ordering a riding dress and two plain day dresses which I thought might serve in Yorkshire without great comment as long as the cost were not known, I got nothing else. When Etienne protested that I had bought no evening dresses I reminded him,

"I have so much here already. I'm sure any one of my evening dresses will do for Thursday."

"But you always wanted to wear something new," he reminded me.

"I remember, but now it seems rather silly. The wardrobe upstairs is simply overflowing with finery much of which I doubt I'll ever wear again."

"You've changed, Leonora."

"Have I?" I laughed. "Perhaps."

On the night of the dinner I entertained the gentlemen before dinner and their wives after, when the gentlemen retired for their port and their heavy political discussion. Politics was no less the subject of conversation in the salon where twice I was forced to intervene between Mrs. Cordery, wife of the Tory member from Aylesbury and Mrs. Aberleigh, Whig both through her father and her husband. Only with the greatest deference to both of them and with consistent changes in the topic under discussion did the coffee hour proceed without open warfare. I later overheard Mrs. Cordery remark on the coarseness of my skin since I had been north, a remark which six months earlier would have sent me flying to my mirror in chagrin. Now it caused me no more concern than when the same lady splashed coffee on the jonquil *crêpe de chine* gown I had chosen to wear. I smiled and assured her I cared nothing for it. In truth I did not. When I had put it on earlier, even this, the least decorative of my evening gowns, seemed outrageously extravagant. I have changed, I thought as the evening progressed, echoing Etienne's earlier remark. And suddenly, I don't know why, I felt happy.

The return of the gentlemen marked an upturn in events. They seemed to have solved their difficulties with far greater aimiability than their ladies. As they entered, I overheard George Canning telling Etienne,

"Your country still has reason to thank you for your actions prior to Waterloo, Lambert. Had we not had the intelligence you obtained for us from your sources we might never have gained the day. No other Englishman could have infiltrated their lines as you did. Though you would accept nothing for your act, believe me we have not forgotten. I still hope that one day you will relent and allow us to raise you to the peerage to show our appreciation."

"That could only be an encumbrance to me, sir. Believe me, it is important to me personally to remain a commoner."

"Important to your self-esteem."

"No, though perhaps in some measure that, too. But a title would be a hindrance to me in the many circles in which I move. Mr. Lambert suits me much better, I assure you. Your personal thanks have adequately repaid me for anything I did."

I was reminded of taunting Etienne for never having served his country and now I flushed at that remembrance. I looked at him and he smiled across Canning's head and nodded as though to indicate the evening was progressing well.

Thanks to our joint efforts and the excellent ministrations of Benoit and the champagne which followed, members of the party remained until after two, and an hour later still found Etienne and me in the salon discussing the evening.

"I wish you had been here after dinner to keep the peace between Mrs. Cordery and Mrs. Aberleigh. I thought they would have each other's eyes out before the night was out."

"Yet they left in the best of spirits. I distinctly heard them promising to call on one another."

"But do you know how much champagne was consumed before that exchange came about?"

"Wine also acts to bring out the worst as well as the best in one."

"Is that why you drink so little?" I asked.

"Perhaps," he mused, "though truthfully I've never cared that much for the stuff or its effects. There are pleasures I prize more."

"And they are?" I pressed.

He thought for a moment as though uncertain whether to continue.

"Good companionship is one of them," he said finally. "And I've seen plenty of that tonight."

I wanted to ask him what the others were but he seemed not to wish to pursue it.

"I thought you once told me you were not at Waterloo," I accused him in mock seriousness.

"No more was I."

"Yet I overheard Canning talking of your acts prior to the battle."

"They were just that, prior to the battle. I had acquaintances in the French camp and I gained some information which was needed. Had I not believed so fully that Napoleon must be crushed I doubt I would have done it. I have French sympathies, you know."

"But was that not dangerous?"

"No more than the dinner here tonight," he laughed.

"I cannot aver there was no danger here tonight."

We held hands climbing the stairs. It seemed natural to do so after our closeness that evening. I was loathe to part from him when we reached my door, and I clung to him for an instant as he quickly kissed me and thanked me for being a perfect hostess. Then he bade me goodnight and entered his room.

I lay in my bed, unable to sleep, tossing and turning until the longing to be with him overcame me and I got up and opened the door to his room.

The candle by his bed was still lit. He was reading. He sat up when he saw me.

"Is something wrong?" he asked quickly.

"No—yes." I stood there, not knowing what to say, but he seemed to understand.

"Perhaps you are afraid, or lonely."

"Yes, that's it. May I sit with you for a moment."

He pushed aside the bedcovers and I sat beside him. I leaned over and picked up the book he had set aside. It was Spenser's *Amoretti*, and I read,

> My love is like to ice, and I to fire,
> How comes it then that this her cold so great
> Is not dissolved through my so hot desire,
> But harder grows the more I her entreat.

I closed the book.

"I think were you to entreat her tonight it would be more a matter of fire to fire."

"Do you mean that?" he asked

"I want you," I said, lying beside him.

"I've wanted you all evening," he replied, dousing the candle.

The act of love which followed was the only possible and natural culmination of our passion. It was obvious that I wanted him. Every breath I drew, every movement of my body, confirmed it, and I had every reason to believe that he wanted me in exactly the same way. We stayed together that night and woke in the morning to love and hold one another again, perhaps more gently this time but no less fulfillingly.

Later that day I remembered an engagement I had made to visit Papa, but it didn't seem important, any more than the Meredith's ball which I cancelled that night. All that seemed important were the hours spent between the cool, lavender-scented sheets which became a cocoon for our love.

So it went all week. Yorkshire, everything I knew and held dear, seemed of little import. I lived only within the orbit of his eye. Every visitor was an intrusion, every moment of his time taken by Cheddell on some matter of business was a deprivation.

I wanted nothing to break the spell which was upon us. I wanted it to last forever. Yet it was I who broke it, unwittingly, unheedingly, irrevocably.

It happened as we lay together one night, quiet and content in those moments after love. Etienne's hand was on my breast, softly tracing a figure round its nipple. I was about to tease him on the shape of his design when he said, quite seriously,

"You've changed, Leonie, changed so much. I never believed you could become such a warm, passionate, sensuous woman. Even in my wildest imagination I would not have thought it possible after that other time. It is a man who has changed you, isn't it? Only a man can make such a change in a woman."

I smiled in the dark, still intent on teasing him, but now I had a different object in mind. When I did not reply immediately, he asked,

"Is it someone from Yorkshire?"

"Yes, he is from Yorkshire."

His fingers stopped their motion. I should have foregone

my jest at that moment but now I was imbued with the anticipation of making up after he discovered his misinterpretation, so that when he asked,

"Is it someone I know?"

I merely replied, "Yes."

There was a pause until he said, as though the words were dragged from him,

"Do you love him?"

"Yes, very much."

He moved his hand away from me and lay quite still and I knew it was time to end the joke, but suddenly he got up and threw on his robe and sat in a chair by the bed holding his head in his hands.

"Etienne," I laughed, sitting up, "don't be so silly—"

"Please, spare me names and explanations. I want none. We have both acted in a rather foolish manner this week and neither of us has given much thought to the others in our lives."

"Others!" I cried. "Just who are the others?"

"You, by your own admission, have found a man who has been able to change you from a shy schoolgirl into a desirable woman and to elicit from you all the passions I sought without success. I have no right to keep you apart."

I was frightened now. What had I done? What had he meant by *others*?

"Etienne, I spoke foolishly—"

"You spoke honestly, just as I should have when I came to see you in Yorkshire."

"There was something you came for, then. It was not simply to see me." I remembered those pauses at the beginning of his visit when he seemed about to speak but did not. "What was it?" I demanded.

"I came to ask you to agree to the divorce we had spoken of before, but somehow—somehow I didn't."

"Why did you want it now?" I asked, fearing his response.

"Phoebe Oliphant and I wish to marry."

"So," I said bitterly, "you were not content with carrying on with her while she was here. It was more than that."

"I'm not sure I would describe it as 'carrying on.' Initially you asked me to be nice to her even though we both knew she detested me. I saw it as a challenge, and then, as she changed, I noticed it annoyed you and quite childishly I wanted to annoy you because you had hurt me. I knew you left London so she would be forced to leave also. It might have been the end of the matter had she not returned to London with her mother to stay with Lady Waitley for the Christmas holidays. They called and—"

"Lady Oliphant was here!"

"Yes, I understand she shared her daughter's first impressions of me but actually we got along quite well. I have been with them several times since. Lady Oliphant knew we were separated, that our marriage had not worked—"

"So she decided you were the one for her daughter," I put in harshly.

"It wasn't quite like that. I made no proposal. I was in no position to, but I came north to talk to you. Perhaps I would have said nothing now had you not told me you had a lover. But all along I realized that there must be some reason for your staying in Yorkshire so long."

I suddenly saw Phoebe as she had clung to him that night. I hated her. I wanted to ask him if he loved her but I could not say the words. I could not bear to hear him say so.

I lay down and turned my back on him.

"I shall return to Yorkshire in the morning. You may send all the papers to me there."

He turned to go, and then turned back.

"You need not worry—financially, I mean. Nor your father, for that matter."

"I don't want your money. As for Papa, perhaps it will do him good to fend for himself. All I want is Pelham."

Chapter V

It was hardly surprising that I felt ill when I got back to Pelham. The return had been nothing like the going. I saw only the worst side of travel, the rutted roads, the poor food, and the general cupidity and animosity of those who waited on me. I longed for Thistle and when she held me at arm's length on my arrival and scrutinized me and then drew me to her and hugged me to her, saying over and over, "Mrs. Lambert, dear Mrs. Lambert, how happy I am to see you," I burst into tears.

She fussed over me in those first weeks and though often I wished to be left alone I was afraid she might misunderstand and I said nothing. She had particularly delicate foods made for me to tempt my palate—milk and egg custards, small filets of sole from the North Sea, fresh peas, sweet and succulent, and raspberries from our own garden—and she scolded me gently when I left most of the food on my plate.

"You must eat. It is so important for you to get nourishment."

But I could not eat. Everything, even Thistle's delicate tea cakes, was unpalatable to me. I felt sick and had an odd, metallic taste in my mouth which would not leave me anymore than would the heaviness of my heart. I wanted to talk to no one. When Dulcie came, anxious for news of London, full of Etienne's praises, I replied in monosyllables, changed the subject often and finally hastened her departure by my intransigent attitude. I rode out on my own for hours at a time, across the lonely wilderness of the moors, for it was only there that I felt in harmony with my surroundings. It portrayed the boundless solitude I felt within.

I waited for the papers I knew would come from Spurrier, Etienne's solicitor, prefacing our final parting. Each day as I arrived home I determined not to look on the hall stand where Thistle placed deliveries, yet each day before entering the parlour my eyes would compulsively be drawn there and I would note, with relief, the lack of any bulky package of papers.

But one day they were there. I came in as usual, but instead of avoiding the hall stand I deliberately walked over to it and there was the large package bearing my name and that of Spurrier as the sender, a man of infallible honesty and equally infallible tenacity. I picked up the package, weighing it in my hands. I had known it would come that day, for that morning I had at last admitted to myself what I had suspected all along. I was going to have a child.

I had first suspected I was with child when I missed my monthly curse, but I put down its absence to the strain of the journey, the lack of rest at night, the general turmoil I had felt within ever since that last conversation with Etienne. When it failed to come for the second month, however, I was forced to admit that nothing but a child forming in my womb could account for it. After all, that was what I had wanted on those nights I had spent with him, the child to seal our union. I, who had the knowledge to prevent such a happening, had taken no steps against it. Rather, I had sought it, not foreseeing the end of that idyllic week. Now my wish had come true at a time when it was clearly my last desire and I had ho one but myself to blame. Well, it was my child, it would always be mine. He had no right to it. He could have other children with that—that—I could not bring myself to even think her name. But my child would bear his name as was his right. I had learned enough of questionable parentage and the suffering it could cause to the child to ever want that to happen again. He could have his divorce after the child was born. Then he could do as he wished. I stuffed the package unopened into my desk.

My body changed but gradually. By the fourth month most of my natural waistline had disappeared, but I was still small and I carried what extra weight I had inconspicuously so that the loose gowns I had always worn in Yorkshire made it unnoticeable. Unnoticeable to all but Thistle, that is. She had continued to fuss over me, insisting on my eating wholesome, appetizing foods and resting more often than usual, and finally it dawned upon me not only that she knew but that she had always known, and I demanded to know how she had discovered my secret.

"I knew the day you returned from London," she said simply. "I saw it in your eyes, just as I had with Mr. Lambert's mother."

"But how?" I asked, mystified. "What is it you saw?"

"I can't say exactly. I'm no poet, but all I can say is it is a look of other-worldliness. I just knew there was something other than you within, that another miracle had begun."

"For a nonliterary person, Thistle, I think many poets might envy your description of my condition."

I wanted no one else to know of it until that time when it could no longer be hidden, but in my fifth month I confided in Dulcie, wanting to make sure she should learn it from no one but me, and I had to bear with her effusions on Etienne's behalf.

"Leonora, he must be beside himself with joy. But will you remain here for the birth? Would it not be better to be with him in London, or will he come north again?"

"I shall be here. I don't know Etienne's plans yet." In fact I had heard nothing from him, nor had I written. But I had had two further letters from Spurrier, both of which lay unopened atop his original package in my desk.

"I am glad you are here today," I took her arm and led her over to my workbox. "You are just the person to show me how to do rose trellis lace. I am quite decided to knit a shawl in that design for the baby, but have such awful trouble with it. Do show it to me again."

Painstakingly she did, and once again I essayed to conquer its intricacies, but either forgetting that the repeat came after the forty-second row, or to slip stitches twice before I knitted, I again fell afowl of its complexities.

I was waiting for her to straighten out my work once again on a brisk October day. I set it aside to examine the Kern Baby the men had made from the last ears of corn they had cut that day. They had woven the sheath, as had been done there from time immemorial, into an intricate spiral design, and a ribbon was tied around the top. Thistle had brought it to me as a sign of fruitfulness and good luck, and I was wondering where to hang it when I heard the sound of wheels on the driveway which signalled Dulcie's arrival. I was glad, for I refused to be conquered by a mere knitting stitch.

"Dulcie!" I called out. "I am in the study. Do hurry and see what is wrong with this shawl again."

I put aside the Kern Baby and lifted the shawl to show the unsightly hole in the last rows of knitting, and waited for her laughing rejoinder. When the door opened, though, it was not Dulcie who stood there, but Etienne.

"Oh!" I cried dropping the shawl, "I thought you were Dulcie—I mean I had not expected you."

He looked at me intently and I waited for him to remark on my condition, but my loose clothes must have disguised it well enough, even from him, for his first words were,

"I don't doubt it. But I had to come north and I decided to stop and talk with you."

So, it was about the divorce he had come. I had not counted on him coming himself. I thought he might write, or send Spurrier or even Cheddell. I had planned to deal high-handedly with them if he did. Now he was here I must decide what was to be done. I supposed it had been too much to hope they would leave me alone until after Christmas, even though I had written to Spurrier explaining that in Yorkshire everything took longer than in London, and Merston, my lawyer, would undoubtedly need time to study the papers.

He bent to retrieve the Kern Baby which had fallen from the table and held it up.

"We used to bring these in as a sign of fruitfulness, I remember."

I looked at him sharply. Did he know? But he had said nothing more than the truth. It was a harvest symbol. I took it from him.

"Do ring for some refreshment. You must be tired and thirsty after your journey."

As he sipped on his ale and I on the milk which Thistle insisted I be served each afternoon, I explained that Thistle had had to visit a sister who was unwell, thinking as I did so that I must be grateful for small mercies. At least she was not there to blurt out the truth until I had time to think of the best course to follow.

"You will stay the night?" I offered, without enthusiasm.

He nodded and I tried to keep the sigh from my voice as I ordered a room prepared for him.

As I dressed for dinner, choosing a loose, empire style

frock which hung straight from my bosom in a style popular some years before, I determined I would myself bring up the matter that night. He must know of the child eventually. It was his, it would bear his name, but I would not permit his interference, only his acknowledgement.

The decision was easier made than carried out. I sat opposite him in the parlour feeling for all the world like Dulcie when she sat beside Salter. I wished he would not look at me so intently. I wished his eyes were not so deep and dark. Most of all I wished Phoebe were in Hades. I began a long monologue on the Harvest Festival and the habit of lighting bonfires and dancing round them, which was said to strengthen the declining sun. I was midway through a particularly convoluted sentence on Mr. Rankin's last sermon describing the harvest blessing, when he cut me off abruptly,

"Do you intend to tell me, or must I ask when your child is due."

I was caught off guard, but in the silence that ensued all I could hear reverberating was his stress on 'your' child.

"Our child, you mean," I said at last.

"So that is why you were so insistent on sharing my bed in London, to make me believe his child was mine."

I had had many conjectures on what he might say when he found out about the child. This had never been among them. I was speechless.

"How dare you!" I said when my voice returned. "Of all the low, disgusting, abominable, hateful things to say, that is the most loathsome."

"If it is mine, why did you not tell me of it. Why did you wait for me to find out?" he asked, unshaken by my scorn.

"Because it will be *my* child when it is born. You may have your own children with your Miss Oliphant, but you may not take this child from me."

"But you want it to be my heir, is that it?"

"You and your damned money. You think to buy everything with it, don't you? Well, you can't. Your heirs can have Oliphant blood, not Fordyce, in their veins. But I insist you rightfully acknowledge this child as yours. I will not allow any question to be raised as to his paternity. The divorce may proceed, but only after the birth. The child is yours. The world will know it is yours."

He eyed me speculatively as though undecided to believe me.

"And what does your lover say about all this?"

"That does not concern you," I replied coldly.

"No, I don't suppose it does really. I just wondered whether it would coincide with his egalitarian ideas, shared wealth, shared wives."

I was too angry to bother to deny that Salter was my lover. If he thought so, what did it matter.

I got up and pointed my shaking hand at the door.

"Get out! Get out of my house this instant! I don't wish to ever see you again—get out and leave me alone."

And when he made no move to leave, I started for the door myself,

"If you won't leave, I will."

He reached the door before I did and stood before it and took my hands. I was crying hopelessly, a trait I hated in myself, yet to which I always succumbed when I least wished it.

"Leonie, forgive me. I had no right to upset you like this. I had no right. It is simply that I was infuriated beyond reason since I saw you this afternoon. I was sure the child was his because you said nothing. I thought you must have wanted it for I knew you knew of the means to prevent it."

"Then you must have known equally well that I did nothing to prevent it in London."

"Why not?" he asked.

"Because I am a fool," I sobbed.

"Well, fool," he said gently, giving me his handkerchief. "Mop up your tears and let us reason together like grown up people on what is to be done for this new member of our race."

Chapter VI

We parted on speaking, if not amicable, terms.

He had been insistent on supplying a London doctor for the lying-in. I was equally insistent I would rely on the services of Sweeting, Sembourne's midwife. I did not give in until he said,

"Since I planted this seed, have I not some say on its coming into the world? Allow me this one extravagance, if you deem it such."

It was an approach which left no grounds for argument.

Dr. Fotheringay, a fashionable London accoucheur, arrived at Pelham in late November, far too soon with the birth nearly three months away. He was short, stuffy and acutely conscious of his own importance in the scheme of things. I didn't know what Etienne had paid him to leave his lucrative London practice for so long a period. I knew it must have been a significant sum, but had I the means, I would gladly have doubled it to have him leave. He plagued me beyond endurance with his daily examinations, the frequent rests he enforced, the meals and medications he prescribed, but most of all by his continuing presence under my roof. He hated being in Yorkshire as much as I hated his being there, but when I suggested that he leave, he adamantly refused.

"Mr. Lambert has engaged me to attend the birth. I will do just that."

"But why so soon? Surely it is unnecessary for you to be here for such a long period of time."

"Mr. Lambert was insistent on that point. The winters here are often most severe, which means the roads will be closed for indeterminate periods and all communications shut off."

I dreaded the prospect of weeks confined to the house with Fotheringay for company. At least now he occasionally went for the day to Harrogate; that might soon be impossible. It could not be, I decided. He was an insupportable bore, besides which the regime he insisted I follow left me little faith in his abilities or my own. I had never felt worse.

I arose one morning feeling decidedly out of sorts. When Dr. Fotheringay sent up a foul smelling draught for me to drink, I dressed and went downstairs in high dudgeon. I called him to my study and gave him twenty-four hours to quit the house, assuring him that I had no intention of availing myself of his medical aptitudes then or in the future. If he refused to leave I promised I would have him thrown out.

He protested vehemently, then he treated me with deference, finally with fury, but to no avail. I held my ground. I would not put up with him for another two, possibly three months, never. It was beyond human endurance.

It was with relief the following morning I watched from my bedroom window as his mountain of luggage was tied to the back of his chaise and his short figure climbed inside. Only when all the dust from its departing wheels had settled once more on the driveway and the sound of the horses' hooves died in the distance did I deem it safe to leave my room. Then I let out a jubilant war cry as I descended the stairs.

Thistle laughed even through her admonitions of my ridding the house of such a fine medical man.

"He was a pompous old nuisance. You know it is so, Thistle. Sweeting knows every bit as much about bringing babies into the world as he does. Now we can plan our Christmas party. It wouldn't have been the same with him here."

I expected there would be recriminations from Etienne, and I decided I would see what doctors could be engaged either from Knaresbridge or Harrogate to prevent his sending a successor to Fotheringay. But soon after my tormentor had left, our first snow storm of the winter began. I was relieved I had not waited a day longer to dismiss Fotheringay. And with the roads closed not even Etienne's scolding could be delivered. By the time the route south was open again, I would have everything arranged and thus forestall him.

The deep snow did nothing to dampen our enthusiasm for the Christmas festivities. The days were filled with preparations of food and gifts. I estimated there would be at least twenty more at the Pelham party this year, for we had taken on additional workers and all the families of both workers and tenants were invited. We decorated the house with yew and holly branches, and hung mistletoe over the doorway. Now that Fotheringay had left I began to eat again, so much so that even Thistle cautioned me.

"But I'm hungry," I said, my mouth full of a fruitcake mixture she had brought to me for approval.

"I only said 'taste,'" she warned.

"Well, it tastes scrumptious."

At night I lay in bed feeling the motions of the baby within. How anxious he was to be born, yet even Fotheringay who, despite his incompetence must have known something, had confirmed it would be mid-February before he arrived. I always thought of the baby in the masculine gender but I found it impossible to choose a boy's name. Etienne occurred to me frequently as a choice and just as frequently I rejected it. If it were a girl I had no such problem. I had always wanted to be Rosalind, and if my child were a girl she would bear that name.

Though the snow drifted and we were cut off from the larger towns, we still managed to clear a way to visit our closest neighbours. I attended church services on Sunday and Dulcie continued her visits. Salter dropped in occasionally though I felt constrained in his presence, I suppose because of the unfounded suspicions of Etienne which I had not dispelled.

Christmas eve was spent in wrapping gifts to be given to the guests at Pelham's Boxing Day party. I could not decide on what to give Mrs. Clayton.

"What do you think, Thistle, would Mrs. Clayton prefer the lace handkerchiefs or the trivet?" I held up both articles for her to examine.

"I am sure she would much prefer the handkerchiefs. They are so decidedly feminine," said a masculine voice from the doorway.

We both spun around.

"Etienne! How on earth did you get here?" I cried.

"Before I answer any of your questions, kindly inform me what you mean, young lady, by dismissing Dr. Fotheringay? I only just found out about it." His voice was stern, but his eyes twinkled.

"I know I agreed to a London doctor, Etienne, but not for three months, and not such a colossal bore in the bargain."

"Now Mr. Lambert," Thistle placated, "you mustn't be angry. I expect he was a good doctor but he was a bit of a fuss budget."

"He was a fuss budget all right," I concurred.

"Look at you, Mr. Lambert," Thistle clucked. "Get off that wet great coat before you catch your death. You're soaked. It must be snowing again."

"How did your coach get through?" I asked.

"I came on horseback."

"All the way from London!"

"No, from Nottingham. The roads were impassable there, at least for any four-wheeled conveyance, so I hired a horse and came on."

"But that must be eighty miles from here!" I protested. "And in such weather."

"It was a good ride and one of which I was sorely in need. I rarely use my muscles as I used to and I'm already feeling the results of it, though nothing that a good glass of Yorkshire ale won't swiftly heal."

"That you shall have, and some cold meats and cheese," Thistle fussed, taking his wet outer garment and looking in such dismay at his wet boots that he immediately sat down and started to remove them. "I had the kitchen prepare my special potato dumplings for dinner so save some of your appetite for those. You know you've always liked them."

Thistle looked from one to the other of us. I don't know what she knew of our relationship. I had never discussed it with her but she knew she could always please me by talking of Etienne's boyhood. Now she looked from us to the mistletoe over the doorway.

"You two shouldn't let my presence hinder you if you've the mind, but in the event it does, I'll leave you alone."

I felt suddenly shy as a barefooted Etienne bent down to kiss me while Thistle beamed. I sensed he did also.

That night at church I pointed out the mistletoe which decorated the altar.

"It is considered a heathen plant in the south and not allowed in the churches."

"But in Yorkshire it is sanctioned since it was officially pardoned at the cathedral in York," he told me.

"I should remember that you are a Yorkshireman," I smiled.

As we listened to the familiar story of the birth of the saviour, Etienne put his hand on my bulging stomach and bent over to whisper,

"This was no immaculate conception."

I took his hand in mine and replied softly, "Perhaps not, but I won't admit there is nothing holy about it."

A strange peace came over me that Christmas, strange because the presence of one whom I had least wanted to know of the birth of my child now gave me the greatest sense of well-being.

Etienne told me that Dr. Macnair from Edinburgh would attend me for the birth and would probably be at Pelham by mid-January. I did not ask if he would leave then, nor did he tell me. He gave himself over to organizing the Boxing Day gathering while I gave in to being coddled and, despite my newfound independence, I recognized how much I enjoyed it at that moment in my life.

On Christmas Day we dined on goose, rabbit and woodcock and finished with Christmas pudding which Etienne said was absolutely the best he had ever tasted. I found the golden ring in my slice which meant I was to be married within the year. Neither of us spoke of it. Carollers came from the village, choosing special carols for me, "Lulla, lulla, thou little tiny child," and "The Five Joys of Mary," and they carried the milly-box lined with sugar and oranges and small figures of the mother and child.

They finished with:

I wish you a happy Christmas and a happy New Year,
A pocket full of money and a cellar full of beer,
And a good fat pig to last you all the year.

Etienne bid them all come in for warm wine punch and fruit cake and insisted on adding some golden guineas to their box.

On Boxing Day it was he who presided over the tenants and workers, making sure there was sufficient food, ale, wine and lemonade, supplying Mr. Duggan from the punch bowl but ensuring that he ate well enough so that he would not be too drunk to get home safely, encouraging young Clayton to finish his year in school and then see him about employment, commiserating with Stott who had had another fall and hurt his right hand, though he admitted to holding a glass very well in his left, toasting the King and Yorkshire and all of those present. He mainly listened— listened to Hodges' desires for increased yield, the men's fears about the corn laws, Mrs. Duggan's tales of woe about her husband, Thistle's concern about the brawn and beef running low, and to all he gave his undivided attention. He listened as though their concern was his only concern and, in a sense, it was. He would remember each one and would do whatever was in his power to help. I sat back and watched and wondered whether I, who could never remember the correct ingredients in a sponge cake, would ever develop that ability.

We dined with the squire and his wife on New Year's day and welcomed in the New Year over a great wassail bowl which contained "lamb's wool," a mixture of ale, roasted apples, sugar and spice, and eggs and thick cream. Salter arrived to announce that the snow had begun to fall again, and though it was early Etienne thought we should leave to ensure a safe arrival home. I could not be sure whether the snow or Salter prompted his decision, though their greeting of one another was cursory.

The snow fell in earnest, and midway to Pelham we became stuck and Etienne got down to help the coachman dig us out. I descended to watch them and, on an impulse, I gathered a handful of fresh snow and threw it at Etienne who retaliated by firing back a volley of the cold diamond dust which settled in my hair and on my eyebrows. He said I looked positively like Mother Carey, the sailor's harbinger of storms. I began to build a snowman, but as I stepped back to view the base I had made my foot slipped into the snow-covered ditch by the road and down I went. As I did I felt a pain and then a warm liquid between my thighs. I cried out, but before I could move Etienne was beside me, lifting me up.

"Are you all right?" he asked tersely.

"Yes," I assured him, "except I feel something strange, something warm and wet."

The look of concern on his face deepened. "The membranes must have ruptured." I must have looked frightened for he added quickly, "It will be all right, don't worry. I'll get you home safely, and we'll take care of everything."

He instructed the coachman to release one of the horses from the harness and gently sat me on its bare back, then climbed up behind me and grasped the bridle.

"Hold me tightly, as tightly as you can. Pretend you're lost in the heavens and I'm the only stable star you can see," and thus we proceeded towards Pelham at a slow but steady pace. I was frightened for I felt something was to happen imminently for which I was suddenly unprepared. I think Etienne sensed this for he held me close and spoke softly and encouragingly as we rode.

At Pelham he carried me over the steps, through the hall and up the stairway, issuing orders as he went for Mrs. Sweeting to be sent for, for the groom to try to get through to Harrogate for a doctor or, failing that, Knaresbridge, for a change of clothing to be brought and a warming pan for the bed and for Betsy to boil water and get fresh cloth ready and then come up with Thistle and be ready to help. I had recently taken Betsy on permanently, considering her a capable girl who would be useful in caring for my child, and though I had not spoken of her to Etienne he had already noticed her and singled her out for the same task.

My linen was changed and I lay in a warm bed wondering whether it had been a lot of commotion without cause for I felt not one whit differently now. Etienne came, having divested himself of his wet coat and boots and wearing a loose, open-necked shirt.

"A girl should have her mother with her at a time like this," he began, "but I'll have to do, at least until Mrs. Sweeting arrives."

I took his hand.

"Sit with me. Don't leave me—please!" I had not meant my voice to contain quite such an air of pleading, but Etienne immediately bent over and smoothed my hair and kissed me, promising,

"As long as you want me, I'll be here."

"I know nothing of what is to happen," I confessed. "My mother died when I was three, and the only one who has ever spoken to me of anything about the married state is Aunt Agatha, and most of what she said was repugnant. Anyway she said nothing at all about childbirth."

"Oh, Leonie!" He squeezed my hand. "It is shameful how little knowledge of importance we give to our children, especially to our girls. We teach deportment, how to please, how to converse, even how to cajole, but let them know nothing of their bodies as though they were something to be ashamed of. We say nothing of our animal instincts and functions, of making love or bearing children, we never speak of them."

"Or of dying," I added.

"That too, that will come for all of us when it is time," he patted my nose, "but your time is not yet. What is happening to you now is a completely natural function, you must re-

· 182 ·

member that. Nature will take its course although we all intend to give her every assistance."

"How do you know of it? Earlier you said the membranes had ruptured, while I didn't know what had happened. Where did you learn this?"

"I lived for some time in America and travelled widely there. There are parts which are very remote, primitive, yet settlers have found their way into that wilderness and have carved out a living there. When their wives give birth, whoever is by must lend a hand. I learned from them, but I learned much more from the Indians whose women give birth often completely on their own and carry on immediately after with whatever is at hand, be it a day's march or raising the crops. From them I learned how truly natural childbirth can be. The physical side of our life is as important, possibly more so, than all the veneer of civilization with which we cover ourselves. What is to happen to you now has happened to women from the beginning of time. If women can come to accept it rather than fear it, accept it willingly and responsively, not with resignation, all will be well. Can you do that?"

"I think I can, if you stay with me."

"I promised I would stay here as long as you want me. Trust me to see that everything is done for you that can be done, and trust me to help you with those things you must do yourself."

"I do."

"Do you understand what is happening now to your body? Has Thistle not spoken to you?"

"Only—" my voice faltered and died away.

"Only what?" he demanded.

"She spoke to me once of your mother."

"That was quite different," Etienne said firmly, looking across the room where Thistle stood instructing Betsy on what Sweeting would need. "My mother's childbirth occurred under the very worst circumstances. It was because of what happened to her that I wished to learn all I could about the process of giving birth."

He explained to me how the cervix must gradually open and while this occurred there would be contractions of the muscles until the opening was large enough for the baby's head to pass through; then, and only then, the mother must bear down with all her might to expel the baby into the world.

"There will be pain, but nothing you cannot bear. I want you to hold my arm when it comes, as tightly as you can, and don't close your eyes, look into mine. Will you promise me that?"

I nodded. I felt warm and comfortable now and was free of the pain of which he spoke.

"Tell me about America," I said.

I learned more of Etienne in the hours that followed than I had in all the months I had lived with him. But then he had never spoken of himself, nor had I ever asked him about his life. I think I had assumed he would be ashamed of it. Then, too, at that time I cared little for him. Now he told me of working his way to America, the colony England had lost, of living in the south among the Creoles of New Orleans where his knowledge of French had swiftly made him accepted. Luck at the card tables had gained him ownership of a cotton plantation in Georgia by the time he was eighteen. He had prospered and then bought into a shipping line plying the Atlantic, the same line on which he had earlier worked his passage. When a series of reverses forced the other owners to put up their shares of the line for sale, he sold the plantation and borrowed enough money to buy them out. By then he felt it necessary to be in England where the ships were being built and where most trade was conducted, and he returned to London, though not as the poor orphan who had left. Since then he had put boats on channel crossings and had diversified his interests into banking and manufacturing.

"Are you glad you came back to England?" I asked.

"You mean, considering my illegitimate birth I would be better off in a new country?" he said without rancour.

I flushed. "Yes," I confessed, "I suppose I did mean that, too, but I also meant with your acumen and enthusiasm perhaps the new world should have been your oyster rather than the old."

"You may be right. I suspect you are, though the power still rests in Europe. It may not always be so, but it does now and I felt it important to be where that power rested."

I winced as a pain stronger than any of those I had felt while he was talking suddenly gripped my body.

"I wish I had the power to bear this birth instead of you," he said fervently.

He rolled back the sleeve of his shirt.

"When the spasms come I want you to grip my arm with all your might, promise me you will?"

I nodded, but when I was next racked by a contraction, he insisted I was only half-hearted in my hold on him.

"Look at me," he ordered. "Look in my eyes and hold on to me. Come along, clasp more than that. That's better."

The muscle contractions grew more intense, but strangely from his arm I felt a flow of strength and confidence, and the dark compassion in his eyes made everything seem bearable.

Mrs. Sweeting arrived at last and examined me to pronounce that all was proceeding as it should, but that it was only a beginning. Then she was taken below by Thistle to be regaled with tea and cold meats. Despite Thistle's insistence, Etienne would eat nothing and he allowed me only a little water to drink from time to time, nothing more than wetting my tongue. He sat bathing my head with a cool cloth dipped in lavender water and read to me from Blake's *Songs of Innocence and Experience*, and Byron's (whom he professed England had treated shamefully) recently published *Don Juan*. He read well; his voice was rich and clear and as he read it was possible to tell from his intonation how he felt about the written word. I became so engrossed and felt so safe that when the groom returned close to midnight to announce that he had been unable to get through to either Harrogate or Knaresbridge I felt no undue concern.

But as the night passed and morning came, and morning turned into afternoon, both my courage and my strength ebbed. As I grew weaker it seemed Etienne became stronger, more persistent, but now there was little time between the ending of one pain and the beginning of the next and I was unsure, even with Etienne's help, if I could survive it.

"Let her have a little brandy." Sweeting passed a glass to Etienne but he pushed it back.

"No, my wife needs all her resources to do what has to be done. She's far better off without that. How far is the cervix opened now?"

"Almost there, Mr. Lambert, about a fraction of a crown to go and then we can get down to bringing this youngster of yours into the world. My, but he's taking his time. He's in no hurry to be sure, keeping all of us cooling our heels this way, but I don't doubt he'll make up for it when he's ready. These seven-monthers need a lot of attention."

Etienne ordered my pillow and top sheet changed and then moved me down in the bed so that my feet rested on the lower bedboard. He explained I would need this when it came to pushing the baby out.

"I hope it won't be long now," I whispered.

"You've been so brave, I know you can do the rest," he encouraged. I lay on my side and he rubbed my back to relieve the pressure and again it seemed the strength and warmth of his hand flowed from him to me.

At last there was a respite from the pain and almost simultaneously Sweeting shouted, "I think she's ready."

I was moved further down so that my knees were bent and outstretched and Etienne held out his arm.

"I want you to use this for support each time you bear down. Press on it as hard as you want."

I felt something wet under my fingers as I held him and I looked to see that I had drawn blood.

"It's nothing," he assured me, rubbing at it quickly, "nothing at all. But you're not looking at me. Come now, I know I'm a sight but not that bad."

Once again I looked into his eyes and at his signal pressed down with all my might.

"That was good, but I know you can do much better," he insisted, and so I did. I pressed until I thought I could do no more, but always when I was about to concede Etienne was there encouraging me to try just once more and then just once more again, and from his dark eyes and his steady arm I drew the strength to continue.

When I was close to giving up all hope of ever seeing my child I heard a shout from Sweeting.

"It's the head, it's coming," and I forgot all my despair in the excitement of the birth. Now I pushed with renewed vigour, though the baby continued to take its time in inching its way through the canal.

"That's it!" Etienne reassured. I felt responding tears come into my own eyes. Now all was activity at the end of the bed, Thistle, Betsy and Sweeting bending over, and at last a cry—loud, healthy, angry, insistent. It was done. I sighed and closed my eyes and held tightly to Etienne's hand. I heard him ask quickly,

"The afterbirth, Sweeting, has it been delivered?"

"Not yet, Mr. Lambert, but it will wait awhile."

"Not too long." There was a note of warning in his voice and I opened my eyes in time to catch a look of concern pass between Etienne and Thistle but then closed them again. I was tired.

"Leonie, Leonie, wake up." I could hear Etienne's voice but it seemed distant. I felt him wiping my face and stroking my hair. He gripped my shoulders. "Leonie, you've been a veritable Joan of Arc but you cannot rest yet. One more thing is demanded of you and that is all, then you may rest. You must push out the lining to your womb on which the baby has been feeding all these months. Don't rest yet, please. Leonie, you must listen to me."

But I was tired and I felt like sleeping and might have fallen into that sleep had Etienne not shaken me, if not forcefully then deliberately.

"I can't. I'm too tired," I complained.

"Not for this," he insisted. I opened my eyes and saw his face leaning over mine and stared up into the eyes I had looked into for the past four and twenty hours. For the first time I saw there fear, raw, naked fear. I remembered the look which had been exchanged between him and Thistle, and I remembered then the death of his mother. He was thinking of that too as his arms grasped mine. I suspect he knew I had guessed his thoughts, for the fear in his eyes became dark and clouded, then he looked away and said briskly, almost matter-of-factly,

"I know, Leonie. You've done a lot but it won't take long now, you'll see. A few more swift, hard pushes should do it and then you can rest all you want."

His hand pressed gently but firmly down on my stomach and despite the calm in his voice I felt the urgency in his hand, as though he would willingly have reached inside me and grasped the afterbirth to pull it from me. I was sure I had no strength left to do as I was bid, but rather than admit it I promised to try.

"That's my girl," Etienne said heartily yet somehow without conviction. "I know you can do it."

I believed I could not, but somehow his touch and his will drove away my lack of resolution. I pushed and strained at something that seemed to have no meaning. The baby had been born after all and from the cries I heard was very much alive.

We worked for what seemed another eternity, Etienne, Sweeting and I to remove the lining, but it seemed irretrievable. Many times I wanted to give up, but always Etienne insisted that I do more, summoning from me efforts I thought impossible. I felt unequal to what seemed an impossible task. At times I felt that fate should have its way, but Etienne was there, making me fight back. I had all but given up when Sweeting cried out,

"There it is Mrs. Lambert, the miserable bugger."

She held it up, a soft, red substance. It looked for all the world like a piece of liver which even a cat might reject. Was this the miserable object which had taken all my life forces? Etienne looked at me and I gave him a wan smile. I saw there were tears in his eyes and suddenly he bent forward and put his head down on my breast and I knew he was crying. I smoothed his dark hair, wet with sweat and obeying all its natural instincts to curl in the nape of his neck, and in the distance I heard the baby's cry. I realized suddenly I had not asked the first question of every mother of a newborn child.

"Etienne, is it a boy or a girl?"

He raised his head and suddenly laughed.

"I forgot to ask."

Chapter VII

We quarrelled over the name for our newborn son. I wanted him to be called Etienne. Etienne insisted no child should be forced to carry his father's name, nor mother's either for that matter. We compromised on David because he had fought against all odds coming into the world. We both liked the name though it had no particular significance for either of us. I insisted, however, that he should also bear Etienne's middle name and my own surname. So he became David Fordyce St. Clair Lambert.

The christening was set for the fourteenth of February, our second wedding anniversary. Etienne sent his yacht to France to bring champagne from that country to Scarborough, from whence it was carried by cart to Pelham for the occasion. He showed no inclination to return to London despite the incessant flow of communications from Cheddell which constantly demanded his attention. I noticed the gravity caused by some of them, but he would catch my look of apprehension and smile quickly and reassuringly and speak of David, knowing to find in him an unfailing object of my interest. And when he found I had been studying French he took to conversing with me daily in that language so that, though I could not speak without error, at least I could speak with ease.

Two days after David's birth he had insisted I dine below and had brought me himself to the table. Thereafter he saw to it that I walked daily, in the house at first, and finally he bundled me up in furs and made me walk with him as far as the gate in the cool, crisp air. By the time Dr. Macnair arrived from Edinburgh to attend me for the birth, I was fully recovered. All that poor, dour man could do was to examine me and pronounce me in good health, something I already believed to be true beyond a doubt. He took it upon himself, however, to severely lecture Etienne and me on the dangers fraught in resuming marital relations too soon, a subject which caused me some confusion but which Etienne promised gravely to observe. I could not tell whether his ready acquiescence stemmed from a desire to please the good doctor or me; had he raised the subject after Macnair's departure I could have assured him that I found the wait tedious. Never did he mention Phoebe or the divorce papers still lying unopened in my desk drawer. For my part, that matter I considered at an end.

Our son's birth brought visitors from the entire neighbourhood bearing gifts and felicitations. I was completely unprepared, however, for the arrival one afternoon of Mr. Lambert and his daughter. I saw Etienne grow pale when they were announced, followed by a look of astonishment as their greeting of me revealed we had met before, for I had never spoken to him of visiting Herenton.

Etienne bowed stiffly in answer to their greeting, but when Mr. Lambert held out his hand he did not hesitate to grasp it warmly.

"My boy, forgive me," Mr. Lambert said. "I am old now and have not many more years to live. The birth of your son reminded me that he is, after all, my great-grandson and I had to see him."

"You give me the greatest pleasure in coming," Etienne assured him, "but this is cold weather for you to be about. Let me get you something warm to drink."

I watched as Miss Lambert greeted Etienne and called him nephew. I knew him to be more pleased with this than any title the realm might bestow on him. She was, after all, his mother's sister, and his heart went out to her on that account if on no other. Before the visit was over it was decided that she should be godmother to our child. George Canning had asked to stand as godfather when he saw him before he left London, Lambert told her, and he would attend the ceremony, roads and weather permitting.

"Mr. Canning, you know him?" she said faintly.

"A good man," Mr. Lambert approved, determined not to be impressed by his grandson being held in such regard by the renowned statesman.

Their visit was shortened by threatening skies, but they promised to return the day before the christening and to stay overnight.

"You have a loyal and devoted wife there, my boy. Take good care of her," were Mr. Lambert's parting words.

Scarcely had Etienne seen them to their carriage before he turned and demanded of me, "You said nothing of meeting them. Where was it and how?"

I told him, though I said nothing of being lost on the moors and certainly nothing of their discourtesy. He must have sensed it though.

"So you sought them out and they cut you."

"Not exactly," I lied.

"But why did you go there?" he asked, ignoring my disclaimer. "If it was on my behalf, there can be no doubt that you succeeded."

"Your grandfather loves you," I assured him. "I knew it

today for the first time. He is set in his ways. His sense of propriety, morality, what is right and what is wrong are engraved in stone. It was a far greater effort on his part to come here today than any similar action on our part."

"I know," he agreed. "But that does not mean I owe you any less thanks for healing this wound."

The intimacy I felt to exist at that moment between Etienne and me and the child at my breast was as binding as steel and as boundless as water.

Canning arrived two days before the ceremony along with two mutual friends with whom he was visiting the north. Papa came, grumbling at the state of the roads and the terrible parochialism to be found this far from London, but he was mollified when a card game was got up between the men and even more mollified when he won, after which he pronounced Sembourne a delightful village and Pelham the prettiest place in it. The Lamberts came the next day, overawed at first by the illustrious company but made to feel immediately at home by Etienne. Soon Miss Lambert had David on her knee and she held him in such a gentle and natural manner that it seemed tragic she had been robbed of the role of motherhood.

Cheddell arrived, invited by Etienne for the christening. Diligent soul that he was, he carried a satchel bulging with papers and was closeted with Etienne for an interminable period, after which Etienne called me aside and told me that he would have to leave for London after the ceremony and that possibly a visit to France might be mandatory. In answer to my look of distress, he assured me.

"I shall be back before you know it. In the meantime grow strong, both of you," and he bent down to stroke the baby's cheek and, as though on an impulse, he turned and kissed me. A month had almost passed since Dr. Macnair's visit, but he made no attempt to come to me the night before he left. There would be other times, I thought, many other times, as I waved farewell to the carriage splashing through the newly-melted snows.

Papa had been invited by Canning to proceed with him and his friends on to Darlington where they were to stay before going back to London. I was alone again. I missed Etienne at every turning, and the house seemed bleak and empty without him, but as March came and the weather grew warmer I was able to get out and ride. As I saw renewal of life around me my own vigour within returned. I had received a short note from Etienne saying that his presence in France was necessary, but since he made no mention of my journeying to London I presumed he would come north when he returned.

I had employed Betsy as David's nursemaid, but my own schedule was set by David's feeding. This did not impede me, however, from taking up active management of the estate again. Dulcie came often to play with David, and at times to simply sit and talk. Salter came too and sometimes they stayed on to dine with me. I preferred it if Dulcie were there when Salter called. I still hoped that he would come to recognize her devotion to him and her intrinsic worth. He had stayed away while Etienne had been at Pelham. Many times I had been on the point of telling Etienne that his suspicions of Salter's role in my life were groundless, but to do so meant reviving that repugnant London denouement and I would do nothing to remind him of it. I wished it to die a natural death. The birth of our child and the intimacy which had developed between us must have convinced him there was no one else in my life, and I preferred to think that it also marked an end to any attachment he had found.

Salter dropped by one day on his return from Knaresbridge bringing David a stuffed toy of such indiscriminate design that we were unsure whether it represented a lion, a dog, a cat or even a seal. After much discussion we decided it safest to merely name it The Animal. We were in the midst of this domestic scene, David busily chewing on The Animal's ear, when the sound of the front door indicated another visitor. I had not expected that visitor, however, to be Phoebe. It was indeed she, elegant, slim and brighter in aspect than ever, accompanied by Francis. Their eyes flew swiftly from Salter to myself in our intimate *tête-à-tête*, and I thought that sight brought a triumphant glow to Phoebe's eyes.

The greeting was effusive on her part, restrained and a little embarrassed on the part of Francis and particularly dubious on mine. I could not forget the last time I had seen her, and now I remembered all too clearly the last time Etienne had mentioned her name.

"But what brings you to Yorkshire?" I asked in as light a tone as I could muster after introducing them to Salter.

"We are staying with the Ladbrooks at Buxstead Park and we thought to come and see you."

"Buxstead Park—but that is in the east riding, is it not?"

"I believe it may be," she replied evasively, "but we enjoyed the ride, did we not Francis?"

Over roads left rutted by the snow and thaw, I doubted it had been such a pleasant journey, and I did not believe that was the sole cause of the discomfort I saw in Francis' eyes.

After they had taken tea and refused an invitation to dine, I began to find their visit heavy going indeed and was relieved when Francis asked Salter to walk out and show him the direction in which his cottage lay, hoping that this would bring an end to the call. Phoebe, however, did not attempt to follow them, and as the door closed behind the two men, silence ensued, broken at last by Phoebe asking,

"You must wonder why we have come."

"I do," I admitted.

"I know we did not part on the best of terms. It is useless to try to hide the reason why. I have come to talk to you about Etienne."

"Oh!" Neither my look nor my voice could have encouraged her, yet she persisted.

"I know that you now have a son and that Etienne, as you say, is the father," I thought to take umbrage at this snide aspersion but decided to hear her out. "You know that Etienne and I love one another. I know that he has asked you for a divorce and that earlier you agreed to it. The child may have caused some change, but certainly not in the way that Etienne and I feel toward each other."

My heart sank. I tried to hide my trembling hands and control my voice as I replied.

"You have seen him—recently—in London?"

"I have. It is because of that that I am here now. I have come to ask you to sign those papers and return them to Spurrier, for the good of all of us."

She saw the protest rise to my lips and held up her hand.

"Hear me out, please. I know that you have a son, a splendid little boy, I saw him. I assure you that he will be taken care of, that he will not be cut out of an inheritance. But you have other interests, as does Etienne. Why should all of us suffer because of one child who, truly, will not be one whit the worse for it?"

"I have no other interests," I insisted, my courage returning and my temper beginning to rise. "If Etienne still wishes a divorce, as you say, then he must tell me so himself, not send a messenger to me bearing such tidings."

Phoebe hesitated, as though unsure of herself for the moment, but when she continued she gave every evidence of perfect sincerity.

"Quite truthfully, Etienne does not know I am here, Leonora. I suspect he would forbid it if he did. You know him, quite rightly, as a man of integrity who believes in doing what must be done, no matter the consequences. He regards his parentage of this child as an obligation, an obligation he owes to the child and, to some lesser extent, to you; an obligation for which he will set aside his own wishes. He will never ask you for that divorce now because of it. Rather he will make it appear that all is forgotten. But I can assure you it is not. It is simply because he will never ask it of you that I am here pleading with you today."

"I refuse to listen to you. I will write to him immediately and ask him whether this is so. I refuse to believe it."

"If you do, I assure you he will reply that nothing is farther from his wishes, particularly if he feels you and the child would be left alone. If, on the other hand, he knows that you will be happy with another gentleman—" she looked in the direction of the window where Francis and Salter could be seen conversing, "if that were the case he is much more likely to tell you he is in favour of proceeding with the action."

"But I do not wish it. I never did."

"Yet you agreed to it before you so conveniently became with child." Her voice was sharp and accusing.

"I agreed to it only because he said his affections were with you. I am no longer convinced that that is so."

"No more will you be," she was openly angry now, "for he is too much of a gentleman to tell you. But I hope you will remember it, though Etienne out of false kindness may deny it a hundred times. He loves me and he always will. He will call you wife but every moment he is with you he will be thinking of me. I know it will be so. I shall, at least, have that to live on. I hope you have the fortitude to be able to live with it."

She was gone, slamming the door behind her, leaving me in a daze through which I vaguely heard them depart. Salter came back but I could not pretend to welcome his presence and soon he, too, left. I was alone at last, able to let the full force of everything Phoebe had said sink into my heart and my brain. I remembered Etienne's love of David. She was right. As a child who had grown to manhood without parents himself he would do all he could to protect him from a similar fate. I remembered, too, his frequent looks of preoccupation while at Pelham, especially when communications had come from London. He had assiduously refrained from mentioning Phoebe's name but perhaps she had communicated with him through Cheddell. I had thought he loved me. I remembered David's birth, but perhaps all that concern had been for the baby, not for me. Since, as she said, he would never admit to wanting a divorce now, all I had to do was to say nothing. But did I want him enough to hold him against his wishes? Did I want to keep him if he did not want me?

I pondered the matter in the days ahead. In fact I was unable to think of anything else, resolving one day to ignore her visit and the next to write to him and demand an explanation. Yet even when I began a letter I knew she was right—he would deny it because of David. I would never know.

I could not sleep, nor could I eat. I began to have difficulty feeding the child. I was nervous and irate. I made up my mind to go to London and then remembered that he was in France. When I put off going I wondered if he had merely told me that to keep me away and I became angry. He would not have the child, I vowed. David was mine. I had borne him, he belonged to me. Even as I made these resolutions I realized that I had made up my mind to give him the divorce.

I arose very early one morning and got the papers from the desk and wrote to Spurrier to proceed with the matter providing Etienne made provisions for his son and agreed that I was to have his custody. I asked that he seek this assurance before any filing in the courts. It was now up to Etienne, I thought as I sealed the envelope. If Phoebe was wrong, if he did not wish for the divorce as she averred, he would undoubtedly come north and challenge me. If, on the other hand, he gave Spurrier his agreement it would prove she had been right in her assertions.

I waited. Spurrier wrote that he had received my letter but that Etienne was out of London. He would have a reply for me as soon as he returned. Was he in France or in Dorset, I wondered. Three weeks passed without a word. Each day I wondered if he were coming to Yorkshire, if he might suddenly burst in demanding to know what I meant by it all, demanding ale of Thistle, and demanding to see his son. I waited.

It was the end of April. It was the same time of year as when he had come north before, but now it was not Etienne who came but a letter from Spurrier announcing that he had shown him my letter, that he had agreed with my terms and had, in fact been more than generous in not simply providing for David but in naming him his heir; that I myself need have no financial worries, that the matter would now proceed without hitch and that I would hear from him in due course. I cried.

I had played into their hands, I thought. Now they would marry without impediment. Even though I might be fault-less in the action, no one would hold it against him. Phoebe would shine in her role as his wife. I hated her. I hated him too. But I resolved he would never have David. He was mine.

I was forced to find a wetnurse in the village for David because my milk had dried up. Betsy took him there twice, sometimes three times a day. I usually walked out to meet them on their return and I began to notice Betsy was often accompanied by a tall, burly young man who never stayed to talk to me but was off whenever he saw me. I presumed she now had a steady boyfriend and perhaps I would soon lose her. I asked her about him but she merely blushed and giggled which confirmed my suspicions. Well, I hoped that her marriage would be more satisfactory than mine.

The Lamberts came quite often to see me, but more especially to see David. I told them nothing of the divorce. They would find out soon enough, I reasoned. They often asked me to visit them, and feeling desperately in need of a change of scene I agreed to go and stay overnight. I could not take David so far from his wetnurse, however.

The visit was a mistake. While previously the Lamberts had refused to discuss Etienne at all, now he was the entire subject of their conversation. It pained me and I could scarcely respond to their effusions. I knew they were disappointed. I counted the hours until I could return to Pelham.

"Where is David? Ask Betsy to bring him to me." I said as soon as I arrived home the next day.

"She's been gone since morning," Thistle told me. "She said she would simply stay at the wetnurse since you were away instead of coming and going. I gave her permission to do so. I thought you wouldn't mind."

"No," I said, removing my hat and feeling suddenly very weary. "I shall lie down but have her bring him to me when she returns."

When I awoke twilight had fallen. It must be late, I thought, but I supposed they had not wished to waken me. I went to the nursery for David but he wasn't in his cot.

Downstairs pandemonium reigned. Betsy was sobbing and Thistle was red-eyed and ringing her hands.

"Mrs. Lambert, you must be calm," she said, pushing me into a chair.

"But I am calm," I argued. "It is you who are not. Where is David?"

They looked at one another and Betsy's sobs became louder.

"What is it?" I asked, my voice rising. "Where is my son?"

"Please, Mrs. Lambert, everything that can be done is being done. Hodges is searching for him and Mr. Salter has taken some of his men to scour the neighbourhood."

"Searching for him, just what do you mean?" I thought my heart would stop beating with the fear that gripped me.

"He has disappeared, but I know we will find him." Thistle started to cry as she spoke.

"Disappeared?" I repeated the word without the least comprehension. "How could a four-month old child disappear?"

"We think he was stolen, but he will be found, everything is being—"

I heard nothing more. I fainted.

Chapter VIII

All the way to London I cursed my gullibility. How could I have been so foolish as to believe Etienne would allow the child to remain with me. He might want Phoebe, but I was sure he wanted David even more. I had seen how tenderly he held him, how he would watch him endlessly. Why had I thought he would let me have him? He knew it would be useless to offer me money. If he wanted the child and the divorce there had been only one option open to him and he had taken it. And I had allowed it to happen. I cursed myself again and again.

Betsy had confessed everything to me. When I had finally got her to stop crying, she had told me that the young man with whom I had seen her walking, and of whom she was obviously enamoured, had asked to be allowed to show the baby to his uncle, old Grisdale over at Four Acre Farm. When two hours passed and he had not returned, she had got a ride out there, only to learn that Grisdale not only had no nephew but that he had never even heard of the young man who claimed this relationship. Further questioning revealed that Betsy had only met the young man after

Etienne had left for London, that no one else in the village knew anything of his background. They simply called him Frenchie, because he spoke with an accent. He had stayed at the Red Lion and had paid his bills, in which manner he had endeared himself to the villagers. Other than that all I could find out was that he had spent some time at sea.

I knew Etienne's yacht had been at Scarborough and I immediately sent Hodges to see whether it was still there. He returned with word that it had just left. The townspeople had remembered it well. No one knew its destination, however.

I reached London in a record thirty-two hours, stopping only to change horses and to allow the coachman and groom to eat. For my part I could eat nothing. I arrived at Grosvenor Square in mid-morning and strode inside to find no sign of Etienne, only Cheddell in his study.

"Where is he?" I demanded, without preamble. I was prepared to shake the information from his solid form if necessary.

"Lady Leonora! I hadn't known you were expected." He got up hastily.

"I am not expected. Where is he? And where is my child?"

He looked bewildered. "Mr. Lambert is at his offices in the city."

"And my son?" I demanded.

"But I thought he was with you," he stuttered. He was either hopelessly stupid or extraordinarily accomplished in the art of histrionics. I could see nothing was to be gained by talking to him.

I stormed back outside, Cheddell at my heels, and instructed my weary coachman who was even then leading the horses away to take me to the city. Then I realized I had no idea where Etienne's offices were. Cheddell, on being applied to, gave me an address on King Street and, ignoring his insistence that I stay and rest while he went for Etienne, I waited for the coachman to reharness the horses and drove off.

I had never been to Etienne's office. In fact I had never been near that part of London except for the time I had searched out a pawnbroker whose establishment, I discovered, was some distance from Etienne's. His office stood not far from the Bank of England and was a large, stately building of six storeys and innumerable windows. As I drew up I thought incongruously of the window tax that must be costing him a fortune, as if that mattered.

On giving a clerk my name I was immediately shown to a large room on the second floor where the clerk whispered to a well-dressed young man at a desk. His eyes immediately travelled to me in askance before he got up and went through a door into another room. I suppose my appearance after a day and a half's travel and no sleep left something to be desired.

Almost immediately Etienne appeared, brushing the clerk and the young man out of his way and holding out his hands to me.

"Leonie, you, in London, I didn't know—" he took one look at me and ushered me into his office.

It was all that Phoebe had told me—spacious, paintings on the panelled walls, the massive desk, soft rose Axminster carpets. It looked more like a state drawing room than an office. He drew me over to a Chippendale chair and urged me to sit down. When I did not do so he put his hands on my shoulders and gently propelled me into the chair.

"Now tell me why you are here?"

His look of innocent concern, his gentle, solicitous manner, the fact that he dared to ask me why I had come made me lose all good intentions I had formed on the way there to talk the matter over in an adult manner.

"You beast! How can you stand there and ask what is

· 204 ·

wrong? You know very well what is wrong! Don't play the poor innocent with me. You monster! You fiend!"

I began crying and wildly striking at him with no avail. He took hold of my flailing hands and I could see only pity in his eyes.

"Leonie! Leonie! Please, tell me what is wrong."

I jumped up, wrenching my hands free.

"I refuse to sit in your iniquitous presence until you return him to me."

My crying increased, racking my entire body until suddenly I had an odd desire to laugh and again my body was racked but with the most peculiar mirth I had ever known, and there I stood, alternately weeping and laughing. I felt him shake me and then I felt a sudden, stinging slap across my face and I became quiet.

"I am sorry," I heard his voice as though from a distance, "but you must listen to me. Leonie, you are not listening."

Again he shook me and I focused my eyes on his face.

"You must understand, I do not know what you are trying to tell me, nor will I learn anything until you calm yourself. Now stop it, do you understand me?"

His words and the shaking I had received were like a dousing of cold water. I felt suddenly all the fatigue, the coldness, the emptiness, the futility of it all. I allowed him to lead me again to the chair and I sat there while he ordered tea for me. Then he poured brandy from a carafe on a nearby carved table and ordered me to drink it.

"Now, tell me, what is wrong?" His voice was soft and gentle. I watched him as he spoke. How could he look so sincerely concerned, I wondered. Was that how he had gained his fortune, by dissembling?

He was strong. He had all the power in his hands. The law would be on his side, not mine. I might never get David back, unless—there was one way I might force him to give up David willingly, I suddenly realized.

"I want my son," I said, clearly, distinctly.

He looked puzzled.

"But our son is with you."

"He was, until four days ago when he was taken from me."

"Taken? How? What are you saying—" Etienne stopped quickly as a manservant brought in a tea tray. He motioned him away as soon as he had poured the tea and handed it to me.

"What are you saying?" he said hoarsely.

"As if you didn't know." I was unable to keep the sob from my voice. He knelt down beside me.

"Drink some of this tea and then I want you to think, very, very carefully and tell me everything."

It was an exercise in frustration, I thought, as the warm liquid flowed inside me, warming my numbed body. I drank the tea slowly, thinking carefully as I did so. It was evident Etienne would admit to nothing, yet only he could have taken the child. Only he wanted him, no one else would do such unconscionable harm. He must know where he was. I would use any means to get him back.

He waited until I was done and then took my empty cup from me.

"Now tell me everything that happened, every detail you can remember, no matter how small. We'll find him, Leonie."

How could he be so cruel! Well, I, too, could be just as ruthless.

"There is one thing you must know. I had not intended that you should ever discover this, but now, I see, I must tell you."

"What is that?" He took hold of my hands. "You can tell me anything, Leonie. Keep nothing from me."

His eyes on mine were full of concern. They were the same eyes which had helped me bear my child. I was not sure I could lie to him, yet unless I did I might never regain my son.

I was forced to look away as I said,

"David is my son, but he is not yours."

I could not bring myself to look at him, but I heard his sharp intake of breath, then a silence broken only by a clock chiming the hour.

"What are you saying?" His voice was stunned, distant.

"Only that you were right when you suspected me of deliberately allowing you to make love to me in London. I was with child when I came. I wanted you to believe it was yours. David was not premature as I pretended. He was a full-term baby, so you see you could not possibly be the father."

"Is it Salter's child?" His voice was harsh beyond recognition.

I could not bring myself to reply. I nodded.

"I see. But why did you do this? You could have told me the truth in the beginning. I would have stood by you until after the child was born. Was it so important to you to pretend he was my heir?"

I said nothing for a minute, then I burst out,

"You know the miseries of being a nameless child."

I began to cry, ashamed of my own duplicity.

"Yes," he replied slowly, "I do."

"Now you know he is not your son, will you give him back to me?"

"I don't have him."

"But you know where he is."

"I believe I do."

He turned away as though he could no longer bear to look at me and walked over to the window to look down on the bustle of King Street.

When he turned back to me his face and voice were completely controlled, yet it was a stranger who said,

"You must tell me everything, Leonora, everything that happened if you want your son back."

I was helpless. He knew where he was, yet I was in his hands. I could do nothing except repeat every detail of what had happened that last day, my visit to his grandfather, Betsy's visits to the wetnurse, the young man she had been seeing who said he was Grisdale's nephew but of whom Grisdale had no knowledge, about Hodges' and Salter's attempts to find him. I faltered as I mentioned Salter's name, but Etienne said nothing except,

"This young man who befriended Betsy, you say he had an accent?"

"I never spoke to him myself. Whenever he saw me, he left. But Betsy said that though he spoke English quite well, he was not English."

"Was it a French accent?"

"You should know. You sent him." I replied in exasperation.

"I care nothing for what you think," he said grimly."Just answer me. How long exactly is it since the child was last seen?"

"Last Thursday," I snapped.

"They've less than a week's start," he said almost to himself. He looked at me closely. "You've had no rest in that time, have you. You had better come back to Grosvenor Square. Leave this to me. I'll find him for you."

He led me downstairs, unprotestingly. I said nothing. I felt nothing unless it was the futility of it all. My son was gone, that was all that mattered. He was gone. Etienne knew where he was, although he would not admit to taking him. Suffice it that he had said he would get him back for me. It still remained to be seen whether he believed me or not, though it would be hard to feign the hurt I had seen in his face. How could he have hated me enough to take the child from me? What had I done to him to deserve such treatment? I may have been indifferent, even callous at times in the beginning of our marriage, but not after. I knew he no longer wanted me, he wanted Phoebe. But I had signed the divorce papers as he had asked. He would be free to marry her. They would have children. Why could he not have left me this one? Why? I had told a terrible falsehood, but it was all I could do. Surely he would no longer want him, believing him to be Salter's child.

At Grosvenor Square I allowed him to conduct me upstairs and instruct a maid to wash me and get clean bedclothes and put me to bed. I heard it, I saw it, yet it was as though it were all happening to someone else.

Even when he came to me with a glass of warm milk and waited until I drank it all, I did so knowing there was something in it and I didn't care. If he wished me dead, as well he might, I thought dispassionately, I would die. He would be free of me then. Even for me it would be a way out.

I lay back and turned my head away from him, trying to ignore his soft instructions for my care. Had Judas sounded so, I wondered as I fell into a deep, troubled sleep.

I awoke with the knowledge that something was wrong, but I still felt the effects of the drug I had been given and I lay without moving for a long time. I recognized the room at last. It was my own at Grosvenor Square. I wondered how I had got there. Then I remembered the journey and, last of all, I remembered the reason for that journey.

Mrs. Dunsmore peaked in at the door and, seeing me stirring, she came to my side.

"Thank goodness you're awake at last, Lady Leonora. I swear if you hadn't awakened today I'd have sent for Dr. Hamilton again. We've been quite worried. He'll be back soon to see you for himself but Mr. Lambert talked to him and he said you were to have complete rest and only light food. I've warm beef broth ready for you."

"I want nothing."

"I'm sorry, Lady Leonora, but Mr. Lambert said I should be insistent if necessary to make you eat. He'll hold me responsible."

"Where is he?" I asked.

"He will be back soon." She fussed with my pillows and drew back the curtains to let in the sunlight. When I showed little inclination to eat the broth the maid brought, she spoon fed me as though I were an infant.

"Where is Mr. Lambert?" I asked again when the bowl was removed.

"He is not here now."

"I know he is not at home, but is he in the city?"

"No, he is away," she replied evasively.

"Send Cheddell to me," I ordered.

"Here! In your chamber?" she looked astonished.

"Here in my chamber," I ordered.

Cheddell entered hesitantly, in obvious embarrassment at being in my bedroom.

"Where is Mr. Lambert? I want the truth and I want it exactly."

"He will return shortly, your ladyship."

"You may dispense with my title. Just tell me what I ask."

"Very well, Lady—Mrs. Lambert, but Mr. Lambert's orders were that you were to stay in bed and rest completely. I was to tell you he would take care of everything."

So, perhaps I had not duped him after all. Perhaps he had decided to spirit him even farther away from me.

"I don't doubt for a moment that those were his orders," I snapped, "but I have no intention of lying here while he takes my child beyond my reach. If you won't tell me where he is, Cheddell, I shall make enquiries on my own. I shall go to the authorities and demand their help. My father has some power. He will help me, I have no doubt."

I suspected Papa would not wish to have anything to do

with the matter. The only communications I had received from him had begged me to return to Grosvenor Square. When he had stayed at Pelham for the christening he had positively fawned over Etienne. Even now, I suspected he would do nothing to upset him in order to preserve his allowance. He was likely to tell me it was better for David to be with his father. Men stuck together. But Papa was not without influence and, if necessary, I would force him to use it on my behalf. Cheddell must have thought so also, for he replied almost immediately.

"That won't be necessary. Mr. Lambert will return soon. He hoped at that time to have his son with him."

"*My* son." My voice was dangerously sharp and he recognized it.

"Your son, excuse me, Mrs. Lambert."

"And where did he propose to find him?"

"In France."

In France, of course, in France!

"And where, pray, in France?"

"In the Dordogne, at Perideux. He has gone to the Château Saint Clair."

"Very well. You may leave now."

As he turned to go, I started to rise from my bed.

"But Mrs. Lambert, you are to stay and rest," he protested. "You are in no condition to get up. Where are you going?"

"To France, to the Dordogne, to the Château Saint Clair."

"I would most certainly advise against it."

"I am quite sure you would."

"You are in no condition to cross the channel. It may be unpleasant, even dangerous there."

I didn't know what he meant by that, but I suspected he told the truth about my condition, though I would not give him the satisfaction of knowing how weak I felt.

"I intend to go, and I will allow no one to stop me."

My determination must have been obvious, for he replied,

"Then at least allow me to accompany you."

I thought for a moment. He was Etienne's secretary. He had his interests at heart. On the other hand, I truly did not know how I would get to the Dordogne, and the persistent weakness in my legs made me doubt my ability to get there by myself even if I knew the way. I believed I was sufficiently astute to see through any subterfuge he might try to make.

"Very well," I conceded. "But you must be ready to leave within the hour."

He bowed. "I shall arrange everything."

PART III

THE CHÂTEAU SAINT CLAIR, THE DORDOGNE

Chapter I

Arriving in Calais was not as it had been that first time. The dock was crowded, and although Cheddell had arranged for private cabins on the packet and saw to it that we were first off and that a coach awaited us for our onward journey, there was no sense of excitement at being on foreign soil, only a sense of dread.

As we crossed the French countryside, green and open, unlike our own chequered landscape, and as we passed through narrow cobblestone streets bordered by dark grey buildings, opening suddenly into a town square of bistros and bakeries, I could think of nothing except how strange and different it all was. Fear gripped me that my baby should be in such alien surroundings.

Cheddell and I spoke little. My worry and lack of rest left me irritable and unwilling to say anything which was not absolutely required. I suspected him of complicity in the matter and felt at no pains to be gracious. It made me watch him more closely than I might, under other circumstances, for I had no wish to be duped. But apart from this cursory surveillance he was not the subject of my thoughts. David occupied that sphere for the most part, though I could not refrain from continually turning my mind to Etienne and his role in this affair and his duplicity over Phoebe. I wondered what proceedings had been taken since I had signed the divorce papers. Cheddell would know but I refused to allow myself to ask him. Not the least of my thoughts concerned the lie I had been forced to tell. I tried to forget Etienne's expression, telling myself he had deserved it. Yet I had seen all too clearly the devastation my words had caused and I would it had not had to be so.

After days of intolerable road conditions, filthy accommodations and often unpalatable fare, we arrived at Perideux, a sleepy village in the Dordogne not far from the Gironde, which, despite its rusticity and somnambulent air, boasted a *mairie* of quite imposing dimensions on a wide boulevard bordered by leafy plane trees. I was all for proceeding immediately to the Château, tired and dirty as we were, but Cheddell insisted we put up at an inn. He must, he asserted, find out for sure that Etienne was there. He directed our coachman to the *Reine Marguerite*, the only inn of any consequence in the town. The coachman, who had kept up a constant harangue throughout the journey in mumbling tones and slurred elisions, suddenly became insupportable to me and I demanded that he not utter another word if he expected a gratuity. Thus it was we drew into the inn yard in perfect silence to be greeted by an excited, tattered small boy who was shortly followed by a brawny groom whose lack of enthusiasm at the extra work we were causing him matched in magnitude the boy's cheerfulness. The groom's surliness increased as Cheddell gave him instructions in deplorable French. I responded to Cheddell with equal ill-humour when he suggested that I wait until he ascertained whether there was room for us, and flounced inside without a word. I was under no misapprehension as to where his loyalty lay, and I had no desire to put it to the test.

It was an inn no better and no worse than many we had encountered crossing France. When my eyes became accustomed to the darkness inside I was aware of the corpulent innkeeper bustling to greet us and his expression of derision at Cheddell's notoriously bad manner of speaking his tongue. We stood opposite the public room where a group of men, obviously locals by their garb, sat drinking together. There was something strangely familiar about the shape of the head of the man whose back was toward me, and I must have stared, for the fellow with whom he was in heated discussion pointed me out to him and he turned. I saw at once, despite his odd, almost quaint manner of provincial dress, shirt sleeves with a leather jerkin and rough textured leggings, that it was Etienne.

He stared at me for a moment, as though deciding whether to acknowledge me or not. It was only when his eyes travelled to Cheddell, still in conversation with the innkeeper who seemed to be deliberately misunderstanding him, that he spoke briefly to his companion before coming into the hall.

"Madame Martin," he said in French, "I had not expected to see you here. What brings you to this part of France?"

I was about to give a spirited rejoinder and a disclaimer to that name in my own tongue, when Cheddell intervened quickly, still fracturing the French language, in his explanation that we were en route to Avignon where M. Martin was to meet us, but we had decided to break our journey at Perideux for a few days since he was not expected there until the following week.

Etienne suggested that we be seated and promised to arrange for our rooms. I noticed that the innkeeper addressed him as M. Falaise and, despite Etienne's simple garb, his tone bordered on the obsequious which made me believe Etienne had not been ungenerous during his stay there.

Soon I was shown to the only room with a private parlour, but not before I had given Etienne a speaking glance and his nod of acknowledgement left me to believe he would soon see me there.

I was not mistaken. I had barely time to wash the dust from my face and hands before there was a knock on the door. Seeing Etienne's familiar face made me, for a moment, forget everything. I wanted to fling myself in his arms and cling to him, but then I saw by his expression that he had forgotten nothing that had passed between us, and I drew myself up and held myself distantly from him as he did from me.

"And where is David?" I demanded, without any salutation.

"I have every reason to believe he is at the Château Saint Clair," he said evenly.

"Then why do you not have him if he is there? And why should he be there? What is all this mystery about? Why are you dressed like a peasant?" My voice rose in exasperation and with the fatigue which was fast overcoming me.

"You are exhausted, Leonora. Sit down. I shall try to explain."

"Please do," I said coldly, sitting on the edge of a straight back chair.

"But first, I must beg you to stay out of sight and not to reveal your name or even your nationality until I have him and can bring him to you."

Was this another of his tricks?

"You promised to explain. Do not demand such promises from me until you do. The life of my child may be at stake. I am entitled to an explanation. I bore him."

"No one could be better aware of that than I," he said quietly and his direct look made me falter.

"I am waiting," I said tersely.

"When you told me David had been taken from you, I immediately suspected a certain man—a man who has no more love for me than I have for him, a man who occupies the Château Saint Clair, close to Perideux. For a long time I have had differences with him and quite recently I was involved in a legal battle which I won but which left our relationship more acrimonious than ever. He is a man capable of committing such a crime against me, believing, as I did, that the child was mine."

I lowered my head to my hands. I was tired, yet that was not the reason. I could no longer bear to look at him as he spoke.

"Are you all right?" he asked.

"Go on," I said by way of reply. "Who is this man?"

"His name is le marquis de Clavel-Grassin."

I had heard that name before somewhere, but where? Then I remembered.

"Was he not so often spoken of when we were in Paris? And did I not ask you then about him and you said his name was of no particular significance?" I asked sharply.

"Perhaps so."

"But it was obviously significant. You must have known him then."

"I have known him since boyhood." His voice grew bitter at the affirmation. "But I did not come to France to discuss him. I came for our—your child. Will you allow me to continue with my plans for his recovery? But I want no word of your arrival to reach the Château. The less known of your presence here, especially by Clavel-Grassin, the better."

Could I believe him? If what he said was true, if the child had been taken by an enemy of his, then I had been wrong in all my actions. But I was not convinced that it was so. I was of a mind to deny him everything, yet he had the upper hand. He was obviously known in Perideux. He spoke the language as a native, even the local dialect. The only person known to me was Cheddell, and he would always be on Etienne's side rather than mine. I was alone. All I could do was bide my time and watch carefully as I waited.

"Very well. But I will give you an ultimatum. If you cannot produce my child within twenty-four hours with whatever method you have conceived, then I intend to go to the authorities here and demand that they take action in my behalf."

He scrutinized me.

"You still believe I took him from you, don't you?"

I saw his dark eyes filled with anguish and the circles beneath them which bespoke his lack of rest. I wanted to believe him. If it was as he said I should never have told that terrible lie. But I remembered Phoebe's visit. I had believed in him before, I had thought he loved me, but no sooner had he returned to London than he had returned to her arms, reaffirming his love for her but saying they were forever separated because of the baby. Well, I had cleared that obstacle now. Everything was simplified for them. I had signed the divorce papers. He had made no protest, he had accepted them. He must have wanted them.

"I don't know what to believe any more."

"No more do I," he said dryly. He turned to go. "I should have preferred more time. I hope you will grant it if it is necessary."

Already he is procrastinating, I thought wearily.

"Another twenty-four hours should be sufficient. You have already had several days. Surely, if you know he is there it is simply a matter of demanding his return. I shall gladly do so if you do not, and I *shall* do so if by tomorrow at this time I do not have my son."

"You shall have him."

He bowed to me, as though to a stranger, a chance travelling companion, someone from whom he was not sorry to part and whom he had no particular desire to meet again.

I supped alone, without appetite. I slept without rest. I awoke early the following morning and, despite Etienne's demand that I remain unseen, I dressed and went below, hoping to see and talk to him again. When he had not put in an appearance by mid-morning, I threw caution to the winds and enquired of him from the innkeeper.

"Ah, M. Falaise. He left early this morning."

"When is he to return?" I demanded.

"That I cannot tell. Since he has fully paid his account here, I do not know whether he intends to return at all."

"But he must!" I cried.

The innkeeper was surprised at my emotion.

"Madame Martin knows monsieur well?" he enquired slyly, no doubt seeking a succulent morsel of gossip to serve up with his *vin du pays* that evening.

But I paid him no mind. Etienne had deceived me again. How foolish I had been to expect anything else. And undoubtedly Cheddell had gone with him. Perhaps even now they had David and were beyond my reach. It would not be.

"I want a chaise—some kind of conveyance, anything— to take me immediately to the Château Saint Clair."

"Ah, so you know monsieur le marquis also?" The innkeeper's interest in me was avid.

"I intend to," I replied grimly. "Don't just stand there, make haste. You'll be well paid for your efforts."

Chapter II

The Château Saint Clair was immense, even from a distance. Its massive, round, yellow sandstone towers dominated the countryside and were in view long before I reached the tortuous driveway which led up the rocky promontory on which it was situated. It must have dated from the Middle Ages. I supposed it was beautiful, yet all I could think as the innkeeper's gig passed through an ancient stone archway and I climbed down into an open courtyard before a great door ornamented with an iron trellis, was that somewhere here in this medieval castle my baby was hidden—hidden, that was, if Etienne had been telling the truth, or if he had not arrived before me to spirit him away. But in a structure of such size and perplexity, if David were still there, how would I ever find him?

I was led up a great staircase to a large, sparsely furnished salon. The ceiling and walls were frescoed with the scene of a cavalry action led by a bold knight bearing a standard. I supposed he was an early ancestor of the present marquis. He soon appeared, though bearing little resemblance in size or mien to the noble warrior, being of slight build, dapper bearing and middling years. Despite his unprepossessing appearance there was a strange familiarity about his facial expression. I felt already acquainted with him, although I knew I had never met him until that moment. I had no time to consider that, however, for now I was confronted by the difficulty and delicacy of my mission. I had, after all, only Etienne's word that this man held David. He seemed so mild in appearance. I noted he was a man of good breeding as he bowed to briefly kiss my hand in greeting. I hardly felt it possible he could have stolen my son. Perhaps it was all another of Etienne's tricks.

"You must excuse me, monsieur le marquis, for calling on you in such an unpremeditated fashion, but I am sure you will understand better when I explain my purpose in being here," I began.

"Indeed, my dear madame?" His dark eyes raked my form and again I had that strange feeling of precognition. Perhaps I had met a relation of his when I was in Paris.

"I am Leonora Lambert, the wife of Etienne Lambert. My baby boy was taken from me some weeks ago in Yorkshire. Evidence indicates that he may have been brought here. I beg of you, if you have any knowledge of him to tell me of it."

I expected shock, surprise, disclaimers, anything but the calm with which he repeated,

"So you are Leonora, Lady Leonora Fordyce, is it not? I have heard of you and long wondered what you were like. Your father is the Earl of Castleford if I am not mistaken?"

I nodded.

"And he allowed you to marry a bastard!" He spat the word at me, and it was I who expressed the surprise and alarm I had been expecting from him. Etienne had spoken the truth about the marquis evidently, for not only was he known by him but clearly quite heartily disliked.

"I did not come to discuss my husband but my child." I replied with equal ferocity.

"He sent you then, rather than come himself. I might have expected that of him. He is no gentleman."

"It is not a question of his sending me. I came. It is altogether different." The only comfort I derived from his words was that Etienne could not possibly have arrived before me. If David was being held in the chateau, then he must still be there.

"I am honoured by your visit, madame, yet you are not the one who can give me what is mine by all that is right, by all that the law refuses to recognize."

He must have been speaking of the lawsuit Etienne had mentioned but I cared nothing for that.

"You admit you have my child then?"

"I admit nothing." He eyed me carefully again. "But perhaps after all we may spend our time well. Your husband is bound to appear now that you are here. Wine, my lady? It is uncivilized to discuss such matters with a dry tongue."

I refused his offer, but he helped himself generously with an experienced hand to the dark, red liquid in the nearby carafe.

"I demand an answer," I repeated when he showed no inclination to speak. "Do you have my son?"

He smiled over the rim of his glass.

"Perhaps. Do get more angry. I think that I prefer you when you are angry. Englishwomen as a rule are too phlegmatic for my taste. But not too angry, though. Ranting women I abhor."

The man was insufferable. I had every reason now to believe David was there as Etienne had told me. Though he had not admitted it, he had not denied it either.

"Please, monsieur le marquis, if you have him have pity on me. I am his mother. What is it you want for his return?"

"Of you, or of your husband?"

"Of either of us. Whatever it is it will be given, I promise."

"Since your husband has not chosen to come, it seems I can deal only with you. What are you prepared to give?"

"Anything you ask."

There was a malicious quality in the way he smiled at me.

"You are no different than any other Englishwoman, I see. There is nothing to which you will not agree. Ladies on the outside, harlots within. Just like his mother."

"She gave her life for her child. I am prepared to give no less for mine."

For a moment I thought my words had had some effect on him, but no.

"I have not said that I have him."

"Then put me out of my misery," I cried. "Either confirm or deny it."

Rather than answer, he countered, "Where is your husband?"

"I don't know," I replied with honesty. I wondered where Etienne could have gone. As much as I had hoped that he had not preceded me to the château, now I wished equally that he was there to argue for me.

"Did he not come to France with you?"

"No."

"Yet you say he did not send you. Where is he?"

I ignored the question. I was convinced this evil little man had David. He must be persuaded to release him whatever the cost.

"You have my child. I want him and I shall have him," I resolved.

"I have not admitted to having him," he repeated with equal determination. It was an impasse. We faced one another and he smiled at me derisively as though daring me to take the next step.

"I know you do. You do have him. I intend to go to the French authorities," I threatened.

"Please yourself," he replied nonchalantly.

I had no wish to leave yet I could think of nothing else to do. I could not search the château room by room. It was enormous. Besides, I doubted he would allow me to wander around at will. As I was deciding whether to go for help or to attempt to cajole my child from him, a seemingly hopeless task, I heard a sharp altercation in the hall below. There were shouts and a sound of scuffling and running footsteps on the stair. I turned in alarm, as did the marquis. The door was flung open by Etienne, no longer in his country garb but plainly, elegantly attired for travelling. He was closely followed by a dishevelled, flustered young groom. I gasped as I recognized him as Betsy's companion.

"Etienne!" I cried, pointing at the groom. "That's the man—the one who said he was Grisdale's nephew. That's the man who took David!"

"I know, Leonora. I just got it out of him."

"Lambert!" My host quickly waved away the groom. "Do come in. I've been expecting you. What took you so long?"

I looked from the marquis to Etienne, then back again to the marquis. Seeing them together I immediately knew why the marquis had seemed so familiar to me. The same dark eyes, the same set to the jaw, the same straight lips, yet on one they amounted to a slighted, malevolent whole while the other bore the same features with assurance and nobility despite the lack of legitimate birthright.

"I can assure you this is not the entrance I had intended," Etienne said grimly, straightening his travelling coat.

"Undoubtedly you had something far more devious in mind," our host murmured.

Etienne ignored him and turned to me.

"Are you all right? Has he hurt you?"

"No," I replied, "but I shall feel much better if I can see David. He must be here. I'm sure of it."

Etienne turned to the marquis who was watching his concern with obvious pleasure.

"So," Etienne demanded of him, "what is it that you want?"

"What is it I want, Lambert? Why, only what is due to me."

"This château, which, as you know and as the French courts confirmed only last month, is mine under the terms of my father's will. I could have had you evicted at that time, but I did not. Give us the boy and it is yours."

"You overlook that I am le marquis de Clavel-Grassin The château is my right. You are nothing but a bastard. I shall always despise father even more in death than I did in life for making it necessary for me to take such measures to procure what is mine."

"Had you applied to me immediately when the will was discovered, instead of simply taking unlawful possesssion of Saint Clair, I would have given it to you. I have no wish, indeed, no need of it. It is yours."

I had listened to this exchange at first without comprehension, but when Etienne mentioned the name of the château I remembered that was his name also.

"You are—brothers? Etienne, is that so?"

He nodded.

"Etienne was my father's name. My mother met him here when she came with the Salters." He faltered at that name, but went on. "It is true that we shared the same father, but I hesitate to call us brothers, for no such feeling ever existed between us as should exist between brothers."

"How true, Lambert, yet despite your lack of legitimacy and consequence how you galled me! To have father bring you here as a child, to dote on you as he did—such an insult to me and to my mother. But he never thought of either of us. Nothing was ever too good for you, his beloved bastard."

"Your mother never had any feeling for my father. After

you were born she considered she had fulfilled her marriage vows in giving him an heir and she left Saint Clair for Paris to enjoy the life of fashion. She even took you with her, leaving him nothing. She would never have come back had it not been for Salter's coming."

"Ah, yes, dear old Salter, his Oxford schoolfellow, and his wife and her charming young companion. How cosy it must have been. How you must have blessed the name of Salter for bringing them together. And you, the result of it all. A love child—I suppose you prefer that to being called a bastard. I remember how I used to sing that out to you. Father never reprimanded you sufficiently for the beatings you inflicted on me for simply calling you what you deserved."

"Beatings! Your mother protected you well enough from my dealing half the hurt I might have. Yet, despite your tauntings, those early years spent here with father when he discovered me in England after my mother's death—those were among the happiest of my life. He loved me as I loved him."

"My only pleasure in the revolution was that it caused him to send you back to England. He bothered little about me. Even when the ruffians occupied the château, I don't think he cared."

"Yet that revolution was responsible for his death. It was such a senseless act of brutality against a man who favoured so many of the revolutionaries' motives. He was an ardent lover of learning, and unlike many other noblemen he favoured using wealth wisely. But that you will never understand."

"I hated him. I shed no tears when he went to the guillotine."

" 'Pleasure perfects the soul,' the Clavel-Grassin motto, yet that pleasure to you is of the basest kind."

"And all the pleasure you ever know is acquiring wealth."

"For the power it can bring, and the good it can bring, I admit I have sought it. But not just to sqaunder or for its own sake."

"Dirty money grubber!" The marquis spat at him.

"This is all so reminiscent of our early days together—quite touching but hardly concerned with the matter at hand. I want the boy and I want him now."

Clavel-Grassin laughed,

"There is nothing you can do, Lambert, is there? This time you are helpless, on your own with no one to come to your aid, on my ground, surrounded by my servants. Anyway," he added abruptly, "I have not said I have him."

"That little game won't work. I have already ascertained he is here and has been for the past week. Had—had things not happened as they did today I would have come to you with the force of the law at hand. Now, however, at the moment you have the upper hand. I have already promised that the château is yours. What more do you want?"

Clavel-Grassin ostentatiously poured himself another glass of wine, noticeably excluding any invitation to Etienne to join him. He drank part of it before saying with cold deliberation, "The château is mine by right. Whatever the law may allow, it is not yours to give. Therefore to give it to me for your son is to give what is mine already. No, that will not do."

"Then what do you want?"

"A controlling interest in your shipping lines—in fact in all your affairs of commerce. You may continue to run them, but I want control."

"How generous of you! But no, I think not. If those are your terms you get nothing, not even the château."

"Etienne, please! The child!" I intervened in terror.

"Yes," Clavel-Grasssin said quickly. "Surely you want your son and heir."

"You admit you have him then?"

"I have him."

"Have him brought here. I must know that it is so."

"Very well. But remember, my servants have instructions to kill your son if I deem it necessary."

"You might be doing me a favour as matters stand," Etienne said grimly.

"What the devil do you mean by that?"

"The boy is not mine."

"Etienne, please!" I said pleadingly.

"Yet it is so, Leonora."

Clavel-Grassin looked quickly from one to the other as I lowered my eyes before Etienne's direct gaze.

"What trick is this you are trying to play on me? If you think I am so stupid as to believe you would travel all this distance to save a child who is not yours, you must believe me a fool. No, Lambert, you must think of something else. No man would do that."

"I have done it."

"I refuse to believe you. You want me to return your child without recompense."

"I have offered to give you Saint Clair. You can hardly call that nothing. In truth, even though the child is not mine, I would not have him left with you. I would not want any helpless child left to your devices. I have told you I am willing to give up all legal right to the château when you return him to his mother. I consider you are well recompensed for your reprehensible deed. Take it and be thankful. If you do not, I shall gain his release legally in the end and assure you are punished. I have the power in France for that. The law will side with me."

"You would give up Saint Clair for your wife's bastard son? No, Lambert, I've heard much of your astute mind in business affairs. This, I am convinced, is an example of how you gain your own way."

"Ask my wife if you do not believe me." Etienne's voice was hard as flint stone. "A woman does not lie about such things."

Both pairs of dark eyes were fixed on me, so like yet so unlike, one with that veiled inscrutability which, I had learned in the past, came to hide their most vulnerable feelings, the other filled with nonplussed amazement.

"No more does she," Clavel-Grassin said slowly.

"It is so," I stammered. I suspect my distraction must have made me the picture of guilt, yet Clavel-Grassin could not believe it to be so.

"No woman of birth would ever admit to such a thing. It is preposterous! You christened the boy, Lambert. You gave him your name. You celebrated his birth."

"As my wife says, though, he is not my son. I would to God he were."

The last came as a cry. It was the anguish in it which seemed to give the marquis pause.

He crossed the room to the book case and returned with an immense volume which he held out to me.

"If you swear on this bible that what Lambert tells me is true, that he is not the father of your child, the boy will be returned to you in exchange for the title to Saint Clair."

I looked down at the black, leather-bound bible. Its gold embossed cross loomed up at me. If I lied what would happen? Would I be struck dead upon the spot? An oath was an oath. One did not lie under such conditions. Yet it was my child this devil of a man held, mine and Etienne's, though the marquis did not know that and I realized he must not know that.

I reached out slowly to touch the book, reminding myself that it was a Roman Catholic bible and I was Church of England. Besides, in this instance, would not God forgive my falsehood?

"I swear it is so." My voice was low, but firm.

"You must say it. Say the words," Clavel-Grassin persisted.

My lips trembled. I felt tears come to my eyes and trickle down my cheeks. The lump in my throat made it difficult for me to speak, but I managed to say,

"Etienne is not the father of my child."

"Who is the father?"

Etienne intervened, "That is enough. Don't torture her any more. You heard what you wanted to know. Now give us the child. I have the title papers with me and I shall sign them over to you."

"This one question and it shall be done. Who is the father? I want to know."

"Jeremy Salter," I whispered.

As Clavel-Grassin pulled the bell rope for a servant to bring David, he chortled,

"It is more than I could have wished for in my wildest dreams. Oh, how fate has favoured me this day. Did I not say, Lambert, that you must bless the name of Salter. Little did I guess how much. To be cuckolded by a member of the family which was the cause of bringing that woman, that slut your mother into this house. It is too perfect."

"Cretin!"

Etienne's face was white. He had seized the marquis and was about to strike him when I cried out, and he turned to me and then thrust Clavel-Grassin from him.

I dissolved into tears and I did not look up until I heard a baby's cry.

"Oh, David, David, David!" I ran to take him from the woman servant who carried him. He looked pale and thin. He still wore his own clothes. I supposed they were the ones he had had on when they took him for they were terribly soiled. But he was alive. That was all that mattered.

I sat hugging him close to me, hardly aware of the two

men concluding arrangements for the transfer of the property, until Etienne came over to look at the baby.

"Poor little innocent," he said softly, gently stroking his cheek. Then he quickly pulled his hand away as though he had remembered that was a forbidden gesture.

"Come along, Leonora, we can go now."

Clavel-Grassin stood holding the papers Etienne had signed. His thin lips were wreathed in a malevolent smile. He tapped the legal documents and said to Etienne,

"I don't know which I am enjoying more, my rightful inheritance at last or your preposterous situation."

"*Cocu!*" he shouted after Etienne as we descended the stairs.

Chapter III

I began to explain, to apologize to Etienne for the wrong I had done him as soon as we left Saint Clair. I tried again at *La Reine Margeurite*, where he found a wet nurse to accompany us to England. Over and over again I tried to explain why I had lied, in the course of that long, tedious journey through France to Calais, brighter than the journey going, for David was safe and growing stronger daily, darker because of the despair in Etienne's eyes whenever I caught him off his guard. Though he continued to be as gentle to David as ever, a reticence had replaced the joy I had always noticed in him whenever he was with the child.

To me, he was kind and solicitous, far more than I might have expected considering what had happened. But he studiously shrugged off all my apologies and refused to listen to my explanations.

"Please," he said in answer to my efforts to right my wrong, "Please, Leonora, don't. Leave the matter alone. Enough has been said already. It is done and in truth, it is better that it is known now rather than later."

"But it is not so, Etienne. I have lied to you."

"How many times have you lied to me?" he said seriously, yet without rancour. "How many times? Our whole marriage has been a lie, but it is a lie which can and shall be set aright."

"You have wanted the divorce all along," I argued hotly. "That is why you refuse to listen."

"It was you who returned the papers to Spurrier. But really, does it matter who wanted it?" His voice sounded tired. "Suffice it that it can be done before it is too late for both of us."

"But, Etienne, please believe me. You must believe me. You must! David is your son. I have known no man but you. I swear it is so."

"Please, Leonora, don't swear to anything more, I beg of you. If it is for my sake you do so, it is unnecessary. I have been a fool throughout this whole affair of ours. I should never have asked you to marry me. You did not want it, and had I been honest with myself I would have admitted that. I cannot be angry with you now. If you protest because of your child, it is still unnecessary. He can take his father's name after you—after the divorce. He need never know anything of all this if you prefer it."

"Why won't you listen? You are his father, you, no one else. Listen to me!"

Helplessly I began to laugh and cry as I had on that occasion once before when I had accused him of stealing the baby, though he didn't shake me as he had then. He held me until I became quiet, but I felt pity rather than love in his embrace.

"Don't, don't. I know you've had an awful time of things but it is all over now. Your child is safe. If you are crying for me, don't. It hurts, I won't deny it, but I have been hurt before and survived. We will soon both be free to make our lives over. The child will be well provided for, I promise that. You, too, and your father. You have no need to worry.

But I beg of you, don't raise the subject again for there is nothing more to say on it."

So it was that whenever I tried to broach the matter, he would abruptly change the subject or, if I insisted on being heard, he would leave. I noticed he began to go to great lengths to avoid being alone with me and, whenever he was in my company he would discuss at great length some inconsequential trivia, or pick up a journal at hand and quote at length from some item of news until Cheddell came or the nurse brought David to me, at which time I could almost feel his relief that the *tête à tête* was over, that the moment had passed when I might again insist on protesting my innocence. Realizing this I, too, began to avoid being alone with him and by the time we boarded his yacht in Calais we were virtual strangers.

I saw my name on her prow and remembered that first journey on her, how he had helped me overcome my sea sickness, how we had stood together by the rails watching the gulls. I stood there alone now, watching their outstretched wings circling the grey waves as the white cliffs loomed closer and closer bringing with them our inevitable parting. I might never see him again, I realized with a sense of emptiness. He had been forced to tell a man he hated that he had been betrayed by his wife and listen to his taunts. He was proud. Apart from the deceit he thought I had practiced, what must that have cost him. He would never believe me now. He would marry Phoebe and all of his love and attention would be hers. He would rename his yacht for Phoebe and she would rearrange his furniture. She would give him children and David would become someone to whom Cheddell sent a bank draft every quarter, just as he did to Papa. I clenched my fists. I wouldn't have it. David, as his son, was entitled to it, but only as his son, not if he was fathered by another. And that was what Etienne continued to believe. I had been wrong to say such a thing, but I had been desperate. Too late I knew how terribly wrong I had been to believe Etienne capable of the heinous crime of kidnapping his child. Now I was paying for my wrong. How dearly I was paying for it.

The ride to London was quiet. Our dinner together that night at Grosvenor Square was even more silent. I made one more attempt to set matters right that evening. Etienne had left the table immediately after dining, pleading pressure of work which had accumulated in his absence. I followed him there and entered without knocking.

He sat at his desk, his head in his hands, but when he heard my steps he jumped up in anger.

"What is it you want of me, Leonora. I have told you I have nothing more to say to you."

"I am well aware of that. I promise I shall not take much more of your time, but I must ask you to hear me out without interruption." I made my voice as clear and distinct as I possibly could, afraid I might break down again and burst into tears when I could least afford to. "David is your son. No, don't," I said quickly as I saw the protests arise on his lips, "I asked you to hear me out. I promise to be brief and to the point. I repeat, David is your son. It is only possible that he is your son for I have known no one else. You are his father. I lied to you because I thought you had taken him from me. I lied to Clavel-Grassin because I thought it was the only way to get David from him. It was wrong to lie, but I did it. Now I am sorry, for I see the harm I have done—to all of us."

"And your lover from Yorkshire, you may remember you yourself told me of him at a particularly intimate moment as I recall. That, too, was a lie I suppose," he said savagely.

I swallowed before replying, "In a way, it was. You were the lover I referred to."

He raised his eyebrows.

"Ah, so now that lover is me, and I am once again the

child's father. And next week, will it still be the same or will you have some other amazing disclosure for me?"

I thought of his maxim: never apologize, never explain. He was right. It was useless to think I could make him understand. The more I said the more convoluted everything became.

I turned to go but he stopped me, drawing something from his desk.

"I almost forgot. This is yours. I had intended to return it to you earlier."

I looked down at the shimmering glow in his hand. It was the emerald necklace he had given to me in Paris, the necklace I had pawned to pay my obligation to Lorimer.

"I don't want it," I retorted bitterly. "It was a present to your wife. It is clear I am that no longer. Give it to—" I could not bring myself to mention Phoebe's name in that connection. "Keep it until you remarry."

"I shall not burden you with it if you have no wish for it."

He dropped the necklace carelessly on the desk where its twinkling, teasing glow reminded me all too well of other places, other days.

"I want nothing from you except Pelham," I vowed. "I shall accept nothing for myself, nor shall I accept anything for David as long as you continue to be convinced that I lie when I tell you he is your son."

Etienne said nothing. His lips moved as though he intended to speak; I waited, but no words came.

At the door I flung back at him in anger,

"You will greatly oblige me by refusing to pay any further sums to my father. He must learn to stand on his own two feet, as I shall."

The sound of the door slamming behind me as I left reverberated through the house and through my head in the days to come. It signalled the finality of the break between us.

PART IV
PELHAM MANOR, YORKSHIRE

Chapter I

"**I** have told Lambert everything about that business with Jerningham, how I pleaded with you to go to Jerningham for me to redeem my note. I told him that you went against your wishes, only to help me, that you believed, as I did, that he had nothing nefarious in mind. I told Lambert you were completely innocent in the matter and that all the wrong was mine. It cost me my word as a gentleman but I told him. I said how heartily sorry I was, for I fear that that is behind the rift between you two. Lambert was surprised, I'm sure of it, though he said little enough. He's not an easy man to explain things to, you know."

"I know, Papa."

I had been helping in the dairy when he came. The maid had been teaching me how to churn butter and my arms still ached with my efforts. I knew I was unkempt for it had rained continuously for the past week, and though I had removed my mud-caked shoes on entering the house in answer to the summons of Papa's unexpected arrival, the hem of my plain worsted dress was still badly soiled. But I had only taken time to call out to Thistle to have a room prepared and I had not stopped to change, for Papa's descending on me in that fashion, with no warning, frightened me. He had to have a reason for coming so far from London. I was sure it was not merely to enquire after my health.

I ran to him and kissed him. It had been so long since I had seen him that I had forgotten the estrangement which had grown between us. I was only glad to see his familiar face. But after greeting me, Papa held me at arm's length to examine with disfavour my untidy hair, my plain, mud-stained gown and stout slippers.

"Leonora!" The word contained all the disapprobation which his face so clearly showed. "Leonora, what on earth are you doing to yourself up here in the wilds of the north. You must return to London with me immediately. As your father I insist upon it."

"Papa, dear, do sit down. You must be fatigued after your journey. And do stop frowning and being bossy. I shall be twenty-one on my next birthday, and if that is not enough to convince you of my independence, I must remind you that I am no longer single."

"I am well aware of that. That is the reason for my visit. God knows I should not choose to come here unless it were essential."

"You are well aware that I am now independent."

"No. I am well aware that you are no longer single, though if things continue as they are going you will find yourself in a worse state, being neither married nor single."

It was not going to be an easy interview and I was grateful for the arrival of Thistle at that moment with refreshments, though I could see Papa disapproved of her easy familiarity as she scolded me for wearing my muddied frock in the house.

"I thought you knew how to train servants better than that," Papa said as soon as she left. "We never put up with such disrespect at Hill Street, or even in the country at Briarsmere."

"Thistle is not a servant, Papa."

"Well, what is she then? Don't tell me she's a surrogate mother to you or I shall take you from here by force if need be. Too much rustication can turn into a disease."

I could not explain my relationship with Thistle to Papa because I had no clear way of describing it to myself. I only knew that without her I could never have got through the past long, difficult months. She had welcomed us back, delighted that David was safe and well, but she had asked no questions either about him or about why Etienne never came. She was simply always there at hand when I needed her. She offered advice when it was sought, never otherwise. She taught me the difficulties and the rewards, though at first I found it hard to believe there were rewards, of learning to survive on a strict budget. I had been unused to accounting for my expenditures. Papa had never demanded it and, after marriage, Cheddell had paid all my bills so I rarely saw them. I had no idea what it was to make do, to have to choose whether to buy seed for planting or replace that part of the barn roof which leaked. Hodges was a great help, though I feared I would have to let him go for I could no longer afford the high wages I had originally set him. He would, however, not hear of leaving. I went to great pains to keep my farm hands, for they needed work, but my economies on the estate caused something of a furor in Sembourne. The villagers believed I still had unlimited wealth and considered it miserliness and eccentricity on my part when I no longer purchased supplies and provisions in prodigious amounts from them, and when I insisted on learning one task after another so that I might know how much I could expect of my workers. Hodges, like Thistle, asked no questions, merely working along side me, instructing me in a way of life I had theretofore only viewed from the outside. I knew that it was essential that I thoroughly understand everything if David and I were to live on what Pelham could provide for us and that alone.

I was grateful that neither Hodges nor Thistle ever brought up Etienne's name, though I would notice Thistle's frown as she handed me the communications which flowed like flakes in a snowstorm from Etienne's solicitor. Spurrier was anxious to bring the divorce proceedings to a satisfactory conclusion, but Etienne was insistent upon monetary settlements being made upon us and I was just as insistent in my refusal. Spurrier was puzzled at my stand. I was sure that to him the divorce was simply another case in his busy practice. His clear legal language deprived the whole matter and its participants of any singularity of being, any emotion, any humanity. He presented me with one set of papers after another for my signature but all contained the monetary settlements to myself, my son and my father for life. When I had first refused to sign them, the amounts had been raised, as though that were the reason. I had written Spurrier a stinging letter, calling him a blithering idiot for deliberately misunderstanding me. I demanded that the money which continued to flow into my account at the bank at Harrogate cease forthwith, and when it did not I instructed the bank to return it. After several attempts to deposit bank drafts in my name, but not before both the banker and Merston, my lawyer from Knaresbridge, came to reason with me to keep the money because of my dwindling resources, pleas to which I resolutely refused to listen, the drafts had at last ceased. Some time later Papa sent me a thousand pounds which I had accepted. Though I had written to him at the time, I was glad to be able to thank him in person.

"It was good of you, Papa, for that was a good deal of money considering you no longer—" I hesitated, for Papa and I had never spoken much of the allowance he received from Etienne, and concluded lamely, "get money from that other source."

"From Lambert, you mean?" Papa admitted boldly.

I nodded. "But you can be assured I put the money you sent me to good use. I bought a Rumford range for the kitchen so now we can have a good oven and a water heater as well. It was expensive but it is such an improvement over the open fire. And I repaired the barn roof, and only just in time. You can probably imagine how much rain we've had from the state of the roads. I can show you where every penny of that thousand pounds went, for I keep accounts now."

I was proud of my achievements and not prepared for Papa's horrified response, "The next thing I'll hear is that you're living on a budget."

"As a matter of fact, I am," I said defensively.

"That's almost as bad as going into trade. It's a terrible thing to see one's daughter, one's only daughter, one's formerly respected, formerly beautiful daughter succumb to such—such mediocrity. I never thought the day would come when I would find myself to have more in common with Lambert than with my own child. At least he understands the importance of money in this world, even though he still refuses to use it as I would. I tried again to put him up for White's but he was adamant against it."

"Do you see much of him?" I asked hesitantly.

"Yes, I see him quite often."

"How is he?"

"Quite well, in fact very well indeed. He looks a great deal better than you, I might add."

It was so long since I'd spoken of him, even heard anything of him other than as the party of the second part in

Spurrier's correspondence. His name was rarely mentioned in the one luxury I allowed myself, a subscription to the *Morning Post*, though I found Phoebe's there from time to time among those attending notable social functions. What was happening between them, I wondered. Was she growing impatient? Would she descend on me again, begging me to agree to the settlement so that the divorce could proceed. It sometimes crossed by mind, though I firmly refused to admit it, that my adamant refusal to accept money stemmed from my wish to stop that proceeding altogether. Looking across at Papa another thought crossed my mind.

"Did Etienne send you, Papa?"

Papa flushed. "He did ask me to talk to you. He tells me you are refusing to accept any of the money he sends you. He says it is a senseless stand you are taking, and I quite agree with him. What you should do is to return to him. Come back to London with me."

"Did he ask you to say that?" I tried to keep the eagerness from my voice.

Papa paused. "No," he said slowly, "not exactly. But you should know that there are awful rumours running rampant in town regarding your marriage, rumours of—I cannot bring myself to say what they concern."

"Rumours of a divorce?"

"Just so. Exactly. You must quash these now, before they go any farther. You must return to him without further delay and put these idle tongues to rest."

"But it is so, Papa. A divorce is imminent. It awaits only the settlement of certain matters before the proceedings will be made public, though it would seem they are not completely unknown already."

Papa was thunderstruck.

"Leonora! I can't believe it. Tell me it is not so. No Fordyce has ever been part of such an action."

"One soon will be. You must get used to the idea. You must also get used to living on a lesser income."

"You mean—" Papa's jaw dropped, "you mean he will take away my allowance after—after that awful thing happens?"

"Has he not done so already?" I demanded.

"No. In fact he increased it and asked that I send you that small sum."

"You mean that thousand pounds was from him?"

"Yes. He asked me to do it since you were refusing the money he was sending to you."

"Had I known I should never have taken it. I might have guessed though," I said bitterly. "I shall certainly refuse any such sums in the future. I intend to stand on my own and support myself and my son."

"From what? From this, this—" Papa waved his hands disparagingly at his surroundings. "From this shabby retreat?" Words seemed to fail him, and he subsided into gloom.

"Pelham may seem shabby and mean to you, Papa. I can assure you it is not so to me. I have few tenants, but they are good. There is ample livestock for the needs of my small household and, if the weather favours me, I shall derive a good return from my corn. Pelham is a good estate; not grand in the manner of Briarsmere, but I intend to make every inch of it pay. Soon it will show sufficient income for all our needs if not for luxuries."

"You talk like a farmer or a tradesman, I don't know which is the worst," Papa lamented. "No lady would ever speak of such things."

"I advise you to do likewise at Briarsmere, Papa," I said sharply, "for I have asked that your allowance be discontinued also. It will be so when the divorce comes about."

"No, Leonora, you cannot do that. What Lambert gives to

me is of no concern to you. It is between the two of us."

"That was part of the marriage settlement that you arranged—a part you never told me of, just as you never told me that Mama's pendant was paste. You have never been honest with me, have you?"

He hung his head. "I wanted to spare you sordid details."

"Yet you did not hesitate to give me in marriage to someone I did not at that time want."

"Forgive me, Leonora, perhaps the divorce is for the best after all, though I fear it is going to hurt you more than it does him. He will become an eligible *parti* once again, while it will be the end of everything for you if you continue to bury yourself here."

"The divorce does hurt me, but not in the way you think."

"I am sorry I made you marry him."

"I was sorry at the time. I hated it at first, but after—"

"I hated it also. I hated having to acknowledge a connection with such an upstart. I felt he should pay for marrying into our family, that is why I took the allowance. I suppose he got what he wanted, for now he is highly regarded. Even Lady Oliphant sings his praises, and you know how choosy she is of the company she keeps."

"I've no doubt she does," I said dryly.

"I dare say the divorce suits him, but what's to become of you? Look at you! You're neither a lady nor a commoner."

"I'm a woman. A woman in my own right, not your daughter nor—nor Etienne's wife. I shall be on my own. Pelham will be my home from now on. My friends are here. They may not be the friends whom you would choose, but I enjoy them."

Papa looked at me quizzically.

"Is there someone here, someone you prefer to Lambert?"

"What makes you ask that?"

"It was a chance remark of Lambert's. He said he thought your future lay here, but I understood him to mean you would not be alone."

"He referred to David, no doubt," I said quickly.

"Is there—someone else? Do you intend to remarry?"

"No, absolutely not."

"There is one fool in every marriage, but I am not convinced in this case it was Lambert." Papa looked at me from head to toe. "No wonder he has become fascinated with that little Frenchwoman."

"What do you mean? What Frenchwoman?"

"Madame Garnier. Do you know her?"

"Slightly. What makes you say he is fascinated with her?"

"He has been seen with her. It is said she is to be co-respondent."

"Co-respondent? What does that mean?"

"There have to be grounds for a divorce, Leonora."

"Oh! Does that mean that he—that she—that they were together?"

"Well, you could hardly expect him to accuse you of infidelity. She is an attractive woman. I can't imagine that he looked upon it as any hardship."

My face must have reflected the sinking feeling which seized me.

"What on earth is the matter, Leonora?"

I ran from the room, pushing past Thistle on the stairs, ignoring her comment that Papa's room was ready. Nor did I descend until dinner was called. I wondered if the law's requirement that there be proof of such wrongdoing made Phoebe feel as low as I.

Throughout Papa's short stay he alternately begged me to return to London with him and make peace with Etienne, or to take on his solicitor to represent me in the action.

"If it is Lambert who wants this divorce you could become

a very rich woman," he reminded me time and time again.

My assertions that I wanted nothing from Etienne infuriated him, so that we parted on less than amicable terms.

He looked back at me before climbing into his coach.

"Think over carefully what I have said, Leonora. You should hang onto the husband you have, for as you look now, so plain and drab, no other man will ever want you."

Chapter II

But Papa was proven wrong, for the month following his visit I was to receive not one, but two proposals of marriage, neither of which I sought, neither of which I accepted.

The first came from Francis Oliphant.

I had not expected him, but when he drove over one day from Buxstead Park, where he was staying with the Ladbrooks, I greeted him with pleasure as an old friend, for he reminded me of the carefree girl I had been in the days of our youth together. Assiduously we avoided all mention of his sister or my husband. I invited him to return before he left Yorkshire, but I had not expected him to reappear so soon as the following morning. He was dressed for travelling and said he had been unexpectedly asked to return to London, but that he had to talk to me before he left.

"I hope nothing is wrong, Francis."

"No, it is just that mother wants me back to talk to Phoebe. You see, she has become secretly engaged, and mother is against it being done in that way. If she wants the man she should wait and announce it publicly. I must say I agree with mother, but I don't understand all of it. I suppose I shall find out in due course."

"Yes," I replied dully. My heart was heavy. I could not bring myself to ask Francis who the man was. I knew. "What are you going to do about it?"

"Talk to Phoebe, I suppose. Perhaps she will see reason. But she is stubborn. She always wants her own way and usually gets it. But I didn't come here this morning to discuss Phoebe."

He came and stood so close to me that involuntarily I stepped back.

"Leonora, all London knows that your marriage is at an end, and that it will soon be legally set aside. As I see it, that leaves the way clear for us to do as we always planned."

"As we always planned?" I questioned absentmindedly. My thoughts were still on Phoebe's secret engagement. She would have him at last, I thought bitterly. Francis was right. She usually got her own way.

"Why, our marriage, of course. You know we always said it would be, ever since we were children together. I've reached my majority now and though my allowance is not very large at the moment, eventually everything will be mine, the title, the estate. In the meantime, I am sure we can manage nicely on what you have, for everyone says if you play your cards right in this business with Lambert you can come out of it a rich woman. Together we would know how to spend his money. Money is to be enjoyed not tied up in useless works."

I hardly heard what he said, except that the divorce was public knowledge.

"Are they really discussing it as openly as that?" I asked.

"Yes. There have even been bets placed on it at White's—how long it will take, how much he'll agree to settle for. Everyone knows he wants it. There's a lot of speculation, for they guess he's just using Madame Garnier to cover up."

So Papa had been right about Madame Garnier, and everyone knew of that also.

"How long is it before it goes before Parliament?" Francis asked.

"I don't know."

"Surely you must have some idea."

"I don't, none at all."

"Well, I see no reason why we can't have an understanding between us now that will leave us free to get married as soon as the matter is concluded. I see no need of an engagement, do you?"

"I certainly don't," I snapped.

"Well, that's settled then," he replied with satisfaction and went to take me in his arms.

"What do you mean by 'that's settled'?" I asked with asperity.

"Our engagement, of course."

"I never agreed to any such thing."

"But it's what we've always wanted, you know it is."

"It may have been at one time; we were children then. We're not children any more, we're adults."

"Of course we are. Everyone grows up."

I looked at his eager, young face, just as set as his sister on having his own way. Not everyone grew up.

"We've changed, Francis. We're not the same."

"I haven't changed," he asserted stoutly. His eyes ran over my plain garb. "You may have in some ways, but not in the ways that count. Once we're back in London we'll take a house. Lady Newbury's is available on Cavendish Square; we'll be able to afford that. You'll get new clothes and look every bit as smart as you did when you came back from Paris. We'll give parties and you'll be the toast of the town again, you'll see."

I looked at Francis' dandified form, his many-caped travelling coat with its bright, shiny buttons, his intricate cravat.

How had I ever been enamoured of him, I wondered.

He went to embrace me again, and I stopped him.

"I am still married, Francis. To talk of either Etienne or myself remarrying is thoroughly premature." I hoped he would carry this word back to Phoebe when he saw her.

"The matter's not at an end," he said on leaving.

"It is as far as I am concerned. Please don't ever mention it again."

But he waved goodbye cheerily enough and I feared my admonition went unheeded.

That was to be a day full of the unexpected, for in the afternoon a letter arrived from London. I knew it was from Etienne as soon as I saw the hand. It was the first time he had written to me directly since that awful last night in London. It was several minutes before I steeled myself to open it.

Dear Leonora,

Do stop being so stupidly obstinate and letting your pride stand in the way of accepting the settlements I have proposed for you and members of your family. To assert you want Pelham and nothing more is ridiculous. It is true that you have made wonderful improvements. I was delighted in everything I saw when I was there. I know it was only done through your efforts. I truly never before believed you had such acumen. You may have had help, but even if you had, it cannot detract from all you have done.

To suggest, however, that you and the child can live on the proceeds from this small estate is unreasonable. You must remember that without ample money the improvements and renovations you made to bring Pelham to some degree of productivity would have been impossible. When you attempt to continue your efforts without such funds, you will discover what I say to be true, if you have not done so already. To borrow money is to bury yourself in a quagmire, for eventually, one way or another, it must be repaid. I feel I need say no more on that matter, for you know the exigencies of it at first hand. You may perhaps be able to eke out an existence for yourself at Pelham, though certainly not in the style to which you have always been accustomed. But if you choose to deprive yourself for some foolish whim of pride, you should first consider the child and his future. I know only too well the difficulties of a boy growing up with questionable legitimacy and without money to boot.

I feel all of this explanation is unnecessary and would not write you now had not Spurrier spoken repeatedly to me of your refusal to accept anything from me. Your stand is ridiculous. Pardon me that I speak plainly, but if you won't listen to me, listen to your solicitor, or to your father. To make a settlement upon you in no way implies that I intend to place any future demands upon you, if that is your fear, nor does it imply any commitment on your part toward me. It is merely a common sense solution to something that has been a difficult situation from the beginning.

In mentioning your father, I am reminded that I must ask your forgiveness for a misconception I formed, one which you allowed me to believe instead of telling me the truth in an attempt, I suppose, to avoid embarrassment to your father. It was a loyal action. I hope he is deserving of it. I speak, of course, of the day I found you at Jerningham's. You were there, as your father tells me, and I have no reason to doubt his veracity for I know what it must have cost him to admit the truth to me, to save him from another of his gaming peccadilloes, not, as I so wrongly concluded, for some romantic interlude. I'm afraid that I jumped to conclusions because, at the time, I was horribly jealous of Jerningham's attitude toward you and I thought the worst. I suppose it no longer makes any difference. I can do nothing more than ask your forgiveness for my stupid mistake.

It is my fondest wish that you will find all the happiness you seek in the future. If you are ever in need of my help, do not hesitate to call on me.

> *I remain,*
> *As ever,*
> Etienne

I did not come down to dinner that night. I sat in my room reading and rereading his letter. At last Thistle brought up a bowl of soup which she was to take away again in the morning, cold and untouched.

I thought over everything he had said. He was right, I knew. For what reason, other than pride, was I depriving David of what was his? He was, after all, Etienne's son. Perhaps one day Etienne would know that. Perhaps when it was too late, when he had another wife, another family. No, he was right, David should not be deprived.

At last I wrote him a short note. It was cold in tone. I knew it was so, deliberately so. I could not write him how I felt for that would again lead to the tears and protestations he had so despised. I agreed that he might set up a trust fund for the child, to be available, should he desire to use it, when he was of age. At that time I would tell him the truth of the matter, the truth to which he, Etienne, refused to listen. He would then be free to accept the money in that fund as his. Until that time I would take nothing for the child and at no time would I take anything for myself.

It was done. I gave the letter to Thistle to have it franked before I changed my mind, and it was gone. The matter was at an end.

I was more grateful than ever for Dulcie's presence. I had seen a great deal of her since I got back. I had heard nothing of Jeremy Salter, of which I was glad, for I had sadly wronged him in using his name as I had. I had assiduously not asked after him, nor had Dulcie ever mentioned him until one day when she was showing me how to make ink with the gallic acid from our oak apples, and with iron sulphate and gum arabic. I was busily beating these together in the mortar while Dulcie readied the small beer and sugar when she said, a trifle too casually,

"Jer—Mr. Salter came back yesterday."

"Oh. I didn't realize he was away."

She put aside the vial she was holding.

"Leonora, I wish you would talk to him. I think he would listen to you."

"What do you mean?"

"He—has a great regard for you."

"No more than for you," I affirmed.

"I know that—that it is more than that."

"Well, if you are right, it certainly should not be." This turn of conversation was distressing to me. I had no wish for my name ever to be linked to Salter's, anymore than I had already so disgracefully done.

"If you mean because you are married, it is known that that is at an end and you will soon be free if you are not already."

"How on earth did you know that? I said nothing of it."

Dulcie saw my hurt and indignation and flushed.

"I should not repeat gossip, I know I should not. Father says it is a most unchristian thing to do. But if you haven't heard what is being said in Sembourne I must tell you. Mrs. Dorling had it from a friend in London, I believe. Anyway she says it is openly talked of there, that there is to be a divorce. It is not your fault, Leonora. Everyone knows you are not to blame. He was a fiend to take your child from you as he did."

I saw how wrong I had been in saying nothing after I returned of what had really happened to David, but I had been unable, then, to talk of anything that concerned Etienne. I suppose I could hardly blame people for drawing what must have seemed an obvious conclusion. But I had to enlighten Dulcie, and I did so without delay. I told her everything—everything, that is, except that one terrible lie. She was my friend, but even to her I could not repeat it, especially to her since I had so shamefully used Salter's name.

"But why, then—why the divorce?" she asked in a hushed voice as I finished. "Or is that also untrue?"

I shook my head. I could not bring myself to reply.

Dulcie took me in her arms.

"Is he blind not to see what a wonderful, loyal wife he has?

Is he no longer satisfied with you? Does he want someone giddy and fashionable? Mr. Lambert seemed such a sensible, sensitive man when I met him, but now I begin to wonder if my impressions were correct. How could he bear to lose you?"

"I don't want to talk of it, Dulcie. Later I may be able to but not now. But Etienne was not the man you wanted to discuss, it was Salter. What is it about him that is concerning you?"

It was Dulcie's turn to look disturbed.

"He has been away in Lancashire. I am sure he has been riding with the machine-breakers, the Luddites. You must have read of their spate of destruction there in these past few weeks. Your husband's mills were among their targets, though unlike the others, his workers seemed willing to lay down their lives for their machines."

I felt stupid. I had been reading the paper but I had glossed over the reports of the machine breaking. My own sowing and threshing machines were now accepted, and since I did not expect to have money to buy any more, it had not seemed to concern me. I did know, however, that severe sentences were being handed down to the offenders, particularly to their leaders. Transportation was not unusual. In certain instances where property or owners were severely harmed, death sentences were given.

"He mustn't, Dulcie, he mustn't. He must be made to see the danger."

"That is why I want you to talk to him. He will listen to you."

I shook my head dubiously.

"I am not at all sure that he will."

But the next afternoon when Salter called on me, I broached the subject.

"You're worried about your husband's property," he accused. "Everyone knows he's in the forefront of this iniquitous move to mechanize our industries and put honest people out of work. Anyway, why should you care any more. Your marriage to him will soon be a thing of the past."

I was startled. So Salter also knew. Yet it might as well be now as later, for Merston, my solicitor from Knaresbridge, had called again only that morning with the revised papers. I had at last signed them and he had sighed with relief saying that in no time at all the matter would be at an end. I knew that to him it was another case, probably a lucrative one since Etienne was paying his fee. I wished I could be in his shoes and regard it in that light.

"You are quite right, Mr. Salter. My husband's property is not my concern. But the fact that you openly defy the law by involving yourself in such dangerous activities, putting your very life in jeopardy, is a matter of great concern to those who think highly of you."

I had expected some political harangue, some talk on the oppression of the masses, anything but the complete change of attitude which came over him at my words.

He took my hand.

"Leonora, Leonora, I didn't know. I dared not allow myself to hope."

Then, to my horror, he dropped to his knees and haltingly asked me to be his wife.

"Please, please, stop. Stop, Mr. Salter, I beg of you and get up. I am sorry I did not make myself clear. You have misunderstood me. I spoke because of Dulcie Rankin's fears for you. She asked that I speak to you. She said you would listen to me."

How stupid I had been. Dulcie had known he would ask me to marry him. She had therefore presumed he would listen to me.

"Dulcie Rankin!" Salter repeated dazedly.

"Yes." Now I had gone this far I could see no point in stopping. "She loves you. You must be blind not to see it. I knew it the moment I first saw her look at you. If you think about it you must realize it also."

"But I—I love you," he said, still in that dazed manner.

"You may think so, but if you seriously consider you must find it is not so. I can never love you and no man wants a woman who loves another. I shall never love anyone but Etienne."

"Why the divorce then? Is it he who demands it? He is mad if that is so."

"It is all too complicated, and I cannot explain it to you." I did not add that Salter was the last person to whom I could explain it. "Suffice that my marriage is at an end, but there is no reason why yours and Dulcie's should not be beginning. She loves you, Mr. Salter. She loves you so much she was willing to give you up to me. She asked me to persuade you to stop your dangerous activities believing if I told you, you would do so. She promulgated this scene between us thinking only of your welfare, of your safety. That latter is a wish I share both for your sake and for hers. Will you not think of her now and of her love for you? You share so many things. She is as concerned for the well-being of the villagers and workers as you are. She shares your ideas even though her father does not. Please promise to think more carefully in the future of those you harm when you involve yourself in these terrible raids."

He stood awkwardly before me.

"I promise to consider my actions. I cannot promise to discontinue them."

With that I had to be satisfied.

Chapter III

It was with utter disbelief that I read in the *Morning Post* not a week after Francis' visit of the engagement of Phoebe Elizabeth Oliphant to Henry George Armbruster Foxcroft of Heath Park, Surrey.

I read the announcement again and again. I could not believe it. When Francis had spoken of Phoebe's engagement, I had thought it could be to no other but Etienne. I had thought that the necessity of the secrecy. But to read that Phoebe was engaged to be married to Harry Foxcroft, the young man she had slighted so despite his admiration of her after that unfortunate accident, how could it be? I had to know. I sat down immediately to proffer my congratulations in the hope that she would reply and tell me everything. From the minute my letter was posted I impatiently awaited a reply.

Salter did not call again, but Dulcie came often. She spoke of everything; only on the matter of Salter was she reticent, though I gathered he called on her. These visits could not have been easy for either of them, given Mr. Rankin's dislike of Salter, but I knew Dulcie would brave even her father's censure for the pleasure of spending time, however little, with Salter. I longed to know what passed between them, but though her voice grew soft whenever she mentioned his name, there was no evidence that anything above commonplaces was exchanged. I was disappointed.

Phoebe's reply to my letter came at last, and I opened it with trembling fingers. She acknowledged my congratulations, saying she had not expected to hear from me after all that had occurred. She continued,

I was so glad you wrote for it gives me the chance to admit honestly how very much I have wronged you and how very sorry I am for it all. I speak, of course, of Lambert. It is true that I saw something of him when Mama and I were in town the Christmas when you first went to Yorkshire. Mama liked him and he liked her. I must admit I was hopelessly attracted to him when I stayed with you at Grosvenor Square, but I think you guessed that. I always thought that was your reason for going to Yorkshire in the first place.

Anyway, seeing him again made that attraction towards him stronger than ever. I did not feel particularly guilty about it for I was convinced that you had never cared for him. Mama, in fact, spoke quite frankly to him and from what he said she guessed that the marriage was over in all but name. Nothing was or could be said between us, but I came to believe, perhaps because I wanted to believe it, that one day we would be together. He said nothing, he could not, but I felt he believed it also. When I learned that you were to have a child, I was furious, partly with envy but mainly because I felt a child would draw him to you and away from me. Because of that I went to Lambert before the child was born and confessed my love for him. He was wonderfully kind and gentle, he took the blame for my feelings upon himself. He admitted that at one time he had thought of me in that light. He had, in fact, gone as far as to ask you for a divorce, but all that was past. You were to have his child. Everything had changed and he intended to do all that he could to put your marriage on a firm footing. In view of my feelings, he said we should not see one another again but he wished me well. He hoped I would marry and be very happy.

I could not put him from my thoughts. I confess that I did not wish you well for I would have done anything to take him from you. That is why I came to Yorkshire. I lied to you when I said I had seen him, that he wanted the divorce but would not ask for it. I thought if you would divorce him he would turn to me. In my own defence, I must admit that I thought you did not want him.

I was wrong about Lambert, for though I wrote to him repeatedly, he refused to see me. Finally I went to his offices in search of him. I'm afraid I made rather a fool of myself. He did see me briefly, but only briefly, and then he talked to me like a Dutch uncle. He told me I was ruining my reputation and that I must not come to him in that way. He told me that he loved you and that he always would, no matter what. When talk began to spread in town of the divorce, I hoped against hope that he would come to me, but then he was being seen about with that Garnier woman. I was horribly jealous. It was then I agreed to a secret engagement with Harry, who had proposed to me with such regularity throughout all of this that I regret to say I had consistently ignored him. I am ashamed to admit that I became engaged to him out of spite, to make Lambert jealous. But when I wrote to tell him of it he wished me joy and said it was the wisest thing I had done, that Harry was an excellent man and would undoubtedly make a fine husband. Strangely enough, Lambert was right. Harry had been so available all the time I had taken him for granted, but when he said we must either publish our engagement or it was off, I knew I did not want to lose him. He may not have Lambert's éclat, but he loves me dearly. There is nothing he would not do for me, and daily I grow to care for him more.

All that I have told you today, I have told Harry. He has forgiven me. I only hope that you can do the same. I greatly regret that any of my actions may have caused the difficulties in your marriage which are bringing about this divorce, though I think not. I know you never wanted it from the beginning. I am sorry you have never known the close companionship and warmth which Harry and I are experiencing. I can only hope that you may find it in the future.

I put the letter aside, my heart still jumping at that phrase, "He told me that he loved you and he always would, no matter what." But that 'no matter what' had not included betraying him. How was it possible to love a woman whom he believed had lied, and lied over such a thing. Had I only known before all that I had just read. But now, what good was it, except to explain the past. Phoebe no longer stood between us, but that awful lie I had told about David did. Then, too, it seemed Madame Garnier was filling that place in Etienne's life to which she had always aspired. All this need never have been if only—if only—but what good was 'if only'? I must learn to accept things as they were, not speculate on what might have been. My married life had been a series of misunderstandings. Nothing I could do would now change anything, of that I was convinced.

The air seemed full of weddings, for before long Dulcie came to me, full of radiance. It must be true that beauty is the lover's gift, for that day she appeared more lovely, more glowing, fairer than I would ever have believed possible. Cinderella at the ball could not have outshone Dulcie as she was that afternoon.

I waited for her to speak, but when she did it concerned the merest trivialities, so that I was forced to interrupt her,

"Dulcie, don't keep me in suspense. You must have news. I can see it written all over your face."

She nodded, blushing, but still hesitated.

"Dulcie, you are the most awful tease. He asked you, didn't he?"

"Yes, he did. How did you know?"

"How could I help but know?"

I led her to the looking glass over the mantlepiece and she laughed as she caught sight of her reflection.

"Yes, he did, Leonora. Jeremy asked me to be his wife, but I intended to say nothing yet. Father is so against him. In fact he has been ranting and railing more than ever lately about Jeremy's political activism, especially since the unrest in Lancashire. For Jeremy to ask his approval now would ensure father's refusal. We must wait until that matter calms down, until father begins to know Jeremy better. I am sure he will come to respect him as I do."

"But Dulcie, the advent of machines is certain. Just as certain is the movement against them until it is recognized by everyone that the machines have come to stay. To fight them rather than making use of them is futile, and dangerous besides."

"Jeremy has a mind of his own, convictions of his own. I shall never control him, nor do I wish to. He sees the machine as evil, and I don't think he will change. But I have asked him to use caution and he has promised to do so. That is as much as I can expect."

I hugged her.

"Dulcie, I am so very, very happy for you. I am sure that all will be well."

"Jeremy told me that he had spoken to you, in fact that he had proposed to you, and that it was you who had opened his eyes to my feelings for him. He said he felt a fool, for afterwards he realized how much he—" she blushed and faltered, "how suited we were to one another. But how did you know that I loved him?"

"Dulcie, sometimes you are such a goose. You've said so a million times."

"Leonora Lambert, I have never said anything of the sort."

"Not in words, but your face has betrayed you every time you looked at him, just as it did today."

"Oh, dear, I hadn't realized it was quite that obvious. Then I am more pleased than ever that I decided to come to ask you to dinner on Sunday evening. I have already asked Jeremy—Mr. Salter—for I want father to get to know him, though nothing must be known of our attachment until the time is right. Do come, Leonora, so that if my preference for Jeremy becomes too obvious, you can attract father's attention. You know how he enjoys your company."

"Dulcie, of course I'll come."

"Oh, Leonora, if only things could have worked out for you as they have done for me."

I smiled, saying nothing, but inside I felt a gnawing pain. If only they could.

Chapter IV

Nothing in life ever seemed to go as I planned or come about as I expected. I had come to Yorkshire to spite a man I believed I hated only to find I loved him. When he became my lover I had teased him in jest only to convince him that it was someone else whom I loved. When my child had been taken from me, I was sure he had committed the crime only to be confronted by a half-brother who despised him sufficiently to do anything within his power to cause him harm. And my subterfuge for regaining my son from Etienne had been unwittingly exploited by that evil little man. I could still feel the heavy leather of that bible, with its indented cross, under my fingers as I swore that Jeremy Salter was David's father. How stupid of me ever to expect to be able logically to explain the web of my actions, all of which at the time had seemed the only course to pursue, all of which had been disastrous.

I was turning all of this over in my mind as I made my way to Dulcie's on Sunday. At least that evening promised no unpleasant surprises. We would enjoy their good, plain fare. I would draw Mr. Rankin into conversation so that the two lovers could have a few quiet words to themselves. I would put in a good word for Salter to show him in as favourable a light as possible to his soon-to-be, albeit unwitting, father-in-law. On this last point, however, I was not overly optimistic, for Mr. Rankin's sermon earlier that day had been on the foolishness of taking the law into one's own hands as men in Lancashire had so recently done. If he were to continue that topic at the dinner table, I was not sure that Salter would be able to restrain himself from taking the bait, new love or no.

I was, therefore, conjuring up some item of interest with which to divert Mr. Rankin's attention should that unfortunate event occur. I remembered reading that when General Wolfe was about to attack Quebec, he had repeated Gray's Elegy to the officers with him, they being greatly affected by the line "The paths of glory lead but to the grave." At the close, General Wolfe had said he would rather be the author of that poem than take Quebec. Knowing Gray's Elegy to be a great favourite of Mr. Rankin's, one which he oft repeated, I felt this anecdote would interest him sufficiently to allow any rancour to cool.

So busy had I been envisioning the evening as it was to unfold before me that I was completely unprepared to find Mrs. Dorling, Mr. Merston and his wife already ensconced at the vicarage on my arrival. I could not think of anyone I less desired to see. My chagrin must have been obvious, for Dulcie hastened to draw me aside to apologize. I am not entirely sure that she realized that Merston was representing me in the divorce, though she might have guessed it. But she clearly was aware that I was totally opposed to Mrs. Dorling, especially since her sharp tongue had been so busy of late with my affairs.

"I am sorry, Leonora, but father invited them to dine with us, not I. I did not discover the fact until this morning. That is why I was unable to attend church. I had to completely revise the menu with three extra places to set at the table. Sometimes, I fear, father is just a little inconsiderate."

"Mrs. Dorling I can understand, though she is certainly no friend of mine, as well you know. But why the Merstons? I didn't realize they were any more than acquaintances of your father."

"No more are they, but it seems that Mrs. Merston is related to Mrs. Dorling and that is why they were invited."

So that was where Mrs. Dorling had found all her information on my affairs, I realized. Well, to look on the bright side, at least they should keep Mr. Rankin occupied and less concerned with Salter. I suppose Dulcie must have been of the same mind, for the evening began well enough, the two lovers being able to converse quietly without attracting attention. I was more than usually silent, answering only those questions directed to me, and even those noncommittally, much to Mrs. Dorling's dissatisfaction. I knew she was dying to draw me out on the subject of my domestic problems and I refused to take her bait. In the end my coldness, together with some clearly admonitory glances directed at Mrs. Dorling by Mr. Merston, discouraged even her impertinence. To escape from such undesirable company, however, I decided to leave immediately after dinner. But it was during the course of that meal that the relative calm of the evening was unexpectedly shattered.

As I had suspected, Mr. Rankin began to outline to Merston the views on the activism of the Luddites which he had expressed so strongly in his sermon earlier that day. I noticed Salter growing restless and, seeking to keep the peace and prevent a confrontation, I plunged into my anecdote on Wolfe and Gray's Elegy. Under other circumstances, I believe it would have worked, but that evening Mr. Rankin was not to be diverted from his topic, for, after hearing me out, he immediately returned to it.

"But Mr. Lambert must have very definite views on all this machine-breaking fiasco. Surely, as one of the country's leading industrialists, he must be very directly involved. What do you hear from him, Mrs. Lambert?"

Mrs. Dorling gave Mrs. Merston a conniving smile and all eyes turned to me. It was so obvious that Mr. Rankin was the only person at the table unaware of my marital problems. I was at a loss how to answer him. I think that Mr. Merston initially spoke with a desire to assist me in my difficult situation, but what he said completely jolted me.

"I believe I have your answer, Mr. Rankin." His tones were, as usual, pompous. "There can be no doubt that Mr. Lambert is totally in favour of the mechanization of our industries. Mechanization, to him, is not a passing whim but the wave of the future. For that reason Mr. Lambert has just purchased the Pearsall Mill outside Knaresbridge. He is planning on installing the very latest power looms there for worsted weaving."

I saw Jeremy Salter's face across the table from me. I was obviously not the only one to be startled by Merston's news. In fact, it was Salter who asked the question which rose to my lips.

"But where did you hear that, Merston? I thought the old Pearsall Mill was in complete disuse."

"So it was until a few days ago. Mr. Lambert came to me and asked me to negotiate for its purchase. Had he waited I think he could have got it cheaper, for Pearsall was desperate to sell, but he wanted it immediately and he didn't quibble at the price. I arranged the sale. I also arranged for its cleaning and whitewashing in preparation for delivery of the machines. They are due to arrive tomorrow."

"You mean he is here?" My voice expressed all the pain I felt in hearing that Etienne was in Yorkshire and had not called upon me. I was oblivious of Mrs. Dorling's all too plain enjoyment at the turn of events in an evening which, heretofore, I have no doubt she would have counted as dull.

"Yes, Mrs. Lambert. But forgive me, I am sorry. I thought you must know of it otherwise I should never have mentioned it."

I shook my head and lowered my eyes, aware that they glistened far too brightly with brimming tears.

"My dear lady, I should not have said a word had I not thought you were privy to his being in the area. I understood that he stayed with his grandfather at Herenton for obvious reasons."

I had seen the Lamberts but a few times since my return. Since they knew nothing of the difficulties between Etienne and myself and since I refused to be the one to enlighten them, it made for a difficult situation. They had, however, got wind of it from another source, for I had very recently received a letter from Mr. Lambert demanding to know the truth of those rumours, a letter which even then lay unanswered in my desk.

"He has returned to London, then?"

"I believe he must have, for all legal matters were settled yesterday and I told him that I would undertake to oversee delivery of the machines. Not that I am overanxious to do so, what with all this unrest, but Captain Redmond and his militia are at hand, should it be necessary to call on them. We'll not put up with any of the shenanigans those ruffians stirred up in Lancashire, I assure you."

I saw both Mr. Rankin and Dulcie eyeing Salter, and, though their expressions were similar in aspect, I knew that one stemmed from righteous admonition while the other was obviously born of worried concern.

Mr. Merston evidently took my own discomfort upon himself for he hastened to assure me.

"I trust you do not consider me unethical in acting for Mr.

Lambert in this matter. I assure you it has nothing what-soever to do with—with that other business. That was at no time mentioned between us."

Mrs. Dorling could not restrain herself.

"That was odd, was it not, Mrs. Lambert, that Mr. Lambert should be here in Yorkshire and not even have the courtesy to call upon you? I had heard there had been some parting of the ways between you, but I should have thought he would have wanted to see his son. That seems only natural."

If looks could have frozen a person for time eternal, mine should have done just that, but Mrs. Dorling was deliberately oblivious to my hurt and anger. She continued unabashed.

"I dare say his other interests call him back to London in such haste. They say he is seen everywhere with that Madame Garnier, sporting an extremely handsome necklace she is. There can be no doubt where that came from. Believe me, Mrs. Lambert, in my opinion you are well rid of him. A French milliner is much more to the taste of such a man than a lady of nobility."

Everything she said disgusted me, yet it I might have ignored it had it not been for her allusion to the necklace. Could that be the emerald necklace Etienne had given me? I thought of my recommendation that he save it until he was to remarry and I became convinced that it must be the emerald necklace. That could only mean . . .

The despair which overcame me at the thought of what that must mean was, apparently, all too obvious. I saw a wreath of malicious satisfaction encircle Mrs. Dorling's sharp features. At that moment I loathed her as I had never loathed anyone before. That loathing evidenced itself in a manner of behaviour which, until that moment, I would have believed myself incapable.

"I'll thank you to care for your own concerns and leave those of others alone. In case you have none to attend to, allow me to be of assistance."

With that I reached for the glass of water at my place and very slowly, very carefully poured it down the front of Mrs. Dorling's peacock blue bombazine bodice.

There was an uproar. Mrs. Dorling screamed. Mrs. Merston hastened to mop at her capacious bosom with a stiff table napkin which had been laced with too much starch. Mr. Rankin repeated over and over "Oh, dear me! Oh, dear me!" as though incapable of any other utterance or action. Dulcie got up in confusion, undecided whether she should, as hostess, assist Mrs. Dorling in her predicament, or obey her instincts as a friend and come to my side. To top it all, Salter, without seeming aware of the confusion at the table, took that moment to explode.

"Bringing those devilish machines to our very doorstep, how dare he! It's a deliberate affront." Salter turned to me. "I'm sorry, Mrs. Lambert, for I dare say at one time you must have thought highly of him, but you no longer need owe him your loyalty. He is not deserving of it. To plant his infernal monsters in our own neighbourhood, at Knaresbridge, bespeaks the contempt in which he so obviously holds us. The man's a menace! He'll be stopped, if it's the last thing I do!"

Chapter V

To think that he had come,
that he had been in Yorkshire not an hour's drive from
Pelham, but he had not come to me. He had not even sent
word that he was in the county. I could not sleep for thinking of it.

The next morning I determined to visit the Lamberts. He
might not have left. Even if he had, they would have first
hand news of him. I set out at a gallop across the moor, but
when I was almost at Herenton I slowed my horse to a walk,
considering what, exactly, I would say and do, realizing the
impossibility of it all. Slowly I turned back. He had come to
Yorkshire. He knew where I was yet he had deliberately not
come to see me. Perhaps Salter was right, perhaps he had
bought the mill and was mechanizing it out of spite, knowing how much Salter would detest it, thinking to hurt me
through him. A confrontation, if he were still at Herenton,
would be pointless and could only hurt me even more than I
was already hurt.

Yet when I got back, I could not rest and I wandered

aimlessly from room to room, unable to settle at any task. I was glad when Dulcie arrived, but one look at her face showed it was far from a social call, for she hastily interrupted my apologies for my conduct of the previous evening.

"Leonora, we have to stop him!"

"What is it? What do you mean?"

"Jeremy. I know he has gone to the mill at Knaresbridge. I was afraid he might. I went over to talk to him and he is gone. They wouldn't tell me where, but I know he has gone there."

"Dulcie, Dulcie! It may not be so. He may have gone—." Frankly I could think of no other place he might have gone under the circumstances.

"You see! You know he has gone there. And you heard what Mr. Merston said yesterday. He probably has Captain Redmond sitting there waiting for them. Jeremy will walk into a trap. I'm sure of it. We must stop him."

"We will. But you mustn't come, Dulcie. That is all your father would need, to find you mixed up in such an escapade to forbid you to have anything to do with Mr. Salter ever again. You can't risk that."

"You may be right," she said doubtfully, "But you can't go by yourself."

"I'll send Hodges. He's to be trusted and he's reliable. Likely as not he'll be there before Mr. Salter has rounded up his men and he can head them off."

"But do you think Jeremy will pay any attention to Hodges?"

I was not at all sure that he would.

"I know. Write him a note. Tell him what it is going to mean to you both if he gets into difficulties over this."

Dulcie wrote so copiously that I had to remind her more than once that she was not writing a novel. He must get the impact of her message immediately for it to be of use. She agreed, but kept on writing for what seemed an age before folding and sealing her letter.

"Is Hodges ready?" she asked.

"I shall give it to him to deliver immediately. Now go home and please do nothing to arouse Mr. Rankin's suspicions."

"I'll try," she worried, "but please tell Hodges to hurry."

"I will."

But Hodges, to my dismay, had gone to look over some sheep and was not expected to return until that night. There was no one else to whom I could entrust Dulcie's note. I had to go myself.

The ride itself was not unpleasant despite the darkening evening, at least I felt no fear until the outline of the mill loomed before me. There was no sign of life, nor had I seen anyone on the road. I hesitated in front of the newly white-washed door before taking my horse around to the side to tie him up out of sight. Then I went in.

Even in the darkness I could make out the tall, angular shapes of the looms as they stood in rows like so many windmills awaiting Don Quixote's lance, yet they were still intact. There was no sign of either their protectors or their destroyers. No sign of anyone except—except for a light shining under the door of what must be the counting house. Was it Salter there, or someone else? I stood undecided. Yet if it was Salter, I was wasting valuable time. Dulcie's note in hand, I crossed quietly to the door and opened it.

"You!" I gasped.

"Leonora! What on earth are you doing here? Don't you realize how dangerous it may be? Don't tell me he allows you to go along on his mad escapades!"

Etienne came from behind a battered, oak desk on which was strewn a number of legal documents.

"Is Salter with you?" he demanded.

· 276 ·

"No. I am looking for him."

"So am I. Since we both have the same object, we might as well wait together."

Etienne's face seemed thinner than I remembered it, yet I could not conceal the delight I felt in seeing him and I had to remind myself of my object in being there.

"I came to warn him."

"Of me?"

"No. I didn't expect you to be here. But I suspect Captain Redmond may come. Salter could be caught. It would be disastrous for him—and for others."

"I see," he said dryly. "Well, I wouldn't want him harmed any more than you, under the circumstances."

"I thought you had returned to London."

"You knew I was here then."

"I heard of it only last night. I dined at the Rankins. Merston was there. He mentioned your visit, that you had bought this mill."

"And Salter must have been of the party also?"

"He was."

"Then undoubtedly he should soon be here. Sit down. Did you come here all alone?"

I nodded.

We sat together in silence. I was acutely aware of his eyes on me, of my dishevellment and my mud bespattered cloak.

"I suppose, like Papa, you are finding me plain and drab," I said defensively after minutes had passed without a word.

"I was thinking you look exceptionally lovely." His voice was low and the words came slowly, almost unwillingly. "How are you?"

"Quite well."

"And how is—how is your son?"

"He is well also."

There followed another silence until he said,

"This business between us will soon be finished. Canning

tells me the special act will pass through Parliament without difficulty, possibly within the next week. After that you will be free."

"And you, too," I reminded him.

"Yes."

"Are you planning to marry Madame Garnier?" I asked before I could stop myself.

He looked at me sharply.

"Does it make any difference whether I do or not?"

"No, of course not. Why should it? As you say, we will both be free to do as we wish."

The silence that followed this exchange was not broken until the sound of muffled voices and heavy footsteps came from outside. Etienne got up, but I forestalled him and stood between him and the door.

"Don't go outside, Etienne, please. They may—they may be in an ugly mood."

"I don't doubt that they are," he replied grimly, "But then, neither is this the happiest day of my life. My mood is ugly also."

"Why did you ever come here, or having come, why do you stay? Can't you understand that they might even kill you?"

"My dear, if I had run away every time I encountered danger, I'm sure that by this time I would be dead from fatigue. Believe me, it is far better to face things in life, however difficult or impossible they may seem at the time. They are hardly as difficult in actuality as the imagination would have them be, except—except occasionally for the unexpected."

His expression was inscrutable but I wondered if he was thinking, as I was, of that which had come between us. I could hear that the men were outside the mill now, and Etienne moved to pass me.

"Don't go, Etienne," I pleaded.

Gently he pushed me aside.

"I'm unarmed. I won't hurt him, I promise you."

The scene inside the mill reminded me of that night in the barn at Pelham. In the torchlight I could see Salter in the midst of the band of men, each armed with some instrument of destruction—hatchets, cudgels, truncheons, rough sticks, even planks of wood. A few of the men were looking at the looms with curiosity but the overall impression was one of outright hostility.

I had all but forgotten Salter and my mission in my anxiety over Etienne, but I suddenly became aware of Dulcie's letter still clutched in my hand.

Salter caught sight of us and came over with a slight smile, of welcome or derision I could not say.

"Well, I see we have an unexpected bonus. The proprietor of this fine establishment and its diabolical inhabitants, designed only to steal the bread from men's mouths, is with us. We are, indeed, honoured."

"Mr. Salter, please." I thrust Dulcie's letter into his hands. "You must read this before you do anything. Please. The soldiers may be here at any moment. I beg you, read it and consider what you are doing. Remember, your future is no longer yours alone."

"Yes, Salter," Etienne drawled, loudly so that he could clearly be heard. "Do consider the future, as you are advised, consider carefully what you are doing. This property and all the equipment in it, the machines I suspect you are bent on destroying—all of it is yours, not mine."

"What trick is this?" Salter was clearly outraged.

"Come with me and I will show you that it is not a trick."

Salter hesitated before ordering the men to desist from doing anything until he returned. Then he followed Etienne and me back into the counting house.

Etienne pointed to the documents on the desk.

"These are the deeds to this mill. They are all in your

name, all legally correct Merston assures me. He drew them up this afternoon. And here are the bills of lading for the looms. I have simply signed these over to you, but I have no doubt they will stand up in any court of law should that be necessary. Raw wool has been purchased, also in your name, for the first output from this factory. It should arrive shortly. If you choose to make it so, there is no reason why this mill should not be operating within the week, and profitable for you and your workers within a month. I shall be more than happy to offer you any advice should you need it, though you seem to be a young man who knows most of the answers."

"This is some trick to save your property. You know we will smash it," Salter responded, but I could tell he was at a loss.

"Do as you will. But you smash your own machines, you hurt me not at all. You can see that for yourself."

Etienne drew the papers across the desk and Salter glanced at them.

"But why? Why are you doing this?"

"Call it a wedding present if you wish. You are to marry, I believe."

Salter looked accusingly at me.

"But it was to be a secret. You told him, didn't you?"

"I said nothing. I came only to bring the letter. Do read it before you make any hasty decisions."

"Should you continue in your mad round of destruction, I should hope you would not involve your wife in your activities in the future," Etienne warned. "It is no place for a woman."

"You would do well to follow your own advice." Salter threw aside the papers. "I don't want your mill. You can't make me take it."

"Don't think of how you feel at this moment," Etienne pressed. "Think of the future. Think of your son."

"You know very well that I have no son. You know very well that I have not had your fortune there, little though you seem to regard it for all the interest you take in your child. God grant that Dulcie and I may have many sons."

I ignored Etienne's bewilderment at Salter's speech, for it was the first time Salter had spoken of Dulcie and I saw my chance.

"But you'll never be able to have sons, Mr. Salter, if they transport you to Australia. You can hardly expect Dulcie to accompany you there. And if any harm comes to Etienne, the law will be harsher still. Your men must not touch him."

"Ever the loyal wife." Salter turned to Etienne who was still in a state of confusion. "What is it about you, Lambert, that you bring forth this sort of devotion in a woman? Never before have I witnessed such loyalty. Even now, with a divorce imminent, when one might expect the greatest virulence on her part, still she thinks of you and your welfare. How do you produce such probity?"

"Are you saying this to taunt me?" Etienne said bitterly.

"To taunt you? What do you mean?"

"You, of all people, to speak of my wife's loyalty!"

Yet Salter was so obviously sincere that I could see Etienne was perplexed.

"Who better than I should know of it. If it were possible to taunt you on it, you may rest assured that I would, for I know it is a subject with which to hurt any man. Your wife has shown nothing but the most earnest desire to protect you and your name ever since she came to Yorkshire. I cannot deny that until quite recently I was attracted to her in a way a man should not be attracted to the wife of another. Never, at any time, did she allow me any encouragement. When I heard of the divorce I thought she might hear me. I confess that I proposed to her but she would not listen. I don't believe you have any idea of the woman you are allowing to break your marital bonds. Though she would not have me, it was she who opened my eyes to a love which had been in front of me for years, my own true love."

"Your own true love?" Etienne was completely nonplussed. "Leonora, what is he saying? What does this mean?"

But at that moment there was the sound of a carriage approaching and I deferred Salter's disclosure, a disclosure I had so often wished Etienne to hear, in favour of Dulcie's threatened happiness.

"Mr. Salter, I beg of you remember that true love now. If the soldiers find you here with these men now, what chance will there be for your life together?"

Even as I spoke, that love entered, followed by an irate Mr. Rankin.

"Jeremy, I waited, you didn't come!"

"Dulcie! But where, I made no promises to come anywhere?"

"I asked you to come as soon as you had my letter."

"I'm sorry, Dulcie," I intervened. "I don't believe he has read it."

"Jeremy, stop them, I beg you to stop them. I have told father everything—"

"My daughter has, young man, and if you think for a moment I would entrust my only child to a wild machine-breaking scoundrel, you are even madder than I supposed."

"But I don't understand," Etienne began.

"I'm not at all surprised, Mr. Lambert. I find it hard to understand myself. But this hothead thinks to become my son-in-law. It is, of course, completely out of the question."

"I am perfectly capable of being a good husband to your daughter. We have similar beliefs, even though you may not share in them."

"I'm delighted to hear that." Etienne had regained his composure at last. "Perhaps, Mr. Salter, you should show Miss Rankin the documents we were discussing. As your future wife she has a right to know, to reject them with you if that is what she chooses." Etienne turned to Mr. Rankin. "I just presented Mr. Salter with the deeds to this mill and its equipment. He now has a basis for putting into action his ideas of assisting the people, constructively rather than destructively. I think, perhaps, we should leave them alone to discuss it."

"I'm not leaving my daughter alone with that—that anarchist!"

"Come, come, Mr. Rankin. It is important that they talk it over together. Although up until a few moments ago I might have shared your opinion of Mr. Salter, I now think he is one of the finest young men I have met. Let me show you one of these new looms. If you have never seen one you will be amazed at how many tedious tasks they can perform."

Etienne propelled Mr. Rankin from the room. As I followed he shut the door behind us.

But the men in the mill had become impatient with the long wait. Seeing Etienne, they feared a trap. Some of them wished to leave, though others would not do so before the job they had come for was done and they were exhorting their compatriots to do likewise. When they hesitated, the more belligerent among them turned their virulence on Etienne.

"There he is, all the wealth anyone could ever want and more besides, and what's the only thing he ever thinks of? Making more blunt and starving us working men into doing it for him. Little enough he cares what happens to us. He'll just get another machine and laugh."

I saw it was Hawly, Betsy's father, who spoke. I saw too, the axe he held, moving compulsively in his heavy hands and instinctively I grasped Etienne's arm.

"Don't be afraid," he said softly, loosening my grip, and he walked over to confront Hawly.

"What you are doing is senseless. If you stop to think of it you will see that. You can break all the machines you want, but it is men's brains which have devised them and which will go on devising them, making them better and stronger and capable of doing more things until at last they'll break you. Can't you see that machines don't operate alone? Machines need men."

"But not many," Hawly growled. "That's why you and the likes of you get them. So you won't need all of us."

"You are quite right," Etienne answered. "But to do things the old way simply to employ more people will result in ruin for all. These looms are good for worsted weaving, but they will not do fine weaving. That must still be done by hand, though I don't promise that eventually there won't be a machine for that also. But people must keep working with the means at hand, and proprietors must devise ways to use their labour. Money must flow. Working people will buy bread, the farmer and the merchant will have their custom. The country will prosper. If you break the means of production, all will starve except for the proprietor who will turn to a more profitable outlet for his capital. Together owner and worker can produce a commodity profitable to both. I have shown that it can be done at my factories in Lancashire. Salter has a chance to do the same thing here."

"Salter wants us to destroy everything."

"I'm not sure of that. I suggest you ask him before you strike the first blow. All of this is his. If it is his wish that you destroy it, by all means do so, but don't do it without his permission. In the meantime, I promised to show Mr. Rankin how these looms work."

Minutes later, as Etienne was calmly explaining to Mr. Rankin and an ever-growing group of onlookers the intricacies of the new power loom, the door burst open to reveal Captain Redmond, pistol in hand, followed by members of his militia.

"Mr. Lambert, sir, you're safe! Thank God! Arrest these men, every one of them," he shouted.

"Captain Redmond, one moment, please. On what charge do you propose to arrest them?"

Captain Redmond's eyes ran over the motley group with their axes and cudgels and turned back to Etienne.

"Why, anyone can see they're out for destruction, Mr. Lambert. They're those, those—Luddites, they call them. Destroyers of honest men's property is what they are. Merston warned me this might happen. They're out to ruin you, Mr. Lambert, no matter what sad story they may have told you."

"Well, if you have been speaking to Merston, he should have also told you that this is no longer my property. I think it is for you to ask the legal owner what he wants done about it. It is for him to decide. It is my understanding that these men are merely here to apply for employment, I am showing them how the machines are operated."

Captain Redmond was speechless and Etienne took that opportunity to turn to Mr. Rankin, also bewildered by the events of the evening though no longer reproving in attitude.

"Mr. Rankin, perhaps you would take Captain Redmond back to Mr. Salter to see whether he has yet reached a decision on what he wants to do."

"Salter, that blackguard!" Captain Redmond at last found his tongue.

"Take care, Captain Redmond," Etienne warned, "You are speaking of the new owner of Pearsall's Mill and Mr. Rankin's future son-in-law."

Before he went off with the captain of the militia, I heard Dulcie's father whisper to Etienne.

"Mr. Lambert, I value your opinion. Do you really think highly of Salter? Would you accept him as a son-in-law?"

"As a son-in-law, very definitely I would," Etienne replied firmly.

When they had gone, Etienne turned back to me. For the first time that evening I saw him unsure of himself. I even thought I saw a flash of fear in his eyes as he asked,

"Will you allow me to see you home?"

Chapter VI

It began to rain again on the way back to Pelham, large, splattering raindrops. Intermittent at first, they quickened into a steady, pelting shower and drummed against the windows and roof of the carriage. The sound was all around, but in the darkened interior all was silence. I could feel Etienne's eyes on me, yet when at last he broke that silence he had turned to look out into the dreary, uninviting night.

"What a bloody fool I've been! By not listening to you I've been hoisted by my own petard with no one to blame but myself. All this time I've been unnecessarily steeling myself to accept a lie, a lie which you told me more than once was nothing but a lie necessitated by circumstances."

He turned back to me.

"Can you ever forgive my stupidity, my obstinacy in refusing to listen to you?"

"There is nothing to forgive. My own conduct was just as blameworthy—thinking you could be capable of stealing our child."

"Perhaps, but I was the one who would not hear you out."

I wished he would hold me close rather than away from me as he did.

"Please, don't let us argue about what is past—who bears the more guilt. I wronged you from the beginning of our marriage. My attitude was unworthy, selfish. When I look back I am ashamed that I treated you so, yet that is in the past."

"Leonie, I believe you persist in blaming yourself to make my intransigence less reprehensible. Explanations and apologies are necessary. Allow me to apologize now for the wrong I have done you."

"It is unnecessary. You know the truth, that David is yours. That is all that matters."

He paused before saying, "Can you give me hope that I may one day regain your respect."

It was said flatly, without emotion. He did not speak of love. It was not what I wanted, not what I waited for. Perhaps the time he had spent with Madame Garnier had borne fruit. Perhaps it was the emerald necklace he had given her as a pledge of his troth. Perhaps the freedom he was soon to gain was now what he sought after all. My throat constricted and my voice was so low, replying that he had my respect already and always would have, that I was forced to repeat my words.

He now knew the truth, the truth which I had expected would change everything, yet he said nothing—nothing, that is, that I wanted to hear. Had I the right to expect more from him? Perhaps not, yet I knew that if he drove away, back to London without me, no longer wanting me, I could not bear the emptiness which would be mine. The ride which had begun propitiously now became insupportable. I started to speak quickly, as to a chance acquaintance, of the good he had done in bringing employment to that neighbourhood.

"I don't deserve your praise, Leonie. My motives were quite selfish."

"Selfish? You gave the mill to Salter, can that be selfish?"

"It was to you I was giving it. I knew you would not take money from me directly. I thought by giving it to Salter I would not only make him see the inevitability of a mechanized future, but that you would benefit from the profit the mill will eventually produce. If necessary, I knew you to be capable and level-headed, able to run it even if Salter were not."

His confidence in me was pleasing, yet I pressed further.

"You mean it was for David, because I took nothing for him? You wanted to assure his future."

"For David, yes, but it was primarily you I thought of always."

I waited, unable to return to my reasoning words of the moment before.

"I don't know if I still have the right to say this after all that has happened, but I love you, Leonie. I shall never love another woman as I love you, as I have always loved you."

It rained still, yet at that moment all was sunshine inside the carriage.

"Etienne! Etienne! You do love me still, then, and not Madame Garnier?"

"Madame Garnier?" He sounded puzzled. "But you know she is an old friend, that is all."

"I was told she was seen everywhere with you in London."

"That is true. Some grounds had to be established for the divorce. She was willing to help."

"I'm quite sure she was." My reply was unnecessarily caustic. I tried to prevent it sounding so, yet I knew I did not succeed.

"Leonie, come here." Etienne drew me close to him. "This is not the time to discuss that lady, though I hope at some

· 289 ·

time you will get to know her and like her as I do. You two have a great deal in common."

"I know that we do." I remembered the day Madame Garnier had told me she loved Etienne, but that I would keep to myself. Etienne was probably right, I would like her if I allowed myself to do so. He was even more right in thinking this was no moment to speak of Madame Garnier.

"It is true then!" he said after kissing me in that way which was so surely his, the way no other man had kissed me.

"What is true?"

"You do love me even though I don't deserve it?"

"You know I do, just as surely as I know that you love me. Did you come to Yorkshire for that reason?"

"No, I saw no hope for that when I came," he confessed. "I came because of my grandfather's distraught enquiries about our marriage. I came only to placate him, for I knew he could never understand. He is so fond of you and David. It was a difficult visit."

"But you did not come to call on me."

"Several times I rode towards Pelham only to turn back. I could not bring myself to call. It hurt too much."

"I know. I rode to Herenton this morning after I found out from Merston that you were here. I could not bring myself to call for the same reason. To think, you might have gone back and neither of us would ever have known the truth, the depth of our feelings for one another."

"Thank God for Salter and his hot head. I expected him. I did not expect you."

"Thank God for Dulcie, for it was she who wanted to warn Salter of the danger. Since she could not go to him herself because her father knew nothing of their engagement, I went in her stead. How my heart jumped when it was you I found there. Can you understand?"

"Perfectly. Yet my elation was quenched by the thought that you came out of love for Salter."

"Just as I misunderstood about Phoebe."

"Phoebe is very happily engaged to young Foxcroft. There has been nothing between us, though when I thought you had found someone else I implied otherwise."

"Phoebe wrote and told me everything after her engagement. You know, she was the reason I returned the divorce papers, for she came to me after David's christening, after you had been called back to London. She told me you had returned to her. She begged me to free you and she succeeded in convincing me it was what you wanted. I should never have signed those papers otherwise. I waited for you to tell me it was not so."

"And I believed that in spite of all that had happened between us it was what you wanted. Proud fool that I am, I could not bring myself to beg you to reconsider."

"Don't change, please. I love you for being a fool occasionally. You are usually so wise, while I am the foolish one."

"If that is the case, you are the wisest fool I've ever known. I have much to learn from you, if you will but teach me."

At Pelham I went inside, leaving Etienne giving instructions to the groom, to be greeted by a distraught Thistle holding David in her arms.

"There you are, Mrs. Lambert! Miss Rankin came looking for you. She told me all about Mr. Salter and the mill. I was so afraid when you didn't return. I feared you might have gone there and no telling what might have happened. The young master must have felt my anxiety for he refused to go to sleep."

Thistle's face was filled with questions which I knew she would never ask, so I began to tell her all that had happened. But I completely lost her attention as soon as the front door opened behind me.

"Mr. Lambert, Mr. Lambert! You here! Well, I never, I never! Let me look at you."

Etienne bent down to kiss her cheek.

"I know, Thistle, I know. My boots are wet and muddy, but I refuse to take them off, even for your fine floors, until I see my son."

Etienne took David from her and held him high above him for a moment, looking up at him intently as though he had never expected to see him again, before settling him on his broad shoulder and gently caressing him. David gurgled and nestled against Etienne's neck, then he reached down to pick from Etienne's waistcoat pocket something which had attracted his attention. It was the emerald necklace.

"I was going to leave it with Merston to give to you—later," Etienne explained hesitantly, half apologetically.

We both watched as David solemnly studied the brilliance of the candlelight reflected through the green gems and then carefully chose one of the cool, clear stones and savoured it with obvious satisfaction.

"Thank you for returning it to me, Etienne. I shall treasure it now more than ever."

How seldom I had thanked him for anything he had done, I realized. He seemed to sense my discomposure at the thought of my ingratitude, for he laughed quickly and put his arm around my shoulders as he turned back to Thistle.

"I am absolutely famished, Thistle, and I am sure that Mrs. Lambert must be also for we have both been much too busy this evening to think of eating. Can you do something about that?"

"Bless me, Mr. Lambert, that I can. Not that at a moment's notice I can put up anything like the feast I'll have for you tomorrow in honour of your homecoming, but you won't be disappointed."

"I don't believe anything could disappoint me tonight."

No matter that I had borne the name of Lambert for three years past, hearing Etienne refer to me then as Mrs. Lambert I became aware of a surge of pride usual in any young bride on being addressed by her husband's name for the first time. At that moment I truly felt myself to be his wife.

Acknowledged, requited love brings with it excitement, joy, ardour, passion. All of these I knew that evening, yet above all I cherished the profound sense of peace that descended on me and that was to remain with me in the years to come.

THE END

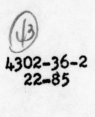

4302-36-2
22-85